THE OTHER WOMAN

A PSYCHOLOGICAL SUSPENSE THRILLER

N. L. HINKENS

Text copyright @ 2020 Norma Hinkens

Published by Dunecadia Publishing, California

ISBN: 978-1-947890-19-0

Cover by: www.derangeddoctordesign.com

Editing by: www.jeanette-morris.com/first-impressions-writing

❀ Created with Vellum

PROLOGUE

*B*ridget wedged the grocery cart between her husband's car and the jacked up red Dodge truck parked in the slot next to her. Fumbling for her keys, her thoughts rewound to the previous evening and the elegantly dressed woman she'd seen exiting her husband's accounting office. Bridget had been telling herself ever since that it didn't necessarily mean what it had looked like. It could have been an appointment that ran late, right? It was almost tax season, after all. But, despite her best efforts to cajole herself, her rational self lingered in a sea of uncertainty, unconvinced of what her heart was so desperate to believe.

Steve had been spending an inordinate amount of time at the office, and less and less time with his family over the past six months. Still, she would need more conclusive evidence that her husband of sixteen years was cheating on her before she confronted him—evidence that he wouldn't be able to explain away with some trite explanation. An unfounded accusation would rock their already faltering marriage.

She pressed the key fob to open the trunk of the car and reached for her grocery bags. Her hand froze midair. She

1

frowned at the unfamiliar tartan blanket lying in there. An ominous pulse began to tap in her temple. It wasn't the blanket as much as the contoured shape beneath it that had stopped her heart in its tracks.

A nervous breath caught in her throat as she set the grocery bags back down in the cart and stretched trembling fingers toward the woolen blanket. With a darting glance over her shoulder to make sure no one was watching, she flicked one corner of it aside. Her ears filled with a steady thrumming of blood at the unmistakable sight.

It was her—the other woman.

1

THE NIGHT BEFORE...

"*H*enry, I need you to watch Harper for a little while," Bridget called from the kitchen doorway to her six-foot-two, fourteen-year-old son, who was busy foraging through the contents of the refrigerator less than forty-five minutes after devouring a stacked plateful of roast beef and mashed potatoes, along with an obligatory stalk of broccoli.

"Why?" he asked, still scanning the refrigerator shelves. "Where are you off to?"

"Dad's working late again. I'm taking him a bite to eat. I won't be long. Please make sure your sister's in bed by eight."

Henry grunted in response, which Bridget took as an acknowledgment of his brotherly duties. His seven-year-old sister, Harper, was tucked away in her room happily preoccupied with the elaborate nail sparkle kit she'd received for her birthday last week. Bridget glanced at her phone. She could still be back in time to tuck her daughter into bed if she left now. Right on cue, Harper stuck her head out her bedroom door. "Where are you going, Mommy?"

Bridget suppressed a grin. Harper's hearing—not to

mention her intuition—verged on supersonic. Not much that went on in the household escaped her curious little mind. "Just going to take Daddy some dinner. Be right back." Bridget blew her daughter a kiss as she grabbed her coat from the wrought-iron rack in the hallway and slipped out the front door, balancing a foil-covered plate of food in one hand.

As she fastened her seatbelt, she smiled to herself, remembering the look of delight on Harper's face when she'd set eyes on her highly anticipated birthday cake—a blue-frosted two-tiered mermaid extravaganza, replete with edible glitter, starfish, and seahorses that had taken Bridget the best part of a day to bake and decorate. But she'd been determined not to disappoint her daughter's ambitious aspirations for a mermaid pool party in November at the local aquatic center. Harper was still relatively easy to please, and quick to express joy in the smallest things, unlike her older brother, Henry, who exhibited an allergic reaction to most of what she said these days.

Bridget grimaced as she started up the car. Henry was a good kid at heart. It was obvious he was desperate for his father's attention. If only Steve would spend a little more focused time with him. That was the whole reason they'd moved out of the city to begin with—to slow the pace and enjoy their kids. Monday was Dr. Martin Luther King Jr. Day and, despite all her coaxing, he still hadn't committed to taking the day off to hang out with them. On the rare occasions when he did come home from work early, he was always multi-tasking, even when Henry tried to strike up a conversation with him. Lack of eye contact told a kid you didn't care. What part of that was so hard for Steve to understand?

Ten minutes later, Bridget pulled up across the street from Bartlett and Hartman where her husband worked and switched off the engine. In the early days of their marriage, she'd often brought Steve something to eat at the office when he couldn't get away from his growing accountancy practice. It hadn't seemed like a chore back then. The chasm between them was widening more rapidly with every passing day. Granted, he was working too much, but she needed to make more of an effort too. Maybe this little gesture would remind him of happier times when simple things like splitting a sandwich had been fun as long as they were together.

As she reached for the plate of food on the passenger seat, a flicker of movement caught her eye. She glanced up to see a dark-haired, willowy woman in heels exiting the building where Steve worked. The woman wrapped a fuchsia scarf around her mouth, partially obscuring her face, and threw a furtive glance up and down the street before briskly descending the steps and disappearing into the parking lot behind the building. Bridget's chest tightened. Even in the shadows, she could tell it wasn't Steve's five-foot-two assistant, Melissa. So who was this mysterious woman, and why was she stealing out of the office like she had something to hide?

Bridget picked anxiously at the foil covering on the plate of food for a moment or two before setting it back down on the passenger seat. What had she just witnessed—was it anything at all, or everything? Was this woman the reason Steve was spending endless hours at the office of late, purportedly working?

Skin prickling, Bridget waited to start her engine until the woman pulled out of the parking lot in a dark-colored Land Rover. There was no way she could compose herself enough to bring a plate of food to her husband now. She was shaken to her core and her mood had soured. Steve would know immediately that something was wrong, and she wasn't ready to confront him. Not yet. First, she needed to clear her head, think about what she'd observed, and then decide what to do about it.

For a while, she drove aimlessly, losing all track of time and sense of where she was going. The smell of the warm meat next to her grew increasingly nauseating, and she rolled down the window, shivering at the icy edge to the night air that matched the chill in her bones. It was well after eight-thirty before she'd collected herself sufficiently to make the return trip home. She couldn't accuse Steve of anything without more evidence. What she'd seen wasn't enough to be compelling. She would make it her business to find out what, if anything, was going on before she confronted him. If what she'd witnessed was what she feared it was, then it was over between them.

Harper's bedroom light was still on when she pulled back into the driveway. Biting back her frustration, she let herself into the house and tossed her purse and keys on the hall table. She opened the door to her daughter's room quietly on the off chance that she'd fallen asleep with her light on. But Harper was still engrossed in her nail kit, the contents of which were scattered across her desk and bed, while a healthy dose of purple glitter twinkled up from the carpet.

"Honey!" Bridget exclaimed. "It's way past your bedtime. Didn't Henry let you know?"

"Nope." Oblivious to her frustration, Harper jumped up and ran to give Bridget a hug. "Look at my nails, Mommy! Do you like them?"

She reached for her daughter's hands and held them in her own, making a show of admiring the sticky, glittery rainbow of color that meandered unevenly over Harper's fingertips.

"They're beautiful," Bridget said. "And now it's time for you to wash up and get off to bed. Don't forget, you have to be up bright and early for ballet in the morning."

After supervising Harper's efforts to scrub up and clean her teeth, Bridget tucked her into bed and then knocked on Henry's door. When there was no response, she opened it and peeked in. Her son was stationed in front of his computer playing Fortnite, yet again, his over-priced headphones successfully drowning out any surrounding sound. Bridget sighed as she looked around at the unkempt space littered with dirty clothes and dishes. He wouldn't have heard as much as a cheep if someone had broken into the house. She might as well have left Harper unsupervised for all the care he'd taken of her. She marched over to him and squeezed his shoulder.

He yanked his headphones halfway off and frowned at her. "Hey! What's up? I'm in the middle of a game with Quinn."

Bridget bit back the reprimand on the tip of her tongue. She didn't want to get dragged into an argument with Henry. Her nerves were too frazzled by what she'd witnessed at Steve's office. Besides, she generally liked it when Henry hung out with Quinn. They'd become friends at the beginning of the school year. He was a good kid, an honors student like her son, and never in trouble. "Just wanted to let you know I'm back, that's all."

Henry gave a thrust of his chin in her direction and adjusted his headphones before turning his attention back to the screen, slipping right back into his ongoing conversation with Quinn.

Bridget closed the bedroom door behind her and was about to head to the kitchen to make a cup of tea when it occurred to her that now might be as good a time as any to do a little investigative work. She slipped into Steve's office and sank down in front of his desktop computer. Her eyes drifted to the silver-framed family photograph on his desk.

She picked it up and studied her husband's face. *What are you hiding, Steve?*

With a resolute sigh, she pulled the keyboard toward her and typed in his password. Maybe she was jumping to a baseless conclusion about the enigmatic woman at his office. After all, Steve had never hidden anything from her throughout the course of their marriage. Surely people who had something to hide from their spouses wouldn't share their passwords, would they? But she and Steve had never kept those kinds of secrets from each other.

While she waited for the computer to power up, she began pulling open his desk drawers and rummaging through the contents. There was nothing of interest inside—miscellaneous cables, stacks of old receipts, cartons of paper-clips, business cards, a couple of old calculators. Next, she turned her attention to the cabinet behind the desk and began working her way through the file folders. In his usual fastidious manner, Steve had organized all their household paperwork into categories. He handled most of the bills online, but he liked to keep a hard copy of items such as appliance manuals and contact information for repair services.

After a few minutes, Bridget closed up the cabinet and sat back down in front of the computer. She clicked on the finder icon and studied its contents, her finger hovering over the Dropbox folder. What if she opened one of the files and Steve tried to access it at the same time from the office? It was too risky. She didn't want to get caught meddling with his files if she could avoid it. She'd rather wait and take a look inside that folder when she knew for certain Steve wasn't working on his computer.

Gritting her teeth, she moved the mouse away from the Dropbox icon and clicked on the Recents tab instead. She threw a scant glance over the Excel spreadsheets and miscellaneous screenshots and notes—all work-related as far as she could tell. She wasn't sure what she'd expected to find. It's not as if Steve would keep a file of evidence on his computer attesting to an illicit affair.

She spent a few more minutes browsing through some old vacation photos before turning her attention to Steve's email. Once again, she came up short—nothing incriminating or even hinting of impropriety. She tapped her sensibly trimmed fingernails on the desk and closed up the computer. Truth be told, she was only partly reassured. Steve was a smart man. Exacting in all his ways, like any good accountant. If he was having a fling, she had no doubt he would make very sure to cover his tracks.

Bridget exited the office and headed to the kitchen to brew a much-needed cup of peppermint tea. As she sipped on it, she browsed on her phone for ways to cover your trail while conducting an affair. She was genuinely shocked to discover the lengths some people went to, and how clever they were about deceiving their partners. Evidently, she was living in a bubble. Cheating 101 involved setting up a separate email account. And saving your lover's number under an alias on your phone was another common strategy to avoid detection. Some went as far as to set up a separate bank account to fund their taboo activities.

Bridget frowned at the screen as she considered this possibility. Steve handled most of their finances—he was the accounting wizard, after all. He could very well have his own bank account for all she knew. An account that would be next to impossible for her to locate. Other things, however, were within her reach. She made a mental note to check his car at some point to see if he was carrying around a change of clothes in a gym bag or something. According to the article she'd pulled up, that would be telling—as would a sudden interest in dressing smarter. She drew her brows together contemplating Steve's attire of late. To the best of her knowledge, he wasn't dressing any differently, but then he'd always dressed well—suits, or sport coats at a minimum. Hardly surprising. He was a professional. She could disregard that particular indicator as irrelevant.

When she'd exhausted all of the websites detailing the myriad warning signs that your spouse was being unfaithful, she began reading an article about what cheaters were really looking for when they went outside their marriage. Her stomach knotted. Was Steve unfulfilled? She'd always thought they had a good marriage—decent at any rate—until recently. Granted, Steve was a workaholic and he sometimes complained about her nagging him about the need to spend more time with his family, but it was entirely justifiable. She was only trying to improve his relationship with his kids, and with her. They had been close at one point. The truth was, they had drifted apart and she missed him.

She was lost in a story about a particularly enterprising husband who used a drone to catch his cheating wife when she heard the front door open. Heart lurching in her chest, she hurriedly closed up the browser on her phone and reached for her cold cup of tea, cradling it in her hands.

"Sorry I'm late," Steve said, setting his briefcase down on the kitchen counter. "Getting into that busy time of the year again."

Bridget raised her brows a fraction. "Already? I thought it only kicked up a notch after Valentine's Day."

"Seems like we're off to the races in January this past couple of years." Steve cast a hopeful look around the kitchen. "Anything to eat?"

"Yours is in the fridge," Bridget replied tersely, swirling her cold tea around in an effort to avoid his gaze.

He pulled out the plate of food she'd driven to his office and back earlier, uncovered it, and set it in the microwave.

"Anyone working late with you?" Bridget ventured.

Steve pinched the bridge of his nose and stifled a yawn. "Just me. That's what happens when you make partner."

"Did you have an after-hours appointment or something?"

He shook his head. "No, just wading through some paper-work. I can blast through it more quickly when I'm alone."

Bridget stood and emptied the remainder of her tea into the sink with shaking fingers. If the other woman wasn't a client, then why was Steve hiding the fact that she'd visited his office after hours?

2

---

*B*ridget smothered a yawn as she tumbled out of bed on Saturday morning. She'd slept in later than she'd intended, which would necessitate a frenzied dash to get Harper dressed in her ballet gear and out the door in time for her mandatory practice for the Valentine's Day performance. Her mood plummeted as her thoughts returned to the strange woman she'd seen exiting Steve's office the previous night, the woman Steve had selectively neglected to mention when he'd told her he'd spent his evening perusing paperwork. Alone.

"I need to get going or Harper will be late for ballet," Bridget said, prodding Steve in the back. "I'll pick up groceries for breakfast on my way back." She hesitated in the bathroom door before adding, "Try and spend some time with Henry while I'm gone. He craves your attention, although he won't admit it."

Steve grunted and rolled over on his side. "All he wants to do is play video games. The kid barely speaks to me anymore. He acts like he can't stand me."

Bridget flashed him a silent glare. *Like father, like son.*

Granted, Henry was a teenager and subject to the occasional hormonal tornado, but she had to admit he'd been particularly biting in his interactions with Steve over the past couple of weeks. It saddened her to think that Henry had come to resent his father for neglecting him, shutting him out in return.

Fifteen minutes later, she pulled the front door closed behind her while Harper skipped over to the car dressed in her pink leotard and matching tights, her ballet bag swinging from her glittering fingers.

"Mom! You have a flat tire!" Harper yelled.

Bridget groaned as she surveyed her Honda Accord in the driveway. The right rear tire was completely deflated. They wouldn't be going anywhere on it in its current condition.

"Miss Martinez said we can't have a part in the play if we're late to practice," Harper wailed.

"We won't be late, honey. We'll take Dad's car instead," Bridget soothed. "Wait there while I grab the keys."

She dashed back inside the house and snatched up Steve's key fob from the kitchen counter where he'd left it lying next to his briefcase. He didn't typically like her driving his Mercedes S-class with sticky-fingered kids and smelly sports gear in tow, but this was an emergency. Besides, he wasn't going into the office this morning, so he wouldn't need it. With a bit of luck, he mightn't even notice she'd taken it if he cracked open his laptop and got engrossed in his work as soon as he got up.

THEY PULLED up at the ballet studio with a scant three minutes to spare. Bridget ushered Harper inside and helped her put on her ballet slippers.

"Good morning, Harper." Miss Martinez beamed at her. "Oh my! Let me see those nails!"

Harper proudly splayed her fingers for Miss Martinez to admire. "Well, that's a very creative look indeed. Come on inside, we're just about to start class."

Bridget gave her daughter a quick peck on the cheek and then headed back out to the car. She had the best part of an hour at her disposal to run to the grocery store and pick up a few essentials. If she was quick about it, she might even have time to go through the Starbucks drive-through on her way back to the studio. She could certainly use a venti latte with an extra shot after that panicked start to the morning.

As she drove, her thoughts drifted back to the raven-haired woman she'd seen exiting Steve's office. She didn't think she knew her, but it had been too dark to say for sure, and her face had been partially hidden by her scarf. It certainly wasn't anyone who worked at Bartlett and Hartman—that much Bridget was certain of. She knew all Steve's employees and made a point of familiarizing herself with their spouses at the annual Christmas party. She wasn't sure how she would go about finding out who the woman was—short of spying on Steve, which would be complicated to say the least. It wasn't like she could leave Harper unsupervised at home every evening and camp out in her car like a private eye in a TV show.

When she reached the grocery store, Bridget took the precaution of parking Steve's Mercedes as far away as possible from any other vehicles. He wouldn't take kindly to a stray shopping cart denting his pride and joy. Inside the store, Bridget pushed all thoughts of Steve from her head and concentrated on working her way systematically down her grocery list, crossing off eggs, bacon, bread, milk, bananas, muffins, and blueberries as she added each item to her cart. After an efficient sweep of the store, steering around the oversized carts that looked like bumper cars and were filled with snotty-nosed toddlers in meltdown mode, she maneuvered her cart toward the checkout, gratified to see that she'd banked enough time to make a Starbucks run. She briefly considered the self-checkout but decided against it. Nine times out of ten, something or other went wrong and she ended up needing assistance anyway. After handing her recyclable bags to the young teenager bagging her groceries, she fished around in her purse for her debit card.

"Hello, Bridget!" a voice boomed out.

She swiveled her head to see Jack Carson, Quinn's grandfather, nodding to her as he walked by with a bag of groceries in each arm.

"Oh hi! Good to see you, Jack." She didn't know the man all that well, but he seemed pleasant enough from the couple of times she'd met him when he'd picked Quinn up from her house. According to Henry, Quinn spent more time at his grandfather's place than at home, as his parents were often either working or out of town. Bridget blew out a frustrated breath as she punched in her debit card four-digit pin. Apparently, Steve wasn't the only parent who barely had time for his kids. She took the receipt from the checker and reached for the grocery cart the teenage bagger pushed toward her.

"Thanks," she said, smiling at him while making a mental note to have a talk with Henry about getting himself a part-time job—anything to curb the amount of time he spent playing video games.

The teen grinned back, displaying a mouthful of neon green braces. "No problem, have a nice day."

Bridget pushed her cart past all the parked cars to the far end of the lot where Steve's Mercedes waited, thankfully, undisturbed by runaway carts, neighboring car doors, or riotous kids, although, for some inexplicable reason, someone had parked a red Dodge pickup truck right next to it. She pressed the key fob to open the trunk and reached for her bag of groceries. For a moment, she stared uncompre-hendingly at the unfamiliar tartan blanket in the trunk of Steve's Mercedes. Her eyes widened in shock as she traced the shape that lurked beneath the blanket. With a strangled gasp, she let the grocery bag slide from her arms back into the cart. A cold sweat prickled across the nape of her neck. Was she imagining it, or did it look uncannily like a body? She darted a nervous glance around. No one was paying her any attention, too busy unloading their groceries into their own cars, and too far removed to see what she was looking at.

She took a quick calming breath, willing herself to muster her courage and peek beneath the blanket. Obviously, it couldn't be a body. Steve must have stashed some tools or supplies in the back of his car.

And then another hideous thought struck. What if it was a duffel bag with a change of clothes like the article had mentioned? This might be the evidence she'd hoped she wouldn't find—proof of Steve's infidelity. Tentatively, she extended a hand and lifted one corner of the blanket. Holding her breath, she peeled it back a few inches. Instantly, her brain filled with static, her legs almost buckling beneath her. She dropped the blanket, and stumbled back a step, hurriedly pressing the key fob to close the trunk. She reached for the grocery cart to steady herself, heaving a few agonizing breaths. *It was her*—the dark-haired woman she'd seen exiting Steve's office the other night! There was no mistaking it. The fuchsia scarf was still wrapped around her neck.

Nauseous, Bridget stumbled her way around the car and climbed into the driver's seat. She locked the door and shrank down in the seat, shaking all over like she was dying of hypothermia. What had her husband done? Her thoughts clambered over one another like a seething mass of cockroaches. She couldn't think straight. She pressed her fists to her mouth to trap the scream that threatened to explode. There was a body in the trunk of the car she was sitting in— *Steve's car.* And not just any body; it was the body of the woman who'd visited Steve last night, the woman he'd lied about meeting.

Bridget moaned softly. Had Steve killed her before he'd come home to his wife and kids? Before he'd sat down at the kitchen table and eaten the meal she'd prepared for him? How could he do such a thing? And why in the world had he killed the woman? Her mind worked furiously, trying to string together some plausible explanation. If they were having an affair, she might have given him some kind of ulti-matum or threatened to expose him. Bridget shook her head free of the ludicrous thought. Steve couldn't kill a woman. It was one thing to suspect her husband of having an affair, but he wasn't capable of killing someone—not the man she knew.

Bridget almost jumped out of her skin at a knock on the passenger window. She stared bug-eyed through the glass, unmoving, as though she'd just been caught with the dead body. But it wasn't a cop or even a security officer staring back at her. It was the young teenager with the neon green braces, rounding up stray shopping carts. Grinning, he held up her bag of groceries. She gaped at him, frozen like a solid block of ice, unable to react.

A confused look flitted across his face. He pointed awkwardly at the bag of groceries in his arms and then at her.

Willing herself into action, Bridget pressed the button to roll down the window. The teenager set the groceries on the passenger seat. "Didn't want you to forget these."

"Thank … thank you," Bridget stuttered. She turned the key in the ignition, wondering how she was ever going to be able to drive without wrecking the car. Trancelike, she plugged in her seatbelt and pulled out of the grocery store parking lot into the flow of traffic. She had no idea which direction she was driving in, and no particular destination in mind. Where were you supposed to go with a corpse in the trunk of your car? She didn't dare stop now that she was on the road. The only safe thing to do was to keep driving.

And then another thought struck her. What was she going to do about Harper? There was no way she could go back to the ballet school and pick her up now. She wasn't going to drive around with her seven-year-old knowing there was a dead body in the trunk of the car. What if the police pulled them over? Her stomach heaved at the thought of Harper witnessing what she'd seen. How could this be happening to her? This kind of thing only happened in movies.

She slowed to a stop at a traffic light, racking her brains over what to do next. She would have to call one of the other moms and ask her to drop Harper home. Her throat bobbed as a new fear surfaced. Was it even safe for Harper to go home? She quickly dismissed the thought. Whatever had happened to the woman in the trunk, Steve would never harm his children. He loved them, despite the distance his workaholic tendencies had created between them.

The car behind her beeped and she quickly jammed the shifter into drive. She hadn't noticed the light turning green. A cold bead of sweat trickled down from her brow. She needed to come up with a plan. She had to get rid of the body.

In a haze of confusion, her brain vaguely registered the Starbucks sign up ahead. As if on auto pilot, she pulled into the drive-through lane. Maybe a heavy dose of caffeine would clear the fog in her head so she could figure out how to proceed.

Swallowing back the bile rising up her throat, she inched forward to the microphone and ordered a venti latte. While she sat in line, she texted her friend, Amanda, whose daughter was also in Harper's ballet class. To her relief, Amanda texted back almost immediately that she was happy to drop Harper home.

Bridget held her iPhone aloft for the Starbucks cashier to scan her payment. Her wrist shook so hard the perplexed employee had to attempt it multiple times before it scanned. Bridget pulled forward to the next window to collect her beverage. Truth be told, it felt like she was operating in some other dimension. It was beyond surreal to think that life was going on as normal all around her while there was a corpse concealed in the trunk of her husband's car. She took the latte from the barista's hand, shaking so hard she spilled several drops on her jeans in the process. Foam dripped from the plastic lid and into the cup holder. Bridget ignored it as she swerved out of the drive-through lane. Keeping the Mercedes clean didn't seem all that important anymore. Not now that it was tainted by the grisly cargo stowed in its trunk.

She tried to think back to what exactly she'd seen. Vacant, unstaring eyes. There was no question the woman was dead. No blood that Bridget could recall, not that she'd looked too closely. How had the woman died? *How had Steve killed her?*

Bridget fanned herself, suddenly feeling nauseous again. Maybe she was jumping to conclusions too soon. It could all have been a terrible accident. Perhaps the woman had returned to talk to Steve and he'd been backing out of the parking lot and knocked her over. He might have panicked afterward. People did incredibly stupid things when they panicked. You never knew how you were going to react to something like this until it happened.

Bridget started to whimper. It was all too horrific to

process. Had she really seen a woman in the trunk of the car? Could she have imagined it? No! That was wishful thinking. She'd clearly seen the fuchsia scarf around the woman's neck.

Her phone rang, jarring her from her bleak thoughts. She glanced at the screen, relief surging through her veins when her dad's number came up. She couldn't talk to Steve yet, not until she'd had a chance to think things through. She'd have to go to the police at some point. There was no way around it. The only question was whether she should tell Steve what she'd discovered first—give him a chance to explain himself. Taking a deep breath, she put her phone on speaker. "Hi, Dad." Her voice sounded distant and tinny, a far cry from the composure she was attempting to project.

"Are you home, Bridget?"

"No, I just left the grocery store. Do you … need anything? I can go back."

"Your mother fell and broke her hip. I'm at the hospital with her. She's going into surgery."

Bridget let out a horrified bleat. "I'm on my way."

She hung up, trying to rein in her panicked thoughts enough to figure out the quickest route from her current location to the hospital. She had no choice but to head straight there. Her parents needed her. For now, the corpse would have to wait.

3

*B*ridget peeled into the crowded hospital parking lot looking around frantically for an available spot. The valet tilted his chin expectantly in her direction, but she ignored him. There was no way she was going to hand over the keys to the Mercedes to a stranger, not with the macabre surprise lurking in the trunk. It was far too risky a move.

Spotting a car backing out, she turned on her blinker and tapped her steering wheel impatiently as she waited for the shrunken, elderly woman behind the wheel to inch her way out. Bridget immediately swerved into the vacated spot, jumped out, and locked the car, checking it twice to make sure every door was secure.

Adrenaline pounded through her as she jogged to the emergency room doors and checked in at the reception. The clerk behind the counter printed her a visitor's badge and directed her to the third-floor surgical waiting room. Inside the elevator, she shuffled nervously from one foot to the other as it made its ascent, and then dashed out once the doors opened.

As soon as she entered the waiting room, her dad stood and greeted her, a relieved look flooding his lined face. Bridget hurried over to him and gripped him tightly, shaking as the shock of everything that had happened began to sink in. "How's Mom?"

"She's okay, honey," her dad soothed, knitting his brows together in concern at the emotional intensity of Bridget's embrace. "She was in a lot of pain when they first brought her in, but they gave her something for it. Now, it's a waiting game. They've already taken her through to surgery."

"How did it happen?" Bridget asked, sinking down in a padded chair next to her dad.

He waved a hand dismissively. "Oh, you know your mother. She was in the garden transplanting something or other she'd been tending to in the greenhouse this past while, and she tripped over the hose." He gave a rueful shake of his head. "I've warned her more times than I can count about that hose laying across the path like that."

Bridget squeezed his shoulder gently. Despite the bravado in his voice, she could see tears glistening in his eyes. "Mom's going to be fine," she assured him. "She's a tough old bird; you know that better than anyone."

He sniffed and nodded. "Indeed I do. But breaking a hip at our age is nothing to sneeze at either."

"How long will she be in surgery?"

"Maybe a couple of hours, with the recovery time and all."

Bridget pulled out her phone and checked the time. "I haven't had breakfast yet. Why don't we go downstairs to the café and get something to eat?"

Her dad got to his feet with a non-committal grunt. "I'm not all that hungry, but I'll drink a coffee with you."

They took the elevator down to the ground floor and seated themselves in a quiet booth in the café with their coffees. Bridget had appraised the unappetizing array of congealed egg croissants and decided to pass on breakfast. The truth was, the very thought of eating anything turned her stomach to mush. It was horribly ironic to think that there was a morgue in the basement of the hospital, and she had a corpse in the trunk of her car. If only there was some easy way to drop off a body anonymously, like you could drop off an unwanted baby with no consequences and no liability. She squeezed her eyes shut at the horror of the odious secret she'd inadvertently uncovered in Steve's Mercedes. It didn't bear thinking about—not yet at any rate. One thing at a time. She'd deal with it after she made sure her mom got through surgery safely. This was turning out to be the worst day of her life.

Her dad reached across the table and covered her hand with his. "Don't take it so hard, honey. Like you said, Mom will pull through this just fine."

Bridget flashed him a melancholy grin. If only he knew how bad things really were. In light of what she'd discovered in the trunk of Steve's car, a broken hip was the least of her problems. But how were you supposed to tell your dad that your husband had murdered a woman he was having an affair with and stashed her body in the trunk of his Mercedes?

"Is Steve coming to the hospital?" her dad inquired.

Bridget's cheeks heated. "I … I haven't called him yet. He's at home with the kids. I asked a friend to drop Harper home after ballet class so Steve will have to be there for her."

"Surely Henry's old enough to keep an eye on his sister for an hour or two."

Bridget squirmed under her dad's meaningful gaze. "If only. He gets so absorbed in those stupid video games, he wouldn't know if Harper was in the house or dancing on the roof."

Her dad let out a disapproving grunt. "Steve needs to man

up and cut him off. A young lad like that should be outside riding his bike or playing ball after school."

Bridget nodded. "I agree. It would be great if Steve would take the time to ride bikes or play catch with him now and again. To be honest, Henry's just doing what Steve models to the kids. He always has his face stuck in front of a computer screen."

Her dad drained the last of his coffee. "Let's go back upstairs and wait. I don't want to miss out on any news. The nurse should be along with an update soon."

A short time later, they were called back to the recovery room. Bridget pulled a plastic chair over to her mom's bed and took her liver-spotted hand in hers. "Hey, Mom. How are you feeling?"

She smiled weakly, her eyes fluttering open and then closed again. "I'm such a klutz. So silly of me not to notice that hose. John always did say I'd end up tripping on it one day. I guess he was right." She chuckled softly as she turned to look at him. "I bet you like that, don't you dear? Being right for once in our marriage."

He leaned over the bed and kissed her on her crinkled forehead. "I wish I'd been wrong about it."

"You're going to need physical therapy to heal from this, Mom," Bridget said. "I can come over and help out at the house until you're feeling better again."

Her mom lifted a hand and flapped it feebly. "Nonsense! You have your own life to lead. You're so busy with the kids and all their activities. You and Steve never stop those wheels spinning. Don't worry about me. John's quite able to drive me to any appointments."

"You can't expect Dad to do all the shopping, cooking, and cleaning, while he's looking after you too—not with his arthritis as bad as it is. I'll take a few days off work and help," Bridget insisted. "Monday's a holiday anyway, and I've got plenty of personal time saved up."

A young nurse bounced into the room and beamed at Bridget and John, before turning her attention to her patient. "How are you doing, Elise? What's your pain level like on a scale of one to ten?"

Elise tinkled a laugh. "I'm so doped up I can't even feel my usual aches and pains. I only wish I felt this good every day."

The nurse grinned as she adjusted a drip line. "That's what I like to hear. We're going to get you transferred to your room now. The doctor will stop by to check on you again once you're all settled in." She nodded to Bridget and John before breezing off to her next patient.

"Why don't you head on home?" Bridget's dad suggested, patting her on the arm as he got to his feet. "I'm sure you've got plenty to do. You can come back later on this evening and check on Mom. Bring Steve and the kids. She'd like that."

"I'm not going anywhere yet. I want to hear what the doctor has to say first."

"He's such a nice, young man," Elise piped up. "Of course they all seem terribly young these days."

ELISE HAD SCARCELY BEEN in her room for five minutes, when Doctor Harris walked in and introduced himself. He lifted the clipboard from the bottom of the bed and glanced at it for a moment. "How are you feeling, Elise?"

"Never better. It's a treat to have a young, good-looking doctor asking about me," she answered with a chuckle.

Doctor Harris smiled politely. "Well I'm happy to report that the surgery itself went well. There was a little intraoperative bleeding, and you are running a bit of a fever. So that's something we'll be keeping an eye on. You take blood thinners on a regular basis, so some bleeding was to be expected. As this was an emergency surgery, we didn't have time to wean you off the medication beforehand." He turned to John. "I understand you're her primary caregiver. Do you have any other questions for me?"

"Is the fever anything to be concerned about?" he asked.

Doctor Harris rubbed his chin thoughtfully. "We'll keep her under observation overnight, just to make sure it's not a sign of a blood clot or anything serious, but it's nothing to be unduly worried about, unless anything changes."

Bridget frowned. "What changes should we be watching out for?"

Doctor Harris replaced the clipboard. "Lethargy, for one, although that's hard to detect when you're still recovering from anesthesia. Any redness or swelling, shortness of breath, chest pain. Let the nurse know right away if she mentions anything along those lines. Other than that, your mother should expect to be getting out of here in a couple of days."

"Thank you, doctor," Elise said. "You did a great job."

"You're very welcome. I'm glad we could put you back together again." He patted her hand and took his leave.

Bridget exchanged a concerned look with her dad. "That settles it, I'm not going anywhere. This place is hopping busy. It's not like they're going to be able to keep a close eye on her."

John rubbed his jaw. "All things considered, it would be good if we stayed put, at least for the next few hours until your mother's out of the danger zone. There's a pull-out bed in the couch by the window so I can sleep here tonight. You should plan on going home in time for dinner, your family needs you."

Bridget gave a distracted nod, the horror of what she'd pushed to the back of her mind resurfacing with a vengeance. Could she go home after this? It wasn't as if she could sit through dinner with her family and pretend there wasn't a corpse in the trunk of her husband's car. She needed to go to the police and tell them what she'd found. But, part of her still wanted to confront Steve first, on the off chance there was some rational explanation for the body in the trunk that she was missing, as unlikely as that seemed. With the dire image stuck in her mind, she pulled out her phone and texted her husband to let him know what had happened to her mom.

As fate would have it, she didn't make it home for dinner. Her mom's fever went up during the course of the afternoon and Doctor Harris was called back in to assess her condition.

"It appears she's fighting an infection," he said. "We can't be sure if she was coming down with something before she went in for surgery, or if this is related to the surgery. Nonetheless, I'm going to prescribe a fast-acting antibiotic and instruct the nurse to check on her at thirty-minute intervals to make sure her fever is subsiding satisfactorily."

In the end, it was close to midnight before Bridget finally felt comfortable leaving the hospital. Her mom's fever had relented, and her dad was worn out and ready for sleep. "Go on home, dear," he said, stifling a yawn. "I'll call you in the morning."

"Love you, Dad." She kissed him on the cheek and padded quietly out of the room, relieved to see that her mom was sleeping soundly at last.

Back outside in the parking lot, Bridget's breathing quickened as she approached the Mercedes bathed in a haunting yellow hue from the overhead light fixture, an unwelcoming shape that housed a horror she had yet to fully grasp. She unlocked the door and slid in behind the steering wheel, gripping it with the raw intensity of someone bracing themselves for a particularly arduous task ahead. Her nose twitched, registering a faint, unpleasant odor. She glanced across at her bag of groceries on the passenger seat. Perhaps the milk had begun to sour, or was it the body?

She swallowed the hard knot constricting her throat. She needed to pull herself together and think this through. It was too late now to go to the police station. It would look suspicious. They wouldn't believe she'd only just discovered the body this late at night after driving around in the car all day. Maybe she should head on home and pretend to discover the body tomorrow morning when it really started to smell. Her brain balked at the thought. *Would* it smell by tomorrow? She didn't know anything about human decomposition—not being much of a crime show buff. Truth be told, she was completely out of her depth.

She lingered a little longer, torn over her decision, before starting up the engine. If she waited until tomorrow to go to the police, it would give her an opportunity to confront Steve first. On the other hand, it might make her a party to the crime. She rubbed her forehead wearily. She couldn't make a logical decision this late at night. Whatever course of action she took, she would take it in the morning and face the consequences that came with it.

---

4

*B*ridget woke the next morning with a vague sense of foreboding. She lay motionless beneath the duvet for a moment or two as her brain kicked into gear, sifting through her muddled thoughts. Her heart jolted against her ribs when she recalled the body in the trunk of her husband's Mercedes. She glanced hesitantly across at the other side of the bed. Evidently Steve was already up and about. She'd taken a sleeping pill when she'd climbed into bed after arriving back from the hospital, terrified she'd end up tossing and turning until the early hours, unable to sleep. Instead, she'd been plagued by nightmares of corpses turning up everywhere she went, from the freezers in the grocery store to the vats in the chocolate factory where she worked as a shift supervisor.

Reluctantly, she slid her feet out from under the duvet and stood, steeling herself to face her family. She needed to get Steve alone for a few minutes and have it out with him. This wasn't something that could wait any longer, not when a body was literally rotting in their driveway. She couldn't hear any chatter coming from the kitchen, or even the low murmur of the television. Maybe the kids were still asleep. Or perhaps Steve had warned them to be quiet and let her sleep in after her late night.

She made her way to the bathroom and splashed her face with cold water, staring at her hollowed-out reflection in the mirror for a long moment. She appeared to have aged in the past twenty-four hours. Hardly surprising, considering everything that had happened in such a short space of time. After stepping into her quilted slippers and belting her robe around her waist, she headed up to the empty kitchen. A note propped up against the still warm coffee maker was the only indication that anyone had beat her to an early morning caffeine fix. She unfolded it and scanned the message.

Taking the kids on a bike ride so you can sleep in. I put the spare tire on your car. We can go to brunch when we get back, and swing by the hospital afterward if you like. S xoxo

Bridget set the note down on the counter and pressed a French Roast coffee pod into the Breville espresso maker. Her heart fluttered in her chest. How on earth could Steve write such a blithe note, and take his kids on a Sunday morning bike ride, when the woman he'd murdered was stashed in the trunk of his car? Only a psychopath could operate in such a detached manner. Bridget dragged a hand through her matted hair. He hadn't mentioned the fact that she'd taken his car yesterday either. Was that significant? Surely, he wouldn't have been okay with her borrowing his Mercedes if he'd known there was a corpse in the trunk. It didn't make any sense whatsoever.

Bridget reached for her coffee mug and took a sip of the bitter, black liquid, willing it to flood her senses and miraculously present her with some kind of insight—some concrete plan on how to move forward. She couldn't put off making a decision indefinitely. It was long past time to notify the police. There was nothing else for it but to forego confronting Steve and call it in. The cops would have to come to her. There was no way she could get back in the Mercedes and drive the body to the police station.

She frowned as she squinted down at the steaming, chocolate-colored liquid in her mug. Who were you supposed to call if you found a body? This wasn't the type of information the average person had at their fingertips. Should she dial her local police station, or 911? Her mind cast about for an answer. Technically, it wasn't an emergency —the woman was already dead. But then again it wasn't exactly a routine situation either. She should probably call for an ambulance too. The police were hardly going to transport a body to the morgue in the back seat of a squad car.

Bridget groaned in confusion as she sank down on her padded dining chair. She could always ask the goddess, Alexa, perpetually on standby next to the phone, bathed in her mystic blue aura. But Bridget had never liked the idea of Amazon documenting her search history in their data base, especially not one that could be interpreted as fishing for information on how to dispose of a body. No, she would do this old school and make a call to her local police station just as soon as she'd mustered her courage. First, she would take care of her other important, if somewhat less urgent, problem.

She pulled her phone out of the pocket in her robe and sent a quick text to her boss explaining the situation with her mom and requesting the following week off work. After sipping on her coffee for a few minutes, she placed a slice of bread in the toaster. It would be best to force down a few morsels of something before she passed out. She hadn't eaten anything at all yesterday—a latte scarcely counted as sufficient nutrition. But when the toast popped up a moment or two later, her stomach roiled at the thought of eating it while a woman's body lay decomposing in the car in her driveway.

Trying not to gag, Bridget tossed the toast in the trash and went upstairs to shower. After letting the hot water pound her tense shoulders for a bit, she toweled off, somewhat refreshed physically, but as emotionally distraught as before. She pulled on a pair of jeans and a T-shirt, determined to make the dreaded call. First, she needed to take one more look in the trunk to make certain of what exactly she'd seen. The police would ask lots of questions—how old the woman was, her ethnicity, if Bridget had noticed any wounds on the body, and so on. Of course they'd want to know how the woman had died, and Bridget hadn't had the presence of mind to check. It had also occurred to her in the shower that she hadn't taken the time to make sure there was only one body under the blanket. As disturbing a thought as it was, a baby or even a small child could easily have been curled up next to the woman.

Hair still damp from her shower, she headed outside, proffering a feeble wave to the neighbor across the street who happened to be pulling out of his driveway. Once he'd disappeared, she walked around to the back of the Mercedes. She took a shallow breath, her legs like noodles beneath her. Her heart was thudding so fast in her chest she was half afraid it would burst. Then Steve would have two bodies to dispose of. How terribly inconvenient for her murdering husband!

She clapped a hand over her mouth to trap the hysterical laugh that hurtled up her throat. It wasn't in the least bit funny; it was a terrifying proposition. The ill-timed humor was proof positive she was close to breaking point.

Darting a glance up and down the street to make sure there were no dog walkers or joggers bound in her direction, she took a quick calming breath, and then popped the trunk and forced herself to look down at the body. A gurgling sound escaped her lips. She blinked in disbelief.

The trunk was empty! No blanket, no sign of a body, no blood. How could that be? Could she possibly have imagined it? No—not likely in broad daylight.

She covered her mouth with trembling fingers, scrunching her eyes shut as she desperately tried to recall what she'd seen. It had been only the briefest of glimpses, but the image was clearly imprinted on her mind. A woman's pale face, shrouded by long dark hair, swathed in a fuchsia scarf. A charcoal and red tartan blanket, pure wool—that much her fingers had detected in the fleeting contact she'd made with it.

Bridget opened her eyes again and stared blankly into the empty trunk of the Mercedes. Was it possible the woman hadn't been dead after all? Maybe she'd hidden in the car to surprise Steve—only pretending to be dead when Bridget opened the trunk—and climbed out later. A ripple of relief ran through her at the welcome thought. But, almost immediately, a shiver skittered across her shoulders as a more ominous possibility presented itself. Steve could have moved the body. He might have gotten up during the night and driven it to some remote location—hidden it in a shallow grave someplace.

The sound of an approaching car startled her. With a gasp, she pressed the clicker to close the trunk and hurried back inside her house. Shaking uncontrollably, she went into the family room and lay down on the couch, hugging her knees to her chest. She stared morosely up at the ceiling. Now what? There wasn't much point in going to the police without a body. Would they even believe her story? The more pressing question was whether or not she should confront Steve. Without the body, he might not admit to anything. She'd watched a documentary one time about a woman who was oblivious for years on end that her husband was actually a serial killer. All the while, he'd been carrying out his gruesome killings in a padlocked shed on their property.

Bridget pulled herself up into a sitting position. What if she confronted Steve and he *did* admit to killing the woman? She pressed her knuckles to her mouth, whimpering small sobs at the thought of Harper and Henry finding out their dad was a murderer. She couldn't make her children suffer like that—branded for life as the offspring of a killer. She would have to move out of the area, change their names, begin again in some other state far from friends and family.

Her phone rang, startling her out of her despondent reverie. She glanced at the screen before answering the call. "Hey, Dad, how's everything?"

"Great, your mother's doing much better this morning. She wants you to bring the kids by to see her."

Bridget swallowed hard, tracing a fingertip through the film of dust on the glass coffee table in front of her. "They … went on a bike ride with Steve. We'll try and swing by later on this morning once they get back. Did you get any sleep at all?"

"A few hours," her dad replied. "You know how it is in these hospitals—it's a revolving door. But I'm not complaining. The nurses checked on your mom regularly. I was happy they didn't take any chances with her."

"That's good to hear," Bridget said. "I texted my boss to let him know I won't be in next week, so I'll be able to help you out with meals, and groceries, and getting Mom into the shower and stuff."

"Thanks, dear. You didn't have to do that, but I appreciate it. The doctor's just stopped by, so I have to go. I'll look for you in a bit."

Bridget stood and rocked back and forth on the soles of her feet. She didn't have a clue what time Steve and the kids had left at, or how long they would be gone. With Harper along for the ride, they wouldn't be able to bike far, maybe to the park and back at best. Knowing Harper, she'd insist on stopping at the swings for a bit too. Bridget ran a distracted hand over her forehead. Should she wait until Steve got back and challenge him about what she'd seen? If she called the police now with her crazy story, and no evidence whatsoever, she might end up being a suspect herself. She choked on the thought. *Evidence! Of course!* She should have inspected the trunk more carefully.

Sliding her phone into her jeans' pocket, she hustled back out to the car. After nervously panning the street, she opened the trunk again and peered inside. She sniffed at the air hesitantly. Was there a faint whiff of something unpleasant, or was she imagining it? With an air of trepidation, she reached her right hand into the trunk and felt around the edges. She wasn't sure what she was looking for, a button, a receipt, some kind of clue like they always seemed to find in the movies. But true to his meticulous self, Steve's trunk was empty.

Frustrated, Bridget pulled out her phone and activated the flashlight. She shone the beam over the fabric as if it might somehow magically reveal a blood stain, or something equally ominous. That's when she saw the long, dark hair lurking in the shadows. She sucked in a sharp breath as her worst fear came roaring back with a vengeance. The nightmare was real. A woman's body had been stashed in the trunk of her husband's car. Overnight, Steve had removed it and hidden it—possibly buried it. But he'd done a slovenly job of hiding his crime. The hair was the evidence she'd dreaded finding. Her husband was a murderer.

5

*B*ridget eyed the single, dark hair with a sense of impending dread. A cold sweat prickled the nape of her neck. This was the part where she was supposed to retrieve the evidence with a pair of tweezers and bag it to avoid contaminating it. But this was real life and she wasn't a detective. What if she botched the job? It would be best to call the police and let them handle it this time. Before she could talk herself out of it, she slipped her shaking fingers into her pocket and yanked out her phone.

A little girl's delighted shriek cut through the morning air. Bridget jolted around in the driveway in terror. *Harper!* In a mad panic, she closed the trunk and stepped away from the Mercedes in time to see her daughter peddling furiously toward her on her miniature strawberry-colored bike, beaming proudly as she raced her dad and brother home. They must have given her quite a head start, or else they'd been peddling backwards since they left the park. Bridget forced her lips into a jovial smile as Harper dismounted and ran into her arms. "Mommy! Mommy! I won."

"Good for you, baby! I'm so proud of you for beating the

boys back home." Her voice wavered, bereft of any real conviction, but Harper was too caught up in her victory celebration to notice.

"Well, look who's awake!" Steve teased, as he pulled up on his bike next to Bridget. She flinched when his arm brushed carelessly against hers.

"That felt good, getting back on the bike again," Steve remarked, stretching his arms out behind him.

Henry skidded to a sudden stop behind his dad.

"What are you doing out here anyway?" Steve asked, his gaze settling on Bridget.

"She was watching for us, weren't you, Mommy?" Harper said, attempting to unbuckle her helmet. Steve leaned over and released the strap for her.

"Like she's gonna stand out here all morning waiting for you to show up," Henry scoffed.

Bridget ruffled Harper's hair and kissed the top of her head gently to hide the flush of guilt heating her cheeks. "Of course, I was waiting for you! Are you hungry?"

Harper gave an emphatic nod. "I'm so starving I could eat everything in the world!"

"Let's get these bikes put away and then we'll go grab some brunch before we visit Grandma." Steve shot a glance Bridget's way as though seeking confirmation. "Any updates?"

"Dad says she's doing much better this morning," Bridget replied, doing her best to sound enthused over the news. "She's looking forward to seeing the kids."

"That's good to hear." Steve opened the rolling garage door and helped Harper mount her bike on the wall rack before coming back outside. "Which car do you want to take?"

Bridget's eyes widened. Her throat constricted and, for a second or two, she feared she wouldn't be able to squeeze the words out. "Mine. It's easier to park in the compact spaces at the hospital."

Steve nodded. "All right. We'll swing by Westside Tires afterward and drop that flat off for repair—they're open on Sundays. You don't want to be driving around too long on the spare."

Bridget slowly released the breath she'd been holding. Her whole body had recoiled against the idea of climbing back into Steve's Mercedes, the metal coffin that, only yesterday, had housed his lover's body.

"I'll just fetch my purse," Bridget said, hurrying up the steps to the front door. Apprehension clawed at her chest, and she briefly contemplated making up an excuse to skip brunch. But she couldn't risk alerting Steve to the fact that she knew what he'd done—not yet at any rate.

When she came back out a few minutes later, Henry looked up from his phone, frowning. "Quinn wants to go to brunch with us. I tried to put him off, but he wouldn't let up."

"Isn't he spending Sunday with his parents?" Bridget asked, unlocking her car. Wordlessly, she handed the keys to Steve, too stressed to drive.

"They're not home," Henry said. "His dad went into the office and he doesn't know where his mom's at. He's bored sick stuck at the house. His grandpa came over, but he fell asleep in front of the TV."

Steve shrugged and exchanged a look with Bridget. "Fine with me."

"All right, he can come as long as he texts his dad and gets permission," Bridget conceded. Ordinarily she wouldn't have hesitated to invite Quinn along, but today was no ordinary day. Her nerves were shot, and her mind was clouded with fear, uncertainty, and the dreadful suspicion that her husband was a killer.

"Tell him we'll swing by and pick him up on the way," Steve added.

"Can we go to Brunch and Munch, *please*?" Harper pleaded, clasping her hands in front of her in her usual dramatic fashion. "I love their pancake animals."

"We'll go anywhere you want today because you won the bike race," Steve responded with a wink.

Bridget fussed nervously with her hair as Steve started up the car. Why was he in such a good mood this morning? Did he think he'd got away with it—that she hadn't discovered what he'd done?

"You're awfully quiet this morning," he commented, as they pulled up along the sidewalk outside Quinn's house.

Bridget cleared her throat. "Am I?" she said, a tad too breathlessly.

"She's worried about Grandma," Harper chimed in. "Aren't you, Mommy?"

Bridget looked out the window and scrunched her eyes shut. If only that's all she had to worry about. "Yes, honey," she replied, suppressing a sob. "I'm worried about her, but I know she's going to get better. It's just going to take a little time."

She shuddered beneath the touch of Steve's hand when he reached over and squeezed her leg. "Your mom will be fine. You know what a trooper she is."

Bridget nodded, not trusting herself to speak—thankful that Harper's explanation of her withdrawn mood had sufficed to bail her out, for now.

Quinn darted down the driveway to their car and sandwiched himself into the back seat with Henry and Harper. At six-foot three, he was an inch taller than Henry, but then his dad and grandpa were both big men too—well over six-foot.

"Thanks for picking me up," Quinn mumbled.

Bridget turned around and smiled at him. "No problem. How are you, Quinn?"

"Better now that I'm out of there." He gave Henry a side-long grimace. "Grandpa's snoring his head off. I left him a note."

"So your parents are both working on a Sunday?" Steve commented.

"My dad is. I don't know where Mom's at—shopping probably."

Bridget tightened her lips into a disapproving pout. She had yet to meet either of Quinn's parents, but she knew from conversations with Henry that Quinn's dad was a worka-holic, just like Steve, and his mom was rarely home. She'd attended the same local high school as Steve, but he'd said they hadn't run in the same circles back then. Still, it appeared they had more in common than they realized. Apparently, Steve wasn't the only absentee parent in these parts. A spark of anger flared in the pit of Bridget's stomach. All this time she'd given her husband a break, making excuses for him to the kids, believing he was slaving away late at the office on their behalf. Instead, it appeared he'd been working on something else entirely. A piece on the side. That is, until something had gone wrong last night and the unthinkable had happened.

Bridget still wasn't sure why she hadn't gone straight to the police when she'd first stumbled on the body, instead of driving around aimlessly trying to formulate a plan. Some part of her had instinctually wanted to protect her husband and prevent her family from being ripped apart by the macabre discovery. But it was too late for that. Steve's infi-delity had already dashed any hope of an intact family going forward. As soon as she got home, she would place the call she'd been about to make when her family had returned from their bike ride and interrupted her. It would be devastating to see the looks on Harper's and Henry's faces when it all came tumbling out, but it had to be done. It was the right thing to do.

At brunch, Bridget pushed a bite-sized piece of scrambled egg around her plate shoving as much of it as she could under a lettuce leaf to make it look as if she was actually eating something. She'd managed to swallow the first bite, but then her stomach had threatened to revolt, and she'd been forced to discreetly deposit several mouthfuls into her napkin after that. Harper chattered away merrily to Steve throughout the course of their meal, while Henry and Quinn carried on a private conversation too low to make out, inter-mittently staring at their screens under the table. As a rule, Bridget would have told them to put their phones away, but she was too distraught to whip up the mettle to enact any of her usual disciplinary measures. She was relieved when Steve finally gestured for the bill and they all piled back into the car to make the short trip to the hospital.

"Are you sure you want to come with us, Quinn?" Steve asked. "I don't mind dropping you home first."

"Nah, I'd rather hang out with Henry. Maybe I can come home with you guys afterward for a bit?" Quinn raised his brows, a hopeful expression lighting up his face.

"I don't see why not," Steve answered, before Bridget had a chance to intervene.

She groaned inwardly, picturing the task that lay ahead. It was one thing to knowingly expose her own kids to a squad car full of police officers descending on their house and seizing Steve's Mercedes, but it was another thing entirely to traumatize someone else's kid in the process. She would have to come up with some excuse to drop Quinn off at his house before they headed home.

By the time they arrived at the hospital, Bridget was a nervous wreck. She'd spent most of the drive going over in her mind what she would say to the police. She'd have to be careful what she told them, or she could end up in trouble herself for concealing evidence. It wouldn't be wise to tell them the whole truth—that she'd known about the body since yesterday. She'd have to concoct a story about discovering the body in the trunk of Steve's car this morning, and then fleeing into the house to compose herself, fully intending to call the police. When she'd gone back out to the car to make sure the woman was dead, the body was gone.

Bridget pressed her fingernails into the fleshy parts of her palms as she and her family rode up the elevator to the surgical ward. The disappearing body story didn't sound very believable, even to her. How could someone have lifted a body out of a car parked in a neighborhood driveway in broad daylight? It would be an extremely risky move. She, or any one of her neighbors, could easily have caught them in the act. Her head pounded with a looming migraine. The police weren't stupid. They'd soon poke her story full of holes with a few well-placed questions.

When the elevator dinged, she pushed all thoughts of the dead woman to the back of her mind and led the way along the corridor to her mom's room.

"Hi, Mom!" Bridget smiled, bending over to kiss her on the forehead. "How are you feeling this morning?"

"All the better for seeing the lot of you," Elise teased. "Come over here, kids, and give Grandma a hug!"

Steve shook hands with John and then sat down in the chair next to him.

Harper leaned over the bed and hugged her grandma as if she were a fragile glass ornament that would crack at the slightest amount of pressure. "I'm sad you broke your leg," she said, plonking down on the edge of the bed.

"She didn't break her leg, dummy," Henry muttered. "It was her hip."

"I'm not a dummy!" Harper protested.

"You leave your sister alone! Get on over here and let me take a look at you," Elise prompted, waving Henry over. "You look like you've grown another inch this week."

He approached the bed awkwardly, fists punched into his pockets. "Hey, Grandma."

"Who's this fine young gentleman with you?" Elise turned to smile at Quinn.

"Uh, I'm Quinn, a friend of Henry's," he said, hoisting one side of his lips up in a tentative grin.

"Well, aren't you the handsome boy with those thick, black curls. I bet all the girls are flocking to your door."

Quinn gave an embarrassed snort in response.

Henry's lips curled into a half-smile. "Girls don't come to your door, Grandma. They snap chat."

Elise raised her silvery brows. "Well, I don't know much about all that snapping and chatting stuff." She waved a hand in the direction of the rolling tray table pushed off to one side. "Why don't you kids help yourselves to a snack? John's been bringing me all sorts of things to eat but, to be honest, I haven't had much of an appetite."

Henry and Quinn immediately swarmed the table and started rummaging through the contents of the brown paper grocery bag that sat next to a vase of flowers.

Harper folded her arms in front of her and stuck out her bottom lip. "There won't be anything left for me. Henry will eat it all."

"I think I might have a morsel for you!" John said with an elaborate wink, rustling something in his jacket pocket.

Harper's eyes widened. She jumped up and darted over to her grandpa as he pulled out a bag of Jolly Rancher candy.

"Hey, not fair!" Henry protested. "She gets all the good stuff."

"There's plenty to go around," his grandpa said. "You just

need to be nice to your sister and she'll dole you out your fair share."

They all laughed at the triumphant smirk on Harper's face as she clutched the bag of candy to her chest.

Quinn's phone beeped and he pulled it out of his back pocket. He frowned at the screen for a long moment, until Henry nudged him in the ribs. "What's up?"

Quinn's perplexed gaze traveled around the faces in the room. "It's … a text from my dad. My mom's missing."

6

*B*ridget's hand flew to her mouth, a thousand dark thoughts colliding in her mind at once. Her tongue felt thick and useless as she attempted to say something—anything.

"What do you mean, she's missing?" Steve asked in a measured tone.

Bridget averted her eyes, terrified of meeting her husband's gaze and reading guilt in it. Surely Jen Carson's disappearance couldn't be connected to the body in his car. She exhaled a sharp breath. No! It was far too preposterous a notion. "How long has she been missing?"

Quinn shrugged. "Dunno. My dad just texted me from work. He was wondering if I was back yet." He exchanged a loaded look with Henry—who cut him a glare in return—and then frowned down at the screen on his phone again.

Bridget surreptitiously observed both boys for a moment. Something was amiss, but she couldn't put her finger on what was so disconcerting about the silent communication that had passed between them.

"Oh dear," Elise said. "This is very worrisome. Bridget,

you and Steve should take Quinn home. I'm sure there's a perfectly reasonable explanation, but it sounds as if his dad needs him."

"We'll come back and visit you again tomorrow, Mom." Bridget reached shakily for her purse. Her whole body was vibrating with fear as the monstrous suspicion that had struck her took root. She let her eyes linger for a moment on Quinn's thick head of jet-black curls. She had no idea what his mother looked like, but the fact that she was missing, and that the body in the trunk of Steve's car had black hair the color of Quinn's, made Bridget sick to her stomach. She shook her head free of the horrifying line of reasoning she was catapulting along at breakneck speed. She was reading far too much into this, jumping to wild conclusions. Quinn's mother had likely gone shopping somewhere just like he'd suspected. There was nothing to indicate otherwise. And nothing whatsoever to suggest that she was the woman Steve had murdered.

They were mostly silent on the drive back from the hospital to Quinn's house. Even Harper seemed to sense that mindless chatter was inappropriate in the interim. When Steve pulled up alongside the curb, Bridget's heart almost leapt out of her chest at the sight of a squad car parked in Quinn's driveway. Why were the police here already—investigating a missing adult who'd only been gone a few hours? It didn't make sense, not unless there was more to the story.

"We should accompany Quinn to the door at least," Steve suggested. "See if there's anything we can do."

Dumbfounded, Bridget stared at her husband for a moment and then gave a wooden nod. Was he genuinely concerned about his missing former classmate, or was he fishing for information? Isn't that what murderers typically did after they committed a crime—hover around the scene and converse with the cops?

"Henry and Harper, you two sit tight," Steve said. "Your mom and I will be back in a couple of minutes."

A tall, broad-shouldered man opened the front door to them before they reached it. "Thanks for bringing Quinn back so quickly." He stuck a hairy hand out to Steve and nodded at Bridget. "I'm Keith Carson."

Bridget mumbled an introduction in response.

"Is there anything we can do for you?" Steve asked.

Keith frowned at his son. "Go on inside, Quinn. Your grandpa's waiting for you."

Quinn scowled at his father and disappeared down the hallway. Keith turned his attention back to Bridget and Steve. He reached an arm behind his head and dug his fingers through his hair in an agitated fashion. "I didn't want to say anything in front of Quinn, but ... they found Jen—my wife."

Bridget's lips parted in trepidation as she waited for him to continue.

At her side, Steve rubbed a hand over his jaw. "Is she ... okay?"

Keith let out a tremulous breath. "She's ... dead."

Bridget shot a sideways look at her husband to gauge his reaction. His jaw was slack, and his face had turned an ashen gray. "What?" he gasped. "I don't understand."

Keith rubbed a finger distractedly over his temple. "Her body was found in a dumpster at the back of the drive-in movie theater on the edge of town."

Bridget let out an involuntary moan. She threw a quick glance at the shrubs on either side of the pathway leading up to the front door, half afraid she was going to be sick.

"I'm so sorry." Steve shook his head disbelievingly. "Do they know what happened?"

Bridget sucked in an icy breath, studying her husband with morbid fascination. If he was feigning shock, his performance was impeccable. He sounded so convincing, an exquisitely smooth blend of shaken and sympathetic.

Keith rubbed a hand over the nape of his neck. "The police said she was murdered. It looks like she was strangled, but it's too early to say for sure." He hesitated, a hitch in his voice. "They don't know when it happened either. I texted her yesterday around noon, but she was out last night when I got home from work." He shuffled his feet, dropping his gaze momentarily. "The truth is, we haven't been getting along all that well lately. She does her thing and I do mine, if you get my drift. I didn't think anything of it when I got up this morning and she wasn't home. I thought she might have spent the night elsewhere or got up early and gone shopping or something. She spends enough time at the mall—money too." He grimaced. "My dad basically raised Quinn."

A police officer appeared in the hallway and cleared his throat in a polite prompt of sorts. "Mr. Carson, we'd like to talk to your son now if you wouldn't mind sitting in on the interview with him."

Keith gave a detached nod before turning back to Bridget and Steve and lowering his voice. "I might ask you to help out with Quinn here and there over the next couple of days. I know how tight he is with Henry, and things are going to get crazy here. The cops have been grilling me for hours already. You know how it is. They always suspect the spouse first." He furrowed his brow. "You'll find out sooner or later, so I might as well tell you—Jen was having an affair. So the police think I have a motive."

Bridget's stomach muscles tightened at the revelation. Yet another coincidence? Or was it possible Jen Carson was the woman she'd seen exiting Steve's office?

"I'm so sorry for your loss," Steve said quietly. "Of course we're happy to have Quinn over any time. Just say the word."

Keith nodded his thanks and went inside the house, pulling the door closed behind him.

Bridget and Steve returned to their car in silence.

"Did they find Quinn's mommy?" Harper piped up the minute Steve turned the key in the ignition.

"She probably went to the mall and forgot where she parked," Henry said with an air of contempt, not glancing up from the game he was playing on his phone.

Steve slid an exasperated glance in Bridget's direction as he shifted the car into drive.

She gave a barely perceptible shake of her head. It was uncharitable of Henry to be so self-absorbed and cavalier about something that didn't affect him directly, but they would have to address it later. After all, he didn't realize yet that his friend's mom had been murdered. And it wasn't as if they could discuss it with Harper in the car. They would have to think carefully about how much, if anything, to divulge to her.

"If Quinn's mommy's lost, she could call somebody on her phone," Harper suggested.

"What if her battery's dead?" Henry chipped in.

"Stop antagonizing your sister," Bridget admonished, the words spilling mechanically from her lips even as her thoughts were spinning in circles trying to make sense of everything that had gone down in the last twenty-four hours. Steve had known Jen from high school. They might have been an item back then, for all she knew. And if Jen had given him some kind of an ultimatum—asked him to choose between his family or her—Steve could have lashed out in a moment of rage and struck her. It was hard to envision her husband deliberately killing her, but it could have been a terrible accident that he'd subsequently tried to cover up.

"I'm sure the police will do their job and find Mrs.

Carson, Harper," Steve said. "It's nothing for you guys to worry about."

"I'm not worried. Neither's Quinn," Henry retorted. "That cow couldn't care less about him."

"Henry!" Bridget exclaimed. "How dare you talk about Quinn's mother like that!"

"You better watch your mouth, young man!" Steve added, narrowing his eyes in the rearview mirror at Henry.

"Or what?" Henry challenged back.

"Or you're grounded, and your phone's mine," Steve growled as he made a sharp U-turn and merged with the traffic onto the main road heading out of town.

"Where are you going?" Bridget's voice rose. "We need to drop off my tire."

Steve scowled. "I've had enough of Henry's attitude. I'm taking you guys home first and then I'll drop off the tire myself."

Bridget slid him a questioning gaze, an uneasy feeling swirling around in her gut. She had a sneaking suspicion it wasn't Henry's attitude, but rather the discovery of Jen Carson's body, that had prompted this sudden change of plan. Where was Steve really intending to go?

7

*B*ridget went through the motions of making grilled cheese sandwiches for the kids' lunch, her mind a million miles away from the cast iron pan on the stovetop. Was it her imagination, or had Steve appeared overly eager to take off by himself? Alarm bells were ringing in her head. What was he up to now? Had he really been carrying on with Jen Carson all this time—their son's friend's mother? It was a nauseating thought. Part of her brain still refused to entertain the idea that her husband could have had anything to do with the body in the trunk of his car, but she couldn't deny what she'd seen. If Steve had accidentally killed his lover, it was entirely plausible that he'd panicked and hidden her body in the trunk. After all, their two families were connected through Henry's friendship with Quinn. The horror of the boys finding out that Steve had killed Jen would have been too overwhelming for Steve to contemplate.

Bridget served up the bubbling cheese sandwiches on plates and called the kids in for lunch as she set the table. After pouring Harper a tumbler of lemonade, she left her and

Henry to eat, and went into the family room to turn on the television. She wanted to catch the midday news in case there was any mention of a woman's body being found. To her horror, it was the lead story. She sat frozen on the edge of her seat as the news anchor shuffled illustratively through the pages in front of her and began reading from the teleprompter.

"Early this morning, police recovered human remains from a dumpster behind the drive-in movie theater in the area of Glenwood Lane and Pine Street. The body was later identified by the county coroner as that of missing thirty-four-year-old wife and mother, Jen Carson."

A picture of a willowy, raven-haired woman standing by the rail of a cruise ship in a strapless white sundress flashed up on the screen. Bridget sucked in a ragged breath as the room began to spin around her. *It was her—the other woman!* In life, Quinn's mother had been gorgeous—the kind of woman men dreamed about having affairs with. Bridget swallowed back the nausea surfing in her throat at the thought of Steve and Jen secretly conducting a lurid affair right under her nose.

"If anyone has any information about Jen Carson's movements in the last twenty-four hours, or any other information that could help police in their investigative efforts," the news anchor continued, "please contact the department at (469) 335-4321 or the City Crime Line at (432) 335-5555."

The camera panned to a dumpster and a cordoned-off street where a reporter was clutching an oversized mike in her fist, waiting to interview the garbage truck driver who'd found the body.

The reporter opened her mouth to speak, but Bridget pointed the remote at the television and switched it off before the woman could begin recounting the details of the grisly discovery. She dropped the remote and buried her face in her hands, awash with despair. She couldn't bear to hear any more. It was all too horrendous to comprehend. What kind of a person murdered someone they were sleeping with? Surely not the father of her kids.

Straightening up after a few minutes, Bridget glanced at the time on her phone. Steve had been gone over two hours. More than enough time to drop off a tire. Maybe he'd decided to wait for it to be repaired. Or maybe he was somewhere burying his tracks. But, what tracks could he possibly be trying to hide at this point? Jen's body had already been discovered. Unless he'd gone to the scene of the crime where he'd killed her to get rid of some other evidence.

Bridget frowned. It seemed odd that he hadn't taken the time to vacuum out the trunk of his car thoroughly. Everyone knew the police could pick up on fibers and hairs, even a skin cell could seal your fate nowadays. It wasn't like Steve, who was so meticulous about everything else in his life, to overlook such an obvious detail. But then again, he must have been under an inordinate amount of stress attempting to cover up what he'd done. And that's when murderers slip up and make the kind of mistakes that inevitably lead to their downfall.

Bridget rocked gently back and forth on her chair, repeating the Crime Line phone number over in her head. She had to do something. If she called in an anonymous tip, she wouldn't have to mention anything about finding the body in her husband's car. Bridget scratched her wrist raw, frantically trying to assemble her thoughts. She would tell the Crime Line she thought she'd seen someone who looked like the woman on the news exiting the building where her husband was working on Friday night. That would be enough to prompt an investigation. The police would likely interview everyone who worked at Bartlett and Hartman. She wouldn't exactly be throwing Steve under the bus, but she'd be pointing the cops in the right direction. If they did their due diligence, they were bound to find out that her husband had stayed late at the office that night and put two and two together. It was enough to appease her conscience. The rest was up to the professionals.

Her fingers trembled as she fished her phone out of her pocket. Before she could talk herself out of it, she punched in the Crime Line number and hit dial, and then abruptly ended the call. She shook her head. This wasn't going to work. First, she needed to iron out a few details. She had to be clear on what she was going to tell the operator. Blurting out everything was a really bad idea and might lead to her inadvertently incriminating herself in the process. She took a quick calming breath and then mouthed each digit as she carefully punched in the number again.

"Mommy!" Harper burst into the room like a tornado. "Can I watch a movie, *please*?"

Bridget quickly hit the end call button and blinked at her daughter, trying to wrangle her thoughts back to the simplicity of a seven-year-old's world. "Did you finish your sandwich?" she stammered.

"Yes."

"All of it?"

Harper gave an emphatic nod. "Henry had four cookies. I only had one."

Bridget gave her a fleeting smile as she got to her feet. "I'll speak to him about it." She handed her daughter the remote control.

"Do you want to watch a movie with me?" Harper's face lit up with a flicker of expectation.

"Maybe later," Bridget replied. "Mommy has some work to do first." She smoothed a hand over Harper's head, and then made her way to her bedroom and closed the door behind her. With a resolute sigh, she sank down on the bed and dialed the Crime Line for the third time. This time the call went through.

"Hello, Crime Line, how can I help?" a male voice said.

Bridget wet her lips nervously. "I ... I need to make sure this call is anonymous."

"Yes ma'am. We're a completely anonymous service. We don't have caller ID, we don't record calls, and we don't want to know any information about you. We'll simply make a note of any information you have and pass that on to the police."

"And ... I won't have to appear in court, or anything like that."

"No, absolutely not. You don't have to make a statement either. All we need is whatever information you have."

"It's about the missing woman whose body was found in the dumpster. I'm not sure it was her, but I think ..." Bridget broke off brusquely, her heart pounding like the thudding of hooves on a hard-packed road. Once she said it, there was no going back. Sooner or later, the police would interview Steve and get to the bottom of what had happened. Her world was about to implode.

"Take your time, ma'am."

"It's just that I could be wrong about this and I don't want to be prosecuted."

"I can promise you that you won't be prosecuted for anything you say on this line. This call is one-hundred-percent confidential. We don't even tell the police if it was a male or a female who called in the tip."

"Okay." Bridget took a butterfly-laden breath before continuing. "Last night, I happened to pull over near Bartlett and Hartman Accounting on Rhode Street to make a call. A woman was exiting the building. She looked like the woman on the news. I can't be certain it was her because it was dusk, and I didn't get a close look."

"What time approximately was this at?"

Bridget hesitated and pretended to think about it. "Six-thirty or seven-ish."

"And was the woman alone?"

"Yes, she walked around to the parking lot behind the building and drove away a moment or two later."

"Did you happen to see what make or model of vehicle she was driving, ma'am?"

Bridget scrunched her eyes shut, picturing the vehicle emerging from the parking lot. "It was a Land Rover, dark, maybe gray or green. I can't be sure."

"No problem. Is there any other information you'd like me to pass along?"

Bridget's nails dug into the fabric of the duvet beneath her. *Yes, please tell the cops that I saw her in the trunk of my husband's Mercedes the next day.* "Uh, no, that's everything." Her voice wavered a fraction. Surely the man on the other end of line had taken enough calls to recognize when someone was lying. But he'd promised her she couldn't be prosecuted for anything she'd said or hadn't said. She would have to take him at his word.

"Thank you, ma'am. I'm going to give you a case number in the event you elect to call back and check on the status of your crime report at any point. Do you have a pen handy?"

Bridget got to her feet and pulled open a drawer in her bed side table. "Go ahead."

She scribbled down the case number and ended the call before sinking back down on the bed in a daze. It was done. Soon, the wheels would begin turning. Her life as she knew it was over. The police would follow the trail like sniffer dogs and, before long, they would come knocking on her door.

8

---

*B*ridget tossed the pen back into the drawer and slammed it shut before walking around to the other side of the bed where Steve slept. Blood like a jungle drumbeat pounded in her ears. She felt like a prowler in her own house. After a moment's hesitation, she slipped her hand beneath the mattress and slid it along the entire length, feeling for anything Steve might have hidden there—a second phone, perhaps? Coming up empty, she yanked open the drawer in his bedside table next. She had no clear idea what she was looking for, but maybe she would stumble across something that would tell her who her husband really was. She rifled skittishly though the drawer contents: a box of Breathe Right nasal strips, some coins, a highlighter, a Swiss army knife, a yachting magazine. Was it possible to identify a cheater or a killer by the kinds of things they kept next to their bed? It wasn't as if they would leave anything incriminating within a spouse's reach.

She lifted out a crumpled receipt and stared at it in her fist for a moment before swallowing back her dread and unfolding it. *The Habit Burger Grill.* Apparently, Steve had

57

recently partaken of a number one meal with a Diet Coke—hardly a criminal activity by any standard. Her fingers froze at the sound of the front door opening. Tossing the receipt back into the drawer, she closed it quietly before smoothing down her hair.

She exited the master bedroom in time to see Steve pull the front door shut behind him.

"I decided to wait for the tire," he explained, before she could say anything. "Thought I'd save you a trip."

"Great, thanks. Did you eat yet?" Bridget asked, aiming for a light and airy tone and failing miserably.

"Yeah, I grabbed a sandwich on my way home." He scratched the back of his neck hesitantly. "I need to go into the office for a couple of hours."

"On a Sunday?" Bridget frowned at him, her suspicions surging to the forefront once again. "Why?"

Steve's gaze flitted from her to a spot on the wall behind her and back. "A client emailed me about a report he needs for a meeting on Tuesday morning. I have to get the numbers together for him beforehand. It's either go in now or on Monday, and you've been bugging me for days on end to take the Martin Luther holiday off with the kids."

"But we agreed weekends were going to be family time from now on. If you want to work on building your relationship with the kids, you can't be gone all weekend. Henry's almost grown and you barely exchange ten words with him during the week."

"I realize that, and I'm making an effort, Bridget," Steve replied testily. "That's why we went on a bike ride together this morning. It was like pulling teeth to get Henry out there, but I persisted, like I promised." He paused and rubbed a hand over his chin. "I'm not going to make working on the weekends a habit again, but this is ... this is an emergency. It's my biggest client."

Bridget opened her mouth and then closed it again. It was obvious he was lying to her. He was a horrible liar. She'd always been able to tell when he wasn't giving her the straight scoop. Her thoughts tumbled over one another in quick succession, her misgivings bubbling up to the surface again. Why hadn't he gone directly to the office after he'd picked up the tire? There was only one logical reason she could think of. He'd made a special trip home first to pick up his own car. He must be planning on cleaning out the trunk and getting rid of any evidence. She glared at him, desperate for the truth, while dreading his answer. "If it's such an emergency, why didn't you go by the office on your way home?"

He gave a nonchalant shrug. "My client just texted me. I was almost home anyway."

Bridget folded her arms in front of her, fighting to keep her composure. "Will you be back for dinner?"

"Yeah, I can pick up some pizzas on my way home if you want."

"Sure," she answered through clenched teeth. "That'll keep the kids happy." And that's all that mattered. It wasn't as if she was going to be able to eat anything. Her appetite had been non-existent ever since she'd found the body in the trunk. She made her way to the family room, flinching when the front door slammed shut.

She picked her way back and forth across the room wondering what she should do, if anything. How long would it take Crime Line to pass the information along to the police? She should have asked the man she'd talked to more questions, but she'd been so nervous she'd blanked out. Hopefully the police prioritized tips pertaining to more serious crimes like murder. But, if Steve was on his way to clean out his car, it might be too late by the time the police followed up. Bridget turned the theory over in her head. If that's what Steve was really up to, it would prove what she'd suspected all along—that he'd murdered the woman she'd seen in the trunk of his car. And he might just get away with it. She needed to find a way to thwart his plan.

Chewing on her lip, she weighed her options. If she followed him, she could video him in the act of vacuuming out his car at some random car wash. The sound of the Mercedes starting up in the driveway sent a shiver through her. She had to make a counter move. If her husband was a killer, someone had to bring him to justice, and right now, she was the only person who knew what he'd done.

Before she could second-guess herself, she snatched up her purse and coat, and strode down the hall to Henry's bedroom. After a quick rap on the door, she swung it open. "Henry!"

Oblivious to her presence, he continued talking and laughing into his headset, eyes locked on the screen in front of him. She marched over to him and waited until he turned his head a few degrees and acknowledged her. "I need you to watch Harper for an hour or two."

He rumpled his brow. "Why? Is Grandma okay?"

"She's fine. I have to run a couple of errands."

Henry shrugged. "Yeah, I got her."

"I want you to check on her regularly, Henry. Don't just assume she's playing in her room. You need to keep a close eye on her."

"I said I got it," he huffed.

Only halfway appeased, Bridget bit her tongue and headed to Harper's room next. Her daughter was happily occupied with her Barbie dolls in her Disney tent, engrossed in some scenario or other that involved an inordinate amount of costume changes judging by the mountain of doll clothes and shoes strewn about on the carpet. "Harper, Mommy has to go out for a bit. If you need anything, Henry's in his room."

"Okay." She smiled angelically up at Bridget.

Bridget blew her a kiss. "And no cookies while I'm gone."

She headed out to her car and reversed down the drive-way, wheeling out into the street. Steve had a minute or two head start on her, but if she hurried, she might be able to catch up with him before he reached the main road. If all else failed, she would drive to his office. At least she would know if he'd been lying to her about where he was going. Stomach churning, she drove as fast as she dared out of the twenty-five-mile-an-hour neighborhood and merged onto the main road.

There was no sign of Steve's Mercedes up ahead. She wished now that she'd downloaded the Find My Friends app on her phone so she could see where he was going. All her friends seemed to keep track of their families that way nowa-days. But she'd never felt the need to keep tabs on her husband before. It had always seemed so intrusive to be able to know where your spouse was at all times—so unnecessary, until now.

As she motored along, she kept a close eye on the road up ahead, overtaking as many cars as she dared when the oppor-tunity presented itself. Her heart jolted in her chest when, at last, she spotted Steve's Mercedes a few hundred feet up ahead in the line of traffic. She slipped back into the slow lane, taking care to keep several cars between her and the Mercedes. Minutes later, Steve turned left at a traffic light. Bridget's heart sank. It was all the confirmation she needed that he wasn't going to Bartlett and Hartman as he'd claimed. She gritted her teeth in frustration when the light turned red as she approached it. For several agonizing minutes, she clutched the steering wheel, palms sweating, until the light changed again.

She turned down the street, her breath coming in ragged bursts as she scanned both sides of the road. Confusion flooded her when she spotted the Mercedes parked outside a coffee shop. She slowed to a crawl, peering warily at the empty vehicle. She'd expected to find Steve at some sleazy, off-the-beaten path car wash, methodically getting rid of any evidence of his crime, not lounging in a fleabag coffee shop called *The Muddy Cup*. What was that about? He could have made coffee at home on their high end Breville espresso maker.

Unless he needed some time to think on his own—maybe he was considering turning himself in. Or was he meeting someone? Her heart began to race. For all she knew, Jen mightn't have been the only woman he'd been having an affair with. She drove slowly past the coffee shop and pulled into a nearby strip mall parking lot. Determined to get to the bottom of what Steve was up to, now that she'd come this far, she climbed out, pulled up the hood of her coat, and began walking back to the coffee shop. To buy herself some time, she pretended to study the array of goodies in the window of the chocolatier next door, all the while peering furtively into the coffee shop. Steve was standing in line at the counter talking to the man next to him who was gesturing back in a perturbed manner. The man said something to him and then turned around to look for an empty table. Bridget gasped. *Keith Carson!*

She stood with her nose pressed to the chocolatier window for several minutes trying to wrap her head around it. Had Keith asked to meet with Steve? Maybe he'd known all along that Steve was having an affair with his wife— which meant he suspected Steve had something to do with her murder. Cautiously, Bridget raised her head and threw another stealthy glance into the coffee shop. Keith and Steve were seated opposite each other at a small corner table now, their untouched paper cups of coffee on the table in front of them. They were talking animatedly, arguing perhaps?

And then another terrifying thought hit. What if Keith, enraged over the affair, had killed Jen and forced Steve to help him dispose of the body? Keith could have blackmailed him into disposing of his wife's body in return for keeping his mouth shut about the affair. Bridget let the idea sit in her mind for a moment. It cast Steve in a whole other light—an adulterer, yes, but also a victim trapped by his own misdeeds in a duplicitous web.

After one final peek through the window, Bridget ducked her head down and sped back down the street to the strip mall where she'd parked her car. She wasn't going to find out anything more by hanging around outside the coffee shop. One thing she knew now for sure, her husband was inextricably caught up in Jen Carson's murder to some degree or another.

9

*A*fter a restless night spent mulling over the possibility that Steve was being blackmailed and worrying that she might have completely misunderstood everything and thrown him to the wolves by calling the tip line, Bridget got up early and brewed herself a strong coffee. She downed the first cup in a few hasty gulps, made a second cup, and then resolutely donned an apron. She'd forced Steve to take the holiday off work to be with the family, so the least she could do was make them breakfast.

With a dogged resolve, she scrambled some eggs and spinach, fried a pound of bacon, made some banana pancakes, and then piled everything into the warming drawer until Steve and the kids showed up in the kitchen, rested and hungry. While she waited, Bridget pulled out her phone and sat down at the island to peruse her news Apps, but her thoughts soon drifted back to the enigmatic nightmare she was embroiled in.

Harper was the first to appear, rubbing her eyes sleepily as she climbed up on a chair at the kitchen table in fluffy kitten pajamas.

Bridget hugged her daughter, and then busied herself making her a plate.

Harper clapped her hands in delight when she saw the pancakes on her plate. "It looks yummy. Thank you for breakfast, Mommy."

Bridget's heart melted. Harper was such a breath of fresh air, always grateful for the smallest gesture of kindness. She reminded Bridget of how Steve had been when they were first married. Over the years, the responsibilities of his job and the long hours had taken their toll on his capacity to appreciate what he had. He seemed too distracted most of the time to notice what she did, even when she went the extra mile. She missed his tender affirmations. But, to be fair, she'd stopped making much of an effort herself.

"You're very welcome, munchkin," Bridget said, as she spooned out a small plate of scrambled eggs and added a pancake and a slice of bacon for herself. She poured Harper a glass of orange juice and set it down on the table. "Did you sleep good?"

Harper chewed on a mouthful of egg, tilting her head to one side as she considered the question. "Well, not really, 'cause Henry woke me up. Can I have some ketchup, please?"

Bridget reached for the bottle of ketchup and squirted a blob on Harper's plate. "Why did Henry wake you up?"

"He was being so loud on his phone."

Bridget furrowed her brow. It sounded as though Henry had been playing online video games during the night again. He wasn't supposed to be on the computer between eleven and seven. She and Steve had a rule that the kids' doors had to stay open at night so they could check on them on their way to bed. Obviously, Henry was getting around their computer curfew. The truth was, he could be playing all night every night if he wanted to and they'd be none the wiser. The master bedroom suite was at the other end of the house to the kids' rooms. At one point, Steve had put some kind of parental control on the computer, but Henry had probably figured out how to get around it.

Bridget tried to keep the frustration out of her voice when she responded to her daughter. "I'll have a word with Henry about it. He knows he's not supposed to be playing video games at night."

Harper slurped her orange juice and licked her upper lip. She set the glass back down carefully. "He wasn't playing games. He was talking to Quinn, and he was *so* mad at him."

Bridget interlaced her fingers around her coffee mug as she regarded her daughter. "What makes you think he was mad at Quinn?"

Harper jutted out her bottom lip. "He was yelling."

"Do you know what he was yelling about?"

Harper picked up her bacon strip and took a bite, then wiped her fingers on her pajama top.

"Honey, don't do that!" Bridget chided, handing her a napkin.

Harper took it and scrubbed it across her lips before setting it down next to her plate. "Henry said, *you don't know it was my dad. Maybe it was your dad.*" She pushed her plate aside and blinked innocently at Bridget. "Samantha in my class says her daddy is the best. But everybody's daddy is the best, isn't that right?"

Bridget traced a fingertip across her brow and nodded distractedly. "Yes, that's true. Everybody has the best daddy for them. Why don't you wash up and get dressed now so we can go visit Grandma at the hospital."

Bridget got up from the table and went to wake Henry. He was curled up beneath his New York Giants duvet, snoring softly, his clothes fanned out on the floor at the foot of his bed. Bridget eyed his phone on the bedside table. She hesitated for a moment before reaching for it and typing in his password. Thankfully, that was another of her and Steve's household rules. They had unlimited access to their kids' passwords to all their electronic devices and social media accounts. She glanced at Henry's phone record. Sure enough, he'd talked to Quinn for over seven minutes at two-forty in the morning.

She set the phone back down and shook Henry awake. "It's almost ten o'clock. Time to get up. We're going to swing by the hospital to visit Grandma this morning."

Henry groaned. "Do I have to go?"

"Yes! We barely got to see her yesterday. It's the least you can do after everything Grandma does for you. I made bacon, eggs and pancakes for breakfast. They're in the warming drawer. Don't go back to sleep."

She exited his room and made her way to the master bedroom.

Steve had just got out of the shower and was digging around for some clothes in the dresser drawers. "Something smells good," he said cheerily, as he pulled a T-shirt over his head.

"Breakfast's in the warming drawer," Bridget muttered, before slipping into the bathroom and closing the door behind her. She couldn't bring herself to look her husband in the face. Whatever he'd done, or not done, he'd been lying to her for the past two days. It was anyone's guess how long he'd been lying to her before that.

When they arrived at the hospital an hour later, Elise was sitting up in bed, chatting and laughing with the nurse on duty.

"Hi, Grandma," Harper said, laying her head down on the bed next to her.

Elise smoothed her granddaughter's hair back from her forehead. "It's so good to see you, my little ray of sunshine."

The nurse turned to Bridget. "Your mother's making excellent progress."

"Not giving you any trouble, is she?" Bridget teased.

"Not in the least. She keeps us all entertained." The nurse chuckled and squeaked off down the corridor in her rubber-soled shoes.

"You're looking good, Elise," Steve said, patting her arm as he sat down in a chair next to the bed.

"I feel good. It must be all those drugs." She squinted up at Henry. "I can't believe they dragged you along with them again today. Don't you have better things to do on the weekend than visit me in the hospital?"

He shuffled his feet awkwardly. "It's okay. I'm glad you're feeling better, Grandma."

Elise pinned a penetrating gaze on Bridget. "You look pale, dear. Are you all right?"

Bridget gave a nonchalant shrug. "I'm fine. Where's Dad?"

"His arthritis is acting up this morning. He'll be in later."

The trill of Steve's phone cut through the sterile space.

"Sorry about that," he said, fumbling to put it on silent. He stared down at the screen, frowning. "Actually, I'd better answer this."

He stood abruptly and went outside the room to take the call. When he came back in, he had a grim expression on his face. "Jack Carson's had a stroke. Keith's here at the hospital with him. He wants to know if we can take Quinn for a bit."

"Of course." Bridget glanced across at Henry for approval, caught off guard to see a scowl flicker across his face. She frowned, wondering again what he and Quinn had been arguing about the other night.

"I'm going to head over to the surgery ICU and pick Quinn up," Steve said, shrugging out of his jacket. "Keith's got his hands full with everything that's going on." He slung his jacket over the back of the chair. "It's about a hundred degrees in here. How can you stand it, Elise?"

"I'm not complaining," she replied. "You know me, I'm always cold."

Steve wiped the back of his hand over his brow in an exaggerated fashion, as he exited the room.

Bridget chatted with her mom for a few more minutes until a second nurse popped her head in. "Can I ask you folks to step out while I give Elise a shot. It won't take long. And the doctor wants to take a quick peek at her incision. If everything looks good, she'll be able to go home tomorrow."

"Sure, no problem." Bridget grabbed Steve's jacket and got to her feet.

"There's a waiting room down the hallway to the left," the nurse added. "I'll let you know when the doctor's finished in here."

Bridget led the kids to the waiting room and sank down in a wingback chair near the door.

"Mommy, I'm hungry," Harper whined.

Bridget widened her eyes. "Already? We just ate."

"Two hours ago," Henry corrected her.

With a bemused shake of her head, Bridget fished a twenty-dollar bill out of her purse and handed it to him. "Go find yourselves a snack. You can head down to the café on the ground floor if you want or look for a vending machine somewhere. Don't be long, and whatever you do, stick together."

"Thanks, Mommy!" Harper chirped, skipping out the door after her brother.

Bridget released a heavy breath and leaned back in the chair. Something dug into the small of her back and she shifted forward again. Dragging Steve's coat out from under her, she felt the rectangular shape of his phone in one of the pockets. Her pulse ratcheted up a notch. With only the tiniest flicker of hesitation, she pulled out the phone and punched in his passcode. If she could find out why Keith and Steve had met at the coffee shop yesterday, she might be able to get to the truth of what had happened to Jen.

First, she scrolled through Steve's contacts. There was nothing listed under Carson, or Jen, or Keith. Next, she opened up Steve's emails and began browsing through them. Her chest tightened until she could scarcely breathe. There it was—an irrefutable testament to her husband's betrayal—a long thread between Steve and carsonj27@gmail.com dating back several months.

*W*ith trembling fingers, Bridget opened up the email thread and began reading the most recent communication Jen had sent to Steve.

Keith definitely suspects something. We need to move quickly. Can you get those assets transferred to my name?

"Look what I got, Mommy!" Harper squealed, bursting back into the waiting room holding aloft a bag of Cheetos and a bottle of Sprite.

Bridget bit back her irritation at being interrupted right on the cusp of deep diving into whatever it was that had been going on between her husband and Jen Carson. She hurriedly stuffed Steve's phone back into his jacket pocket, and eyed the offending items Harper was gleefully displaying, grimacing inwardly at the sight. Henry knew his sister wasn't ordinarily permitted to snack on such poor nutritional choices, but it was her own fault—she'd sent them to look for a hospital vending machine, after all. "You're one very lucky ducky it was Henry who took you and not me because I'd never have let you buy that junk," she said in a tone of mock disapproval.

Harper nodded, a broad smile breaking out across her face at the realization she was going to be allowed to keep the forbidden snacks.

A moment later, the door opened again, and Steve walked in, Quinn trailing behind him. "Ah, here you all are," Steve said. "The nurse told me to let you know the doctor's finished so we can go back in now."

Quaking on the inside, Bridget hurried over to give Quinn a hug. "I'm so sorry about your mom, and your grandpa."

When she released him, he stuffed his hands into his pockets and pressed his lips together, striking an oddly indifferent pose. "Thanks."

"Let's go say goodbye to Grandma, and then we'll get you kids home," Steve said, reaching for his jacket.

Bridget averted her gaze. She didn't need to read any more of the emails to know what she was dealing with. Jen and Steve had been carrying on an affair right under her nose. It sounded like Steve might even have been planning to leave her. Had he been helping Jen move assets around—preparing to set up a new life with her? Bridget's heart began to pound with fear at the implications. What if he'd hidden their money and left her penniless? He was the one with the head for numbers, and she'd always trusted him implicitly with their finances. A stupid mistake that might cost her dearly now that it seemed their marriage was on the verge of collapse.

WHEN THEY PULLED up outside their house, Bridget's heart lurched at the sight of a squad car parked at the curb. It was already happening. The City Crime Line had wasted no time relaying the tip she'd given them. Two men climbed out and strode toward them. The plainclothes officer nodded a greeting. "Mr. and Mrs. Hartman, I wonder if we might have a word with you."

Steve frowned. "What's this about?"

The officer directed a meaningful look at the kids. "It might be better if we spoke inside."

Henry and Quinn exchanged a wary look. Once again, Bridget had an inkling there was something amiss between them, but she couldn't figure out what it was.

"Uh, sure," Steve said, leading the way to the front door.

Harper slipped her hand into Bridget's and tugged on it urgently. "Why are the policemen here?"

"I'm not sure, honey. But it's nothing for you to worry about. Why don't you go to your room and play with your Barbies for a bit?"

Steve led the detectives into the family room while Bridget shooed the kids down the hallway to their bedrooms. "Don't come out until we come get you," she warned them.

She joined the men in the family room and sat down on the other end of the couch from Steve. She kept her eyes averted, not wanting to catch her husband's gaze. She was half-afraid Steve would be able to pick up from the guilt in her face that she was the reason the police were here. She couldn't help wondering if the officers could tell from their body language that something was awry between her and Steve. Why else would a husband and wife not sit together hand-in-hand to hear why two police officers had shown up unexpectedly at their house?

"I'm Detective Wright," the older man began. He gestured to his companion. "This is Officer Lopez."

Bridget nodded in the direction of the young, muscular officer with the square jaw and almond-colored eyes. She squirmed under his scrutiny, even though he proffered her a warm smile. She could feel the weight of guilt grow heavier in the room, and she suspected her face was not masking her emotions well.

"What can we help you with?" Steve asked in a brisk, businesslike tone.

Bridget seethed inwardly at his insolence. He must have some inkling why they were here. Surely, they could see straight through him. She wet her lips nervously as she ran through her options. This was her chance to get everything out on the table and tell the police about the body she'd seen in the trunk of Steve's car. But that would open up a whole other can of worms that might implicate her for concealing evidence, or worse—the police might suspect her of being involved in Jen's murder. Better to wait and let the police get to the bottom of things on their own.

"I understand you were working late last Friday night, Mr. Hartman," the detective said.

"Please, call me Steve, and yes, I work late most nights."

"We received an anonymous tip that a woman who looked like Jen Carson was spotted leaving your office building. Did you happen to see her?" The detective sat back with an expectant expression on his face. He had the air of a seasoned veteran, comfortable waiting as long as it took for the truth to bubble to the surface.

Steve blinked several times, the color draining from his face. Clearly, he hadn't expected this. Bridget could sense he was scrambling to find a way out and coming up short. Any lies he told now would only affirm his guilt. After a long, uncomfortable silence, Steve cleared his throat. "As a matter of fact, she stopped by my office briefly."

Detective Wright drew his brows together, giving a slight nod, as though approving of Steve's decision to come clean. He pulled out a note pad and pen from his pocket and flipped it open. "What time was this at?"

Bridget stared at the carpet in front of her feet. *Six-forty-*

five. She'd been there too. Of course, she had no intention of sharing that information with the police.

Steve folded his arms and frowned. "I couldn't say for sure. Somewhere around seven. I worked for another couple of hours after she left."

Detective Wright looked across at Officer Lopez as if to make sure he was tracking, and then turned his attention back to Steve. "What was the nature of her visit?"

Bridget squeezed her hands together in her lap, feeling the sting of tears in her eyes. One email had told her all she needed to know about the nature of Jen Carson's visit with her husband.

Steve rubbed a hand over his jaw. "She … wanted some advice."

Officer Lopez leaned forward and smiled, dimpling his fresh-faced cheeks. "What kind of advice are we talking about?"

Steve threw him an irritated look, before making a point of addressing Detective Wright. "She needed some financial advice. I'm an accountant."

Detective Wright jotted something down in his notebook. "And why did she come to you for this advice?"

Bridget gritted her teeth. *Why indeed, Steve? Let's hear you explain that one away.*

Her husband's forehead was beginning to glisten with a sheen of sweat. "I knew her from way back in high school. She put in a good word for me when I applied for this job— she knew Ken Bartlett who founded the company. It turned out well for me, I worked my way up to partner. Naturally, I felt I owed her a favor. I told her if she ever needed any financial advice to come to me."

"And so she did," Detective Wright said in a contemplative tone. He tapped his fingers on his knee for a moment and cast a curious glance at Bridget as if assessing how much of

N. L. HINKENS

this was news to her. "Was your relationship strictly business?"

Steve rubbed the back of his neck. "Yes, of course. What are you implying?"

The detective leaned back and raised his palms in a placating manner. "I'm only here to gather the facts, Steve."

"And I'm giving them to you. Like I told you, I was returning a favor by helping her out with some financial stuff."

Detective Wright flipped over a page in his notebook. "Can you be a little more specific about the type of financial advice she was looking for?"

"Why's it important?" Steve retorted, the expression on his face darkening.

"In light of the fact that she was murdered later on that evening, it could turn out to be very important."

Steve gave a resigned sigh. "She was worried her husband was moving assets around and trying to hide money from her. They weren't getting along particularly well."

"Yes, her husband mentioned she was having an affair." Detective Wright pinned his gaze on Steve, the disarming smile on his lips at odds with the steely glint in his eyes. "Did you know about that?"

Steve shook his head in a bewildered manner. "No. She told me Keith was having an affair."

"Did you believe her?"

Steve shrugged. "I didn't know her well enough to say either way. Or Keith either, for that matter. At any rate, it was irrelevant to the advice she needed."

"That's debatable. Were you aware that Jen brought nothing of monetary value into the marriage? The assets she was trying to protect weren't hers to begin with."

Steve narrowed his eyes. "None of which has any bearing on the advice I gave her. I wasn't suggesting she do anything illegal. She just wanted to make sure Keith didn't leave her penniless in the event they divorced."

Detective Wright gave a thoughtful nod. "I see." He snapped his notebook shut, before getting to his feet. "Thank you for your time, Steve. That's all the questions we have for now. You've been very helpful."

He pulled a business card out of the sleeve on his notebook and held it out to Bridget. His eyes bored unsettlingly into hers. "Please don't hesitate to call me if you think of anything else at all that might assist us in our investigation."

*A*s soon as the officers left, Steve announced that he had to go to the office, purportedly to catch up on the work he hadn't managed to complete on Sunday. Bridget wasn't fooled. She'd been married to him long enough to know that he'd been badly shaken up by the cops' visit. No doubt, he needed space to clear his head and finesse his story going forward.

Bridget shivered and hugged her arms tightly to her body, Detective Wright's words lingering in the air.

Please don't hesitate to call me if you think of anything else at all that might assist us in our investigation.

Of course, she had something that could assist them. Something that would immediately trigger a full-scale investigation into her husband, not to mention generate a warrant to search their house and even seize their property—the Mercedes at a minimum, possibly their computers and phones. Child Protective Services might even come for their children if they were both detained. Did Detective Wright know she was the person who'd called in the anonymous tip, or was she just being paranoid about the pointed look he'd given her as he'd handed over his card? Was she over-analyzing his parting words, or had he wanted to let her know that he knew she was hiding something?

She needed to calm down and think rationally. The Crime Line employee had assured her repeatedly that she would remain anonymous—there was no way for anyone to track her down. Detective Wright had simply been going through the motions. *Don't hesitate to call* was nothing more than police jargon, the same generic remarks they made to everyone when they handed over a business card. But Bridget wasn't going to give the police anything else—not when she was no longer sure of Steve's role in all of this.

If Keith had blackmailed him into disposing of Jen's body, then her husband was every bit the victim Jen had been—at least concerning the murder. The affair was another matter altogether. She couldn't risk muddying the waters any more than she already had. She'd wait until the cops unraveled the tangled case on their own steam and got to the truth of what had happened.

Glancing at her phone, she let out a groan when she noticed how late it was. She hadn't defrosted anything for dinner—not that she was in the mood to cook anyway. Maybe she could run into town and pick up something instead. She made her way down the hallway to ask the boys what they wanted, slowing her pace when she detected raised voices coming from inside Henry's room.

"How would I know why the cops are here?" Quinn snapped, a defensive edge to his voice. "Do you really think I'm dumb enough to tell them your dad was doing my mom?"

"I dunno. Maybe you felt sorry for your dad now that your grandpa's sick and all."

"Don't be stupid. What difference does that make?"

"You tell me," Henry growled back.

"I swear to you it wasn't me who called the tip line."

"Whatever," Henry retorted. "Let's play Fortnite."

Bridget drew a shallow breath through her nostrils and let it out again slowly. Keith must have told his son the police had received an anonymous tip. And of course, Henry would suspect Quinn was behind it. After all, it sounded as if the boys knew all about Jen's and Steve's affair. Had they found out about it from Keith? Bridget rubbed her brow. It made no sense that Keith had asked the man who'd been sleeping with his wife to look after his son. It seemed to fit with her new theory that Keith had killed his wife and blackmailed Steve into getting rid of the body. Maybe he was counting on Steve being beholden to him for every little thing from now on.

Bridget took another quick breath before opening Henry's door and peeking in. "What do you boys want for dinner? I'm going to run into town and pick up something."

"Pizza, Hawaiian," Henry called out from under his desk where he was busy plugging in a slew of wires.

Bridget moaned in protest. "We had pizza last night."

"Panda Express, then."

"Is that all right with you, Quinn?" Bridget asked.

"Yup, great, thanks."

She hesitated, her hand resting on the door handle. "Have you heard anything more from your dad about how your grandpa's doing?"

Quinn shook his head. "Dad said he'd pick me up when he was done at the hospital."

"Okay, keep me posted. You're welcome to spend the night. Henry, keep an eye on Harper for me. I'll be back shortly."

She was getting into her car when she heard a vehicle pull up alongside the curb. Turning to look over her shoulder, she spotted Keith Carson climbing out and waving to her.

"How's your dad doing?" she forced herself to ask as he

approached. All the while her stomach twisted as she wrestled with the grisly supposition that had been preying on her mind. Had Keith Carson murdered his wife?

Keith grinned. "You can ask him yourself." He gestured to his car. "They discharged him already. I'm driving him home. Turns out it wasn't a stroke at all, just low blood sugar. The knucklehead forgot to eat."

Bridget walked over to the car and leaned down to the passenger window. "Hi, Jack. Glad to hear you're feeling better. You gave everyone a scare."

He eyed her with a circumspect look and waved a meaty hand dismissively. "Yeah, the doc tells me it was low blood sugar."

Bridget stretched a sympathetic smile across her face. "Well, it's easy to forget to eat when you're under stress. I'm … sorry for your loss."

"Thank you." Jack pressed his lips tightly together, his face a mask of suppressed emotion.

Bridget moved away, loathe to upset him any further. He didn't look like the type of man who enjoyed displaying his emotions, especially to a virtual stranger. She wondered what he would think if he could read the suspicions in her mind about his son. Maybe he had his own suspicions, and the stress of it all had caused him to pass out.

"Quinn's inside," she said, turning back to Keith. "The boys are playing video games. I was just going into town to pick up some dinner. You're welcome to join us if you want."

"Thanks, but I should be getting home. Dad's worn out. And there's—" He broke off and whooshed out a breath. "As you can imagine, there's a lot to take care of. So many loose ends. And with the police breathing down my neck, interrogating me every step of the way, it's been hard to find the time or the motivation to tackle anything."

"Of course," Bridget replied, the words sticking in her

throat. Doubt stirred inside her once again as she saw the emotion in his face. Maybe it was wishful thinking on her part suspecting him of being his wife's killer. What if it really was Steve? She had the power to give Keith some closure, to let him know that she'd seen his wife's body in the trunk of her husband's car. Was it unconscionable of her to try and protect her own interests by continuing to conceal evidence, to wait until the police figured things out for themselves?

But she had her two children to think of. If she and Steve were both arrested, Henry and Harper would essentially be orphaned, something she was not willing to let happen. Her parents were too elderly to care for their grandchildren properly, and Steve's parents had passed away years ago. Whatever the cost to the Carson family, she would keep her mouth shut about finding the body in the trunk of her husband's Mercedes. Ultimately, Steve would pay the price for whatever he'd done, but she wasn't going to suffer for his crime along with him.

TUESDAY FLEW by in a blur as Bridget helped her parents get settled back into their house. She made a trip to the store and brought back a cart full of groceries to restock the refrigerator and pantry, and then cooked up a pot of chicken noodle soup and prepared a lasagna. While her mom napped, she and her dad went through the house together, moving hazards such as fringed rugs and unnecessary decorative furniture in an effort to enable her mom to more easily navigate from the bedroom to the family room on her new walker. They installed an elevated toilet seat in her bathroom and replaced the bathroom mat with a rubber-backed version to make sure she didn't slip.

"It still looks dark in here to me," Bridget remarked dubiously, after she'd replaced a couple of burned out lightbulbs.

"You might want to get another lamp or two, Dad. Mom's eyesight isn't the best."

"I have some extras stashed in the garage," he said. "Your mom decided she didn't like the ones in the guest bedroom anymore so she made me haul them out of the house. But, of course, I wasn't allowed to dispose of them, if you can believe that."

Bridget chuckled. "Don't worry about it now. Mom will probably sleep most of the day. You'll have plenty of time to look for them later on when I'm gone. Speaking of which, whatever you do, don't try and bathe her if I'm not here. With your arthritis, you won't be able to catch her if she slips. I've taken the week off work so I can help out with everything."

By the time Bridget left her parents' house later on that afternoon, she was physically and emotionally spent. She could use a nap herself, but the kids would be home from school by now and Harper would need help with her homework. Besides, she needed to make more of an effort to supervise Henry's computer time and make sure he was working on his school assignments and not just goofing off.

Her heart jolted when she rounded the corner into her street and saw a squad car parked outside her house yet again. Dread circled in her stomach like a gathering storm. She hoped the police hadn't knocked on the door with the kids home alone. Considering the fact that Henry wouldn't hear a thing with his headphones on, Harper might have answered the door, only to find a uniformed officer and a detective staring down at her.

Bridget swerved into the driveway and yanked on the handbrake, trying to settle her jangling nerves before she clambered out. She wondered how much progress the police had made in the investigation overnight. Had they found evidence of Steve's and Jen's affair? If they were here to confront him about it, then he was definitely a suspect.

"I'm afraid my husband's at work," Bridget said stiffly, as she approached the front door where Detective Wright and Officer Lopez had positioned themselves, waiting patiently for her.

"Actually, it's you we'd like to speak with, if you have a few minutes," Detective Wright replied in a disarming manner.

Bridget's stomach churned with apprehension as she opened the door and led them into the family room. This couldn't be about the anonymous tip. Were they going to ask her if she'd known about the affair? Did they suspect her of covering up for something Steve had done?

"Go ahead and make yourselves comfortable," she said, flinching at the wobble in her voice. "I'll let the kids know I'm back."

Truth be told, she needed a few minutes to collect herself. She was running on adrenaline at this point after only picking at her food for days. She stuck her head briefly into the kids' rooms and let them know she was home, before making her way to the master bathroom. After splashing some cold water on her face, she smoothed down her hair and appraised her reflection. A nerve twitched in her face, betraying the terror writhing around inside her. Maybe she should have told the police she wanted a lawyer present. Too late now. She wished Steve was here. It was all his fault to begin with, why should she have to handle this on her own? Bridget leaned on the sink and let out a beleaguered sigh. There was nothing else for it but to head back out and face the music.

Seated in an armchair in the family room, she arranged a neutral expression on her face, tilting it expectantly toward the officers. "What can I help you with?"

"As you know," Detective Wright began, "we had an anonymous tip that Jen Carson was seen exiting your husband's office building on Friday evening."

Bridget gave an indifferent shrug. "He's already explained to you that Jen met with him to get some financial advice."

"Right." The detective nodded thoughtfully, rubbing a hand over his jaw. "The thing is, we've been reviewing some CCTV footage outside the building and it appears that your car was parked on the other side of the street when Jen Carson exited the building."

*B*ridget swallowed the uncomfortable knot that had formed in her throat. Officer Lopez was staring intently at her, the disarming smile that usually rested on his lips at odds with the quizzical gleam in his eyes. Her hands shifted restlessly in her lap as her brain raced ahead, trying to guess where Detective Wright was going with this. Was he hinting that he knew it was her who'd called in the anonymous tip? Or was it more insidious—was he implying that she had something to do with Jen Carson's death?

She startled at the sound of the front door opening. Seconds later, Steve burst into the family room, a thunderous look on his face. "What's going on here?" His eyes darted between the officers and Bridget.

She blinked up at her husband, disconcerted by his opportune arrival. How did he know the police were back? Had they called him? Her head began to throb at a terrifying thought. Maybe they were going to arrest her, and they'd asked Steve to come home to be with the kids.

"Why don't you take a seat please, Steve," Detective Wright said in a placating tone. "I'll explain everything."

Steve clenched and unclenched his fists, before complying and sinking down in the chair next to Bridget. As if reading the question in her eyes, he leaned over and murmured in her ear. "Henry texted me about the police car parked outside. I didn't realize you were home."

"I just got here," Bridget mumbled in return.

Turning his attention back to the officers, Steve said through gritted teeth, "I would have preferred if you'd stopped by my office and talked to me directly with any follow up questions, instead of traumatizing my family like this."

A flicker of pity zipped across Detective Wright's face. "As a matter of fact, Steve, it was your wife we wanted to talk to. We reviewed some CCTV footage outside Bartlett and Hartman to determine what time Jen Carson exited the building on Friday." He paused, a taut expression on his face. "In the process, we discovered that your wife's car was parked on the road opposite your office at the exact time Jen Carson left."

Steve blinked, his brow rumpling as he digested the information. He swiveled his head and threw a disbelieving look at Bridget, before turning back to the detective. "I … don't understand."

Detective Wright rubbed his chin thoughtfully. "That's why we're here. To try and understand exactly what your wife was doing outside your office on Friday night." He raised his brows expectantly at Bridget.

The room spun slowly around her. She couldn't help noticing that Officer Lopez's permanent smile had slipped, replaced by a leaden look. Kind of like how she felt inside. Detective Wright had begun picking at the threads of the case and everything was beginning to unravel, only now she was implicated in it. "I … I did stop by the office briefly," she stammered. "I brought my husband some dinner. I took off again a few minutes after Jen Carson drove out of the parking lot."

Steve stared at her with a look of utter bewilderment. His lips parted, but he closed them again, as if deciding against mentioning the fact that she hadn't actually delivered a meal to him.

The door to the family room opened and Harper peeked in before darting across the room to Bridget. "My tummy hurts," she whispered in her ear.

Bridget picked her up and cuddled her in her lap, burying her face in her daughter's hair to buy herself a moment or two to compose herself. "Mommy will just be a few more minutes, and then I'll get you something for your tummy."

Harper snuggled into her chest, and promptly closed her eyes.

Officer Wright cleared his throat. "Do you remember what time you dropped dinner off with your husband?"

Bridget averted her eyes. "I … realized when I pulled up at the office that I'd left the plate of food in the kitchen."

A wide-eyed Harper wriggled upright in her lap. "No you didn't, Mommy! I saw you carrying it."

Bridget's cheeks flushed. "Yes, well, what I meant to say is that I thought I'd forgotten it, and in my confusion I drove all the way home before I remembered that I'd put it in the trunk of the car." She kept her eyes fixed on Detective Wright, only too aware of Steve's indignant gaze boring into her. She could sense the gears in his brain whirring as he put two and two together. She'd been parked outside his office on Friday evening. She'd seen Jen Carson exit the building. Someone had called in an anonymous tip to the Crime Line. It didn't take a genius to figure out who it was.

Harper squirmed down from her lap. "I'm going to play in my room."

Bridget brushed a strand of hair out of her daughter's face. "Are you feeling better now?"

Harper gave a breezy nod and bounded out the door.

Detective Wright leaned forward in his chair, a troubled look on his face. "Bridget, you said you drove off a few minutes after Jen Carson exited the company parking lot. You didn't happen to see which direction she drove in, did you?"

Bridget swallowed down her mounting trepidation. Surely, they didn't imagine for one minute that she'd stalked Jen and killed her in a fit of rage over her dalliance with Steve. "If you're asking me if I followed her, I didn't."

Detective Wright raised his brows. "Did you have any reason to follow her?"

"What's that supposed to mean?" Steve cut in.

"I'd prefer if you let your wife answer the question," Detective Wright replied, his tone unruffled but unwavering.

Bridget wet her lips. "I admit, it threw me off at first, seeing a woman exit the building. I knew Steve was working late alone. I ... wasn't sure what to make of it at first. But I didn't follow her. I went straight home." She hesitated before adding in a remonstrative tone. "I'm sure you've already deduced as much from the CCTV footage."

Detective Wright didn't react to her cloaked reproach. Instead, he flicked through his notepad, as if to recap what he'd gathered so far. "I'm sure you can understand our position. This is a murder investigation, and you two were the last people to see Jen Carson alive, as far as we know—"

"You mean other than her killer," Steve interrupted angrily.

Detective Wright dipped his head in acknowledgment.

"Like I said, you were the last ones to see her alive, as far as we know. Naturally, that raises some questions."

"I didn't lay a hand on her," Steve said. "I told you she wanted some financial advice. And that's what I gave her. Are you really suggesting that my wife followed her and killed her?"

The detective scratched his temple. "Do you think that's a possibility, Steve? Would she have any reason to?"

A deep flush crept up Steve's neck. He stood and gestured to the door. "I'd like you to leave now. We've been as helpful as we can possibly be, and I don't like your insinuations."

Detective Wright tilted his chin in Officer Lopez's direction and got to his feet. "We appreciate your cooperation."

"No, I don't think you do," Steve shot back. "If you've anything more to say to either me or my wife, you can inform our lawyer."

Detective Wright betrayed no surprise at the acrimonious turn in the conversation. "If you feel you need to retain a lawyer, you're certainly well within your rights." He nodded to Bridget. "We'll see ourselves out."

As soon as the front door closed behind them, Steve wheeled and glared at Bridget. "Do you want to tell me what's going on? Have you been spying on me?"

Bridget gulped, contemplating her answer. *Yes, and I know you met with Keith Carson after Jen was killed.* "What do you mean? Of course not! I made you dinner and I was going to drop it off at the office. I wanted to do something nice for you, like the old days, remember those?"

"You wanted to do something *nice*? Is that what you call tipping off the police to the fact that Jen was at my office on Friday night?" Steve's lip curled in disgust. "Don't even bother denying it. I know it was you who called the Crime Line."

Bridget's voice broke as salty tears pricked her eyes. Her

mind flashed back to the email thread between Steve and Jen. "What was I supposed to think when I saw that woman leaving your office? You've been working late for months on end. You rarely spend any time with the kids or me anymore. You've been obsessing over something. Why wouldn't I think you were having an affair when all the signs pointed to it?"

"I can't believe you're accusing me of cheating. I've never been unfaithful to you," Steve said, sounding deflated all of a sudden. The emotion seemed to have drained from him, leaving only sadness in its wake. "I know things haven't been great between us lately. Work's been extremely stressful. We're short staffed, not to mention the fact that we're getting into tax season again. The company's numbers don't look good. We may even have to lay some people off. So yes, I'm worried and distracted—worried and distracted about how I'm going to take care of my family."

Bridget rubbed her hands over her face. A momentary wave of guilt washed over her. He sounded so genuine. Could there be another explanation for all of this, something she was missing? Maybe Steve had borrowed money from Keith, and then Keith had blackmailed him into getting rid of Jen's body.

"I'm sorry," Bridget answered wearily. "It's just that we don't talk anymore, and I didn't know what was going on at work. If you'd just opened up to me, I wouldn't have suspected you of having an affair. But, when you were obviously hiding something from me, I just …" She shrugged, helplessly. "Naturally, I thought the worst when I saw Jen leaving your office."

Steve nodded, his expression softening. He stepped toward her and folded her in his arms. "It's my own fault. I should have told you what was going on with the company. I was trying to protect you. I didn't want you worrying about it, but all I've done is made you worry about far worse things

N. L. HINKENS

than losing my job. I love you, Bridget. I would never intentionally do anything to hurt you. You do believe that, don't you? I need you to believe me. We have to support each other from now on, we need to have each other's backs. The police are sniffing around looking for someone to pin this murder on. If we're not on the same page, it makes us look suspicious."

Bridget's thoughts flashed to finding the body in the trunk of Steve's Mercedes. He still wasn't coming clean with everything. If he hadn't killed Jen, why had he agreed to get rid of the body? And why had he secretly met with Keith at The Muddy Cup? She had to keep him talking now that he was finally opening up to her. At all costs, she had to get to the truth. "Do you think there's any chance Keith could have murdered his wife?" she whispered, not wanting Harper to inadvertently overhear her if she made another unexpected appearance.

Steve sighed and rubbed a hand over his scalp. "I can't say I haven't asked myself the same question, but it's hard to believe he would kill his own son's mother."

"Did Jen ever mention that she was afraid of him?" Bridget asked.

"Not to me. She was more worried about him trying to hide the company's assets prior to their divorce. It was his money after all—well, his dad's to begin with. His dad founded the company, but Keith has taken it to new heights since—tripled its value."

"So Jen married into money," Bridget said softly

The furrow between Steve's eyes deepened. "I suppose that does give Keith a motive. Jen was attempting to secure half their assets—enough to bring the company to its knees."

13

*T*he following day passed in a dizzying haze as Bridget divvied up her time between making sure her parents had everything they needed to aid her mom's recovery and trying to keep her own family life operating as normally as possible under the circumstances. In between school runs, she spent several hours helping her mom get dressed and ready for the day, and then picking up groceries and prescriptions, as well as preparing lunch and something for their evening meal.

Keith was back at the police station being interviewed again, with no end in sight to the interrogations, and he'd asked if Quinn could come home with Henry after school and stay with them for the next few days. "I hate to put you out," he explained to Bridget over the phone, "But my father's still recovering from his little episode, and he's not up to driving."

"It's no trouble at all," Bridget assured him, fighting to keep the quiver out of her voice. She told herself she was doing it for Quinn's sake. Her feelings toward Keith Carson fluctuated wildly between pity and suspicion, guilt and revulsion. Some part of her desperately wanted to believe that he had killed Jen, only because it was immeasurably preferable to the alternative—that her husband was a cold-blooded murderer.

For once, Steve made it home in time for dinner. They were all seated around the table finishing up the pot roast and mashed potatoes Bridget had fixed, when the doorbell rang. Steve pushed his chair out from the table and stood. "I'll get it."

"Way to get out of the dishes, Dad," Henry sneered.

"It's hardly child slave labor to ask you to rinse and load a few dishes now and then," Bridget scolded, as she got to her feet and began to clear the table. "I bet you have chores to do at your house, don't you, Quinn?"

He shrugged, looking sheepish.

"No, he doesn't," Henry scoffed. "They have a house-keeper who comes every morning. Maria does everything. Quinn doesn't even take out the trash."

"Do too," Quinn protested, his cheeks reddening as he lifted his plate and carried it over to the sink.

Henry snorted and started stacking up dishes. Harper grabbed an armful of condiments and carefully carried them over to the refrigerator. Bridget wiped down the table, contemplating the ongoing air of hostility between the boys. She wished Henry would be a little more empathetic given the fact that his friend had just lost his mother.

A moment later, Steve reappeared in the kitchen doorway and motioned urgently to Bridget. She made her way over to him, an uneasy feeling stirring in the pit of her stomach.

"Who's at the door?" she whispered.

"It's Detective Wright and Officer Lopez." Steve gestured to the family room. "They want to talk to us again."

Bridget pressed a hand to her cheek. "What about the lawyer?"

"I've put in a call." Steve grimaced. "He hasn't responded yet. We might as well hear them out. We don't have to say anything."

A cold shiver ran across Bridget's shoulders. The food she'd eaten lay heavy in her gut. She tried to reassure herself that this was merely another routine visit, but she couldn't quell the nagging possibility that the police had found some new incriminating evidence. She threw a glance over her shoulder to make sure the kids were still busy cleaning the kitchen. "Don't forget to sweep the floor, Harper," she called to her, before following Steve down the hallway to the family room.

Detective Wright and Officer Lopez got to their feet and nodded in greeting when she entered the room.

"Sorry to disturb your dinner," Detective Wright began.

"We were just finishing up," Bridget replied, refraining from returning the smile gracing Officer Lopez's lips.

"I assume there's been a development," Steve said stiffly.

Officer Lopez cleared his throat. "We've recovered some more CCTV footage."

"That sounds promising." Steve raised his brows and waited for him to continue. Instead, Officer Lopez turned to Detective Wright. "Do you want to show them what we've got?"

The detective pulled out an iPad and slid his finger across the screen before balancing it on the coffee table between Steve and Bridget.

At first the image was so murky that Bridget couldn't make out anything, but once her eyes adjusted, she realized she was looking at a dumpster. Her heart flinched beneath her ribs. The time stamp indicated that it was recording at

2:37 am on Saturday morning. It must be the dumpster where Jen's body had been discovered. She pressed her fingertips to her lips, not wanting to watch what she feared was coming next, but unable to tear her eyes away from the grainy footage.

For several minutes, nothing happened, and then, all of a sudden, a Mercedes pulled up next to the dumpster. The driver's door opened and a tall, dark male figure wearing a balaclava stepped out. He threw a furtive glance up and down the street and then hurried around to the back of the vehicle and reached into the trunk. Bridget watched in horror as the man trudged toward the dumpster with what appeared to be a body wrapped in a blanket slung over one shoulder. He maneuvered the lifeless body over the side of the dumpster and shoved it in. Stepping back, he rubbed his hands on his pant legs as if in some misdirected attempt to erase the evidence of his crime.

After a moment's hesitation, he peered inside the dumpster, and then reached in and moved something around, presumably in an attempt to cover up the body. When he was satisfied with the job he'd done, he closed up the trunk of the Mercedes and drove off.

The screen turned black, and Bridget swallowed down the fear rising up her throat. It was impossible from the shadowy footage to read the license plate number on the vehicle, but it was likely the police were already working on ways to enhance it. Time seemed to stand still as she waited for someone in the room to break the grip of terror that had rendered her speechless.

Detective Wright picked up the iPad and switched it off. Bridget remained frozen in place, staring mutely down at the carpet as she went over the footage in her mind again. Had she really just watched her husband callously toss Jen Carson's body into a dumpster? The figure had moved with agility, a youngish man, and around Steve's height. A tiny sob slipped through her lips. Slowly, she turned her head to look at her husband. He was white as a sheet, a dumbfounded expression on his face as he addressed the officers. "Why are you showing us this?"

Bridget shivered at the hard edge her husband's voice had taken on. Was it the voice of a killer, who'd lurked beneath the surface all this time?

"Steve," the detective said in an overly patient tone. "You were one of the last people to talk to Jen Carson before she died. You also happen to drive a Mercedes. Is there anything you want to tell us?"

A ruddy flush crept up Steve's neck. "I didn't kill her! That's not my Mercedes. It was parked here in my driveway last Friday night. My wife can attest to the fact that I was asleep in bed all night. Are you actually going to try and pin this murder on me?" He gritted his teeth. "I've nothing more to say to you without my lawyer present."

The detective pursed his lips. "We just want to get to the truth. It's my job to interview everyone who had contact with Jen Carson the night she died and follow the evidence wherever it leads. And so far, the needle's pointing in your direction."

"Actually, Steve," Officer Lopez piped up. "What we'd really like to do is clear your name. Would you have any objections if we impounded your car?"

Steve shot him a look of disgust and threw up his hands. "What am I supposed to say to that without sounding guilty? I've got nothing to hide, but it'll be a complete waste of your time, not to mention awfully inconvenient for me."

"I can appreciate that," Detective Wright was quick to reply. "But Officer Lopez is right. It's important that we eliminate you as quickly as possible so we can concentrate on finding Jen's killer. I'm sure you want that as much as we do."

Steve rubbed his jaw, a thunderous expression on his face. "Do what you have to do. She was my son's friend's mother— of course I want her killer locked up. How long is this going to take?"

"A week or two at most." Detective Wright got to his feet. "We'll notify you as soon as your vehicle has been released." Without a moment's delay, he pulled out his walkie-talkie and began issuing instructions to dispatch, along with the address of where to pick the vehicle up.

"Can I get anything out of my car, my charging cord, sunglasses?" Steve asked.

"I'm afraid not," Officer Lopez said, his smile firmly fixed in place once again.

"We'll wait in the squad car," Detective Wright said with a final nod to Bridget.

After the officers took their leave, Bridget stared woodenly across the room at her husband, wondering how he could possibly have found it in himself to cold-heartedly toss Jen Carson's body in a dumpster. It must have been him— same height, same vehicle. It couldn't be a coincidence. The police certainly didn't think so. Had he killed her too? She shivered as she pictured Steve with his hands around Jen's neck, the same hands that had so lovingly cradled their children at birth.

"I'll check on the kids," Steve said abruptly, and stomped off to the kitchen before Bridget had a chance to say anything.

Fifteen minutes later, a tow truck pulled up outside the house. Bridget watched through the window as the stocky, bald driver exchanged a few words with Officer Lopez before proceeding to winch Steve's Mercedes onto the back of his truck.

When the detectives finally drove off with the tow truck tailing them, Bridget sank back in her armchair and scrunched her eyes shut. It wouldn't take forensics long to confirm that Jen Carson had been in the trunk of Steve's car. After that, they would come for him, handcuff him, and drag him off like the criminal he was. Because however deeply he was involved in this sordid plot, he was involved—that much she was certain of. Her life, and the lives of her children, would never be the same again. She'd started the wheels of this investigation turning by placing that anonymous call to the City Crime Line. But she didn't regret it. She couldn't envision living with a murderer, or even a man who'd been an accessory to murder, for the rest of her life. She couldn't continue to break bread with someone who'd discarded another human being like a piece of trash in a dumpster. Justice had to be served. Steve must pay for what he'd done.

Bridget grimaced when she pictured Quinn's reaction to the news. He would turn against Henry entirely—hate him for it. Her children would be ostracized in the community. But losing their childhood friends would be the least of their worries. They were about to lose their father—the man who'd patched up their skinned knees, taken them for ice cream sundae breakfasts, challenged them to water hose fights, and chased monsters out from under their beds. They would be both gutted and humiliated. They might have to move out of the area entirely. People did terrible things to the families of murderers; they could become scapegoats for all sorts of rage and violence bubbling just below the thin veneer of social civility.

She startled out of her depressing thoughts when Steve came back into the room and sat down opposite her. "That wasn't me in the video. You do believe me, don't you? I wasn't having an affair with Jen Carson. Someone's setting me up. I need you to have my back."

"Of course," Bridget said, dropping her gaze under his intense stare.

Her words sounded hollow even to herself, and for good reason. She knew Steve was lying. She'd seen Jen's lifeless body in the trunk of his car before he'd dumped it.

*T*he following day, Bridget's worst fears were realized when Steve was arrested and read his rights. She swept a trembling hand over her forehead as she stood helplessly by, watching the arresting officer escort her husband out of their house to the waiting squad car. Forensics had made swift work of determining that Jen Carson's body had been in the trunk of Steve's Mercedes. It remained to be seen if they would formally charge him or question him and release him. Steve's lawyer had assured them the evidence was flimsy at best, consisting of nothing more than a single hair in the trunk of his Mercedes.

A hair I could easily have removed.

Bridget pressed her lips tightly together, fighting the waves of remorse that intermittently washed over her. Would she live to rue her decision?

She leaned against the front doorframe, one arm wrapped protectively around Harper who'd buried her head in the folds of her skirt. Henry and Quinn hovered uneasily in the background, observing the squad car as it pulled away with Steve staring dejectedly out the window at them.

"Okay, everybody inside," Bridget ordered, eying the smattering of neighbors who had gathered on their porches to gawk. Word had spread quickly through the neighborhood that Steve's Mercedes had been impounded. No doubt his arrest would unleash an even bigger storm of speculation about his involvement in Jen Carson's death.

The kids sat back down at the kitchen table and retrieved their abandoned mugs of after-dinner hot chocolate.

"Mine's cold, Mommy," Harper whined.

"Shut up, Harps," Henry growled. "Nobody cares about your stupid hot chocolate. Dad's been arrested, don't you get it?"

Harper's face crumpled and tears began to trickle down her cheeks. "Why did they take Daddy away?"

Bridget reached out and patted her hand. "We'll find out soon enough. Don't worry, Mommy will sort this out."

She glanced across at Quinn who was frowning at his phone. "I expect your dad will pick you up later on this evening," Bridget ventured. "I'm sure the police will let him go now that they've made an arrest."

Quinn and Henry exchanged a tense look. The knot in Bridget's stomach tightened. Whatever had been putting a strain on the boys' relationship before Steve's arrest this was only going to become worse now. How was Quinn supposed to feel toward a friend whose dad had killed his mother?

She got to her feet with a weary sigh. "Okay Harper Hartman, it's way past your bedtime." She took her daughter by the hand and led her to her room, tucking her into bed without even bothering to make her clean her teeth. Somehow it seemed like a trivial endeavor in light of the fact that, after tonight, Harper would quite possibly be growing up without a father. On that somber note, Bridget closed her daughter's bedroom door and made her way back down the hallway. She came to a sudden halt outside the kitchen door at the sound of Quinn and Henry arguing again.

"I told you my dad didn't do it," Quinn hissed.

"You heard what he said," Henry countered.

"He didn't mean it."

"Well it wasn't my dad, either," Henry spat back. "The cops don't know squat."

"They wouldn't have arrested him if they didn't have any evidence," Quinn said. "The man who killed my mom was driving a Mercedes. And they impounded your dad's car. What does that tell you? Face it, Henry, your old man's a killer!"

"Get out of my house, punk!" Henry yelled back.

Bridget heard a scuffle and then the sound of a chair crashing to the floor. Sprinting into the kitchen, she grabbed hold of her son's arm. "Henry! Leave him alone!"

With a final shove, he released Quinn and glowered at him, his chest heaving.

"I think it's best if I take you home now, Quinn," Bridget said. "Why don't you call your dad and let him know. He's probably already on his way back."

With a wary scowl in Henry's direction, Quinn pulled out his phone and tapped out a text. He stared at the screen for a minute and then read out his dad's response. "On my way home. Maria's there."

Bridget locked eyes with her son. "I'm taking Quinn home. Go to your room. And no computer."

For a tense moment, he stood glued to the spot, towering over her, before abruptly turning on his heel and disappearing out of the kitchen.

Bridget grabbed her keys and purse. "Let's get you back to your dad, Quinn. It's been a long day." She took a quick peek into Harper's room to make sure she was asleep, and then headed out to the car.

As they drove, Bridget toyed with the idea of digging for more information on what the boys had been arguing about. "You understand why Steve's been arrested, don't you, Quinn?"

He scratched the back of his hand nervously. "Yeah, I knew it was either him or my dad who killed Mom."

"Let's not get ahead of ourselves. There's no evidence that either of them killed her. It's all … circumstantial."

"I know what I saw," Quinn muttered.

Bridget threw him an alarmed glance. "What do you mean?"

"Dad told me weeks ago that Mom was having an affair, so I started following her." He turned away and stared out the side window. "She went to your husband's office, a bunch of times."

Bridget gripped the steering wheel tighter. "Your mother needed some financial advice. Steve was helping her out."

"That's not what my dad said. He told me they were trying to steal the company out from under him. They were gonna run away together." He let out a shuddering sigh. "I'm not sorry she's dead. She didn't care about me."

Bridget took a shaky breath. "I'm sure that's not true, Quinn. Your parents may not have been getting along, but your mother loved you very much."

"Not if she was planning on running off with your husband." He threw her a sheepish glance as they pulled up outside his house. "I'm sorry you're stuck in the middle of this, Mrs. Hartman. You've always been kind to me."

Bridget smiled back at him, her eyes brimming with salty tears as she switched off the engine. "This must be difficult for you and Henry to navigate, but you're always welcome at our house. Henry's just stressed right now about his dad being arrested."

"Thanks, Mrs. Hartman," Quinn said as he opened the car door.

"I think I'll just have a quick word with Maria before I leave," Bridget said, climbing out of the car after him. "I want to explain what happened."

Quinn shrugged. "If you want."

She followed him up to the front door and waited while he rummaged around in his pocket looking in vain for his key. "Shoot, hold on a minute." He walked over to a nearby planter and tilted it to one side, retrieving a spare key from beneath it.

"Maria!" he called out, as he opened the door and led the way to the kitchen. "Someone's here to see you."

"I'm in the laundry room," a throaty, female voice called back.

Quinn steered Bridget through the kitchen and down a step into a spacious and airy laundry room with a small office at one end. He introduced her to Maria, the house-keeper, before retreating to his room.

"I just wanted to explain what happened and why I had to bring Quinn back home all of a sudden," Bridget said wringing her hands. "I'm sure you've heard already that my husband's been arrested."

Maria listened attentively while continuing to fold linens in breathtakingly deft and expert maneuvers. "Yes, Keith called me a few minutes ago." She stopped folding for a moment and fastened a perceptive gaze on Bridget. "Do you really think your husband did it?"

Bridget spread her hands in a gesture of helplessness. "I don't … I don't know what to think. I didn't even know he was having an affair with Jen to begin—"

Maria let out a snort. "If your husband was having an affair, I can tell you it wasn't with Jen Carson."

Bridget's mouth dropped open. "What do you mean?"

Maria placed a hand on her ample hip. "I've worked for the Carsons for over fifteen years. Jen confided in me. Keith was unfaithful to her several times, but his latest affair was the proverbial straw that broke the camel's back. She'd made up her mind to leave him, and she told him so a couple of weeks ago. As she'd predicted, he was beside himself with rage. He threatened to kill her, and not for the first time." She leaned against the dryer and lowered her voice a tad. "Jen told me she thought Keith was having her followed."

Bridget blinked uncertainly at her. She wasn't about to throw Quinn under the bus and tell Maria he'd been following his mother. "Did you inform the police about the threats?"

Maria reached for a towel and folded the corners together with impeccable precision in a single flick of her wrist. "I did, but Quinn told them it was his mother who was having the affair and threatened his dad. Keith turned that boy against his mother a long time ago." She shook her head sadly. "Quinn was furious with her."

Bridget digested the news in silence for a moment or two. Keith had been the obvious suspect from the start. The spouse always was. But it didn't change what she'd seen—what Maria didn't know—that Jen Carson's body had been in the trunk of Steve's car. He'd sworn he hadn't had anything to do with her murder. He'd even suggested someone might be setting him up, but that was a stretch. Isn't that what guilty people always said? They tried to blame everyone else around them. Keith might very well have hated his wife, and couples on the verge of divorce were often angry at each other. Empty threats were commonplace, but they didn't usually end in murder. Bridget's thoughts tumbled around in an endless loop of confusion, as she considered first Steve, and then Keith, as Jen's potential murderer.

"Why are you telling me this, Maria?" she asked, in a hoarse whisper.

The housekeeper's face softened. "One child has already lost a parent. I would hate for your children to lose a parent too, for no good reason. I don't know if your husband's guilty or innocent, Mrs. Hartman, but I do know that Keith Carson swore he'd kill his wife if she ever tried to leave him."

15

---

*B*ridget twisted the ends of her hair nervously as she contemplated Maria's words. More than anything, she wanted to believe her husband was innocent of this horrific crime, that he hadn't strangled a young woman with his bare hands like the monsters featured on Dateline or Unsolved Mysteries. But, despite the animosity Maria had observed between Keith and his wife, the only evidence so far pointed in Steve's direction, as Detective Wright had noted.

Bridget wondered what else the housekeeper might have overheard that could prove useful. "Maria, did you ever hear Quinn and Henry arguing about what happened? It's just that I've caught them fighting about it a couple of times now, and I'm curious how much they knew about what was going on."

Maria pursed her lips. "Can't say I did, but once when Jack, Quinn's Grandpa, came to pick him up, I overheard Quinn telling him that his mom was cheating on his dad, and how much he hated her. He was extremely angry, kicking the furniture and everything. His grandfather had his hands full trying to calm him down. It's a crying shame. Like I said before, I blame Quinn's dad for turning him against Jen." She glanced up at the clock on the wall above the washing machine and let out a gasp. "I need to get going. I'm babysitting my granddaughter tonight and I can't be late. It's my son's anniversary."

She threw Bridget an apologetic look as she escorted her to the front door. "I don't mean to appear rude by kicking you out. And thanks for taking such good care of Quinn. He's very fond of your family."

Bridget waved goodbye and walked down the pathway to her car, mulling over everything she'd learned from Maria. It seemed Quinn had been living in an unhappy household, one in which none of the adults in his life paid him much attention at all, with the exception perhaps of his grandfather.

But nothing Maria had said threw much light on whether or not Jen and Steve had actually been having an affair. Maria didn't seem to think that was the case, but it was possible Jen had finally had her fill of her unfaithful husband's liaisons and decided it was her turn to have a fling on the side. And who better to have it with than an old friend from high school?

Despite what Quinn had told her, Bridget found it hard to believe that Steve had actually been planning on running away with Jen. He was far too responsible to bail out on his business after becoming a partner and investing so many years into building it up. And, even though he rarely had much time to spend with his kids, she knew he loved them too much to give up on them. Bridget choked back a sob. According to him, he loved her too much to give up on her too. But could she trust him?

When she pulled into her driveway a short time later, she sat in the car for a moment or two wiping away the tears dangling from her eyelashes. She still hadn't heard anything from Steve since his arrest that morning. She only hoped the lawyer he'd engaged was down at the station working on his case. Maybe he would even manage to get him bailed out tonight. Bridget had no idea how these things worked. She'd never had any dealings with the criminal process before—she'd never even gotten a speeding ticket.

Steeling herself, she climbed out of her car and made her way back inside the house. To her relief, Harper was still sleeping soundly, her chestnut waves fanned out around her flushed forehead. Bridget tucked the blankets in and smoothed a hand over her daughter's forehead before closing the door gently behind her and going to check on Henry. She found him lounging on his bed scrolling through his phone. Bridget cast a quick glance at the computer screen on his desk, gratified to see that it was dark, and then sat down on the edge of the bed next to him. "Did you get all your homework finished?"

Henry gave a disgruntled nod.

"What are you doing now?"

"Nothing."

Bridget sighed. "I know you're worried about Dad—"

"Too late for that," he snapped back.

"What do you mean?"

Henry glared at her. "He's guilty, Mom! He killed her!"

"Honey, we don't know that—"

"*I* do!" he yelled, tossing his phone aside and jumping up. "I know he did it!"

Bridget's heart jolted in her chest at the flash of anger in his eyes. "What do you mean? How can you possibly know that?"

He screwed up his lips and turned away. "Never mind. Forget I said anything."

Bridget placed a concerned hand on his arm. "Henry, if there's something you know, you need to tell me."

He kept his gaze averted. "Dad cheated on you, Mom. And I hate him for it. That's all you need to know."

"Don't say that. You know you don't mean it. Whatever he's done, your father still loves you very much." She hesitated, before adding, "And me."

Henry snorted. "Yeah, right. That's why he was helping Jen steal the company's money and running away with her."

Bridget furrowed her brow. "I don't know where you heard that, but it's not true. Dad was only advising Jen on her financial options if she went through with the divorce."

"That's not what Quinn's dad said."

Bridget grimaced. "Keith was upset that Steve was helping Jen sort out her finances."

"You just can't accept it, can you?" Henry scowled and reached for his phone. "I'm going to bed."

Bridget got to her feet resignedly. "We'll talk about this in the morning when tempers aren't so frayed. Goodnight, son."

She closed the door quietly behind her and padded past Harper's room back down the hall to the kitchen. After pouring herself a glass of water, she sat down at the table and opened up her laptop. The police had confiscated Steve's desktop computer, laptop, and phone when they'd arrested him, but she could still access his Dropbox folder online. She needed to try and find out exactly what he'd been helping Jen with, and whether or not there was any truth to the rumor that they'd been planning to run off together.

She pulled up the Dropbox URL, typed in Steve's login information, and began scanning the long list of files looking for anything that wasn't business related. Clicking on a folder marked *personal,* she held her breath as it opened up to reveal several subfolders. She skipped over the folders labelled *photos*, *miscellaneous* and *kids*, hesitating at the one titled *insurance*. Why was Steve storing insurance information in a personal file on his Dropbox? She moved her mouse over the icon, but to her frustration the folder was password-protected.

Chewing on her lip, she tried a couple of combinations they commonly used, but to no avail. Next, she typed in all of their birthdays. As a last resort, she keyed in their wedding date. Her jaw dropped when the folder popped open. Bridget stared transfixed at the screen, her eyes scouring the documents contained in the folder. They were listed by date, so she began with the earliest one.

SENDER: K_Carson@CarsonConsulting

Don't involve yourself in this. I know Jen has been to see you so don't even bother denying it. I'm sure your wife would be very interested to know what's been going on between you and Jen. I'm warning you now to stay out of my business.

SENDER: SteveHartman@BarlettandHartman

Nothing's going on between Jen and me as you well know. And I'm not involving myself in your business. I'm simply advising Jen as a friend on her options.

SENDER: K_Carson@CarsonConsulting

I could make things extremely uncomfortable for you. I'm not going to warn you again.

SENDER: SteveHartman@BarlettandHartman

Are you threatening me? Because if that's what this is, I won't hesitate to go to the police. Jen said you threatened to kill her. You can hardly blame her for filing for divorce after everything you've done.

.   .   .

SENDER: K_Carson@CarsonConsulting

Jen's been moving assets around. There's a large chunk of company money missing. She couldn't have pulled this off without help. Maybe you actually think you can have it all, my company and my wife. I won't hesitate to take you down if I find out you're behind this.

SENDER: SteveHartman@BarlettandHartman

You're completely paranoid. I'm not interested in your company, or your wife.

SENDER: K_Carson@CarsonConsulting

You have a very unhealthy interest in my money and my wife. I know all about it. You'll live to regret it.

SENDER: SteveHartman@BarlettandHartman

What did you do to Jen? Where is she?

SENDER: K_Carson@CarsonConsulting

We need to talk things over. Meet me at The Muddy Cup on Main Street and Fifth tomorrow. I'll text you a time.

BRIDGET SANK BACK in her chair, her brain whirring to make sense of the series of emails between Steve and Keith. *The Muddy Cup.* That was the day she'd followed Steve. Had he done something illegal? Had he helped Jen steal money from her husband's company? It was hard to believe he would risk his own company's reputation by falsifying another company's accounting records and hiding assets. One thing was for sure, she'd been right to suspect that Keith was threatening Steve. There was no telling how far he'd pushed him. Especially if Steve had accused him of harming Jen.

Bridget closed up her laptop and began pacing, going over in her mind everything she'd learned. At least Steve had had the sense to keep a copy of the incriminating emails—*his insurance folder*. He might need that to prove that someone other than himself had a motive to kill Jen. Surely Steve must have told his lawyer by now about the existence of the emails. In and of themselves, they wouldn't amount to enough evidence to convict Keith of murder, but it would be enough to induce the police to take a closer look at him as a suspect.

Bridget glanced at the clock on the wall. Why hadn't Steve or his lawyer contacted her yet to let her know what was happening? She reached into the sink for a sponge and began wiping down the counters in an effort to keep calm. When she was done, she retrieved a broom from the mudroom. She was sweeping the crumbs and Cheerios into a dustpan when a tiny clinking sound caught her attention.

Kneeling down, she spotted something gleaming up at her through the debris. *Quinn's house key!* He must have dropped it when he was helping clean up the kitchen the other day. Her fingers closed over it. Maria, the Carsons' housekeeper, only worked in the mornings. Bridget sucked on her bottom lip, toying with a risky idea. She could stop by the house when Keith was at work and Quinn was at school and do a little investigating of her own. Her heart raced as the brazen notion took root. Maybe she'd find the evidence she needed to prove her husband's innocence and expose the true killer.

16

*B*ridget was dropping off groceries at her parents' house the next day when Steve finally called. With trembling fingers, she pressed the phone to her ear, steeling herself for whatever he was about to hit her with.

"Hey, it's me," he said, an anguished crack in his voice.

"Are they letting you go?" Bridget asked breathlessly.

"My lawyer's working on it. The cops can't keep me here much longer. They haven't charged me with anything, yet."

Bridget chewed on her fingernail, debating whether or not to tell him she'd found the emails between him and Keith in his Dropbox folder. They didn't prove either man's guilt or innocence. Maybe she should wait and see what Steve had to say for himself first. "Do the police have any other suspects?"

"I don't know." He let out an aggrieved breath. "They're not telling me anything. But I know who killed her."

Bridget dropped her voice to a confiding whisper, not wanting her parents to overhear the conversation. "Who?"

"Keith, of course. He'd threatened to do it before. Jen told me it was only a matter of time before he took her out. She was afraid for her life; she'd made arrangements to leave town."

Bridget fell quiet for a moment, wondering if Steve had secretly been planning on leaving with Jen. Of course, he'd hardly admit that to her. And she had no way of proving it— unlike his meeting with Keith which she'd witnessed first-hand. It was time she got some answers on what was going on between the two men. "Why did you meet Keith Carson at that coffee shop the other day?"

There was a charged silence on the other end of the line for a long moment, and then Steve asked. "How did you know about that?"

"I followed you. I knew you were lying to me about where you were going. What business did you have with Keith Carson?"

Steve exhaled loudly. "It's not what you think. Jen didn't like the financial advice I gave her. She hired some shady accounting firm to move some assets offshore. Keith found out about it and thought I was behind it. He wanted his company's money back. I told him I didn't know where it was, but he didn't believe me."

"Did he threaten you, or blackmail you at all? Steve, if you did something, even if you just helped to cover up—"

"I swear to you, I had nothing to do with Jen's murder! Look, I've got to go. My lawyer's signaling to me. I was just calling to warn you that Detective Wright's coming by the house again later on this afternoon. He wants to talk to Henry. If I'm not back by then, you need to sit in on the interview."

Bridget frowned. "Why does he want to interview Henry?"

"Apparently, the Carsons' housekeeper told Detective Wright that Quinn and Henry overheard a heated argument between Jen and Keith. The housekeeper claims Keith was threatening Jen, but Quinn says it was the other way around. The police want to hear Henry's side of the story."

Bridget grimaced. She wasn't keen on the idea of dragging Henry into the situation, but what choice did she have? "All right, I'll make sure he's home. He has practice later on this afternoon, so the cops will have to come right after school if they want to talk to him."

Steve hung up and Bridget slipped her phone back into her purse.

"Everything all right?" her dad inquired, joining her in the kitchen where she was staring into space.

She rubbed her fingertips slowly across her forehead. "I hope so. The police want to interview Henry about an argument he overheard between Jen and Keith."

"I'm sure it's nothing to worry about," her dad soothed. "It might even help Steve's case."

"I just hope Henry agrees to cooperate. He's convinced his father and Jen were having an affair." Her lip trembled. "And he really believes Steve killed her."

"Oh, honey, I'm so sorry." Bridget's dad pulled her into a hug and squeezed her tightly before releasing her. "You should go on home and take care of your family. I'll make your mom a bite to eat. Let me know how the interview goes."

"Thanks, Dad." Bridget slung her purse over her shoulder and headed out to her car, queasy at the thought of her four-teen-year-old son being interviewed by the police. She wondered briefly if she needed to retain a lawyer for him too. She hadn't thought to ask Steve about it. But, if Detective Wright only wanted to ask about an argument Henry had overheard, he'd hardly need counsel for that. If the cops pressed him to make a statement, or appear in court as a witness, she would revisit the issue.

At three o'clock, she picked the kids up from school.

Henry was his usual prickly self, while Harper chatted away merrily, almost as though she'd forgotten that her father had been handcuffed and taken away by police the previous day.

"Mommy, look what I drew!" she said, pulling a colorful butterfly out of her backpack.

Bridget stole a glance over her shoulder. "That's beautiful, honey. Did you have a good day at school?"

Harper let out a petulant sigh. "Well, it wasn't very good because Ainsleigh and Samantha said Daddy was a bad guy."

Bridget tensed. So it had already begun. She'd expected her children to become targets, sooner or later, but it still cut to the bone to hear the cruel barbs Harper's classmates were throwing at her. "Well, that's not very nice of them."

"It's true though," Henry chimed in.

"No, it's not!" Harper said, sounding indignant.

Bridget shot her son a warning glance. "That's enough, Henry."

He shrugged and turned to stare out the window.

When they reached the house, Bridget made Harper a snack and then sent her to her room to play.

"I need to talk to you, Henry," Bridget said, sitting down at the kitchen table next to him where he was methodically working his way through a plate of microwaved cheesy nachos.

"Yeah, what?"

"Detective Wright's going to stop by later on this afternoon. He wants to ask you a few questions."

Henry stopped chewing and threw her an alarmed look. "What about?"

"I think he wants to ask you about an argument you overheard at Quinn's house—between his parents."

Henry narrowed his brows. "I don't want to talk about it."

Bridget pinned a gaze of pained exasperation on him. "It's important, Henry. And it could help your dad."

He seemed to consider this for a minute. "You mean the cops think Keith might have killed her?"

Bridget nodded. "He's still a suspect. Maria heard him threatening Jen on more than one occasion."

Henry answered with a careless shrug. "They were always arguing. Doesn't mean anything."

The doorbell rang and they locked eyes for a fleeting moment.

"That's probably Detective Wright," Bridget said. "Just be civil. I'll stay in the room with you, And remember, you don't have to answer anything that makes you uncomfortable."

She opened the door to see Detective Wright and Officer Lopez standing on the front step.

"Is your son home?" Detective Wright inquired, slipping off his sunglasses. "We'd like to ask him a few questions about an incident he may have witnessed at the Carsons' house."

"Come in," Bridget replied stiffly.

She led them through to the kitchen where they both shook hands with Henry, before seating themselves at the table. Detective Wright pulled out a notebook and smiled genially at Henry. "I understand you're good friends with Quinn Carson."

Henry shot a wary look at Officer Lopez before responding. "Used to be."

Detective Wright raised a sharp brow. "I can appreciate that this situation must be very difficult for you both."

Ignoring the comment entirely, Henry jerked his knee up and down, waiting on the detective to continue.

"Did you ever hear Quinn's parents arguing?" Detective Wright asked.

Henry frowned. "Yeah, I guess. I mean, they were always arguing."

"What did they argue about?"

"Money and stuff."

Detective Wright tilted his head questioningly, like a predator sniffing the air for a hint of blood. "Stuff?"

Henry's cheeks reddened. "Who was cheating on who, that kind of thing."

"Did you ever hear Keith Carson threaten his wife?"

"He said he'd kill her if she tried to leave him."

Detective Wright jotted something down on his pad. "I talked to Quinn earlier. He mentioned that you two followed his mother to your father's office."

Bridget sucked in an icy breath. It was news to her that Henry had accompanied Quinn.

Henry squirmed uncomfortably in his seat. "It was Quinn's idea. His dad told him his mom was having an affair. Quinn wanted to know who the guy was."

Detective Wright nodded thoughtfully. "I assume you were both pretty shocked when you found out that Mrs. Carson was visiting your dad?"

Henry shifted his jaw side-to-side. His eyes flipped to Officer Lopez and then to Bridget. She smiled reassuringly at him.

"Yeah, I guess," Henry conceded, a note of repressed anger in his voice.

Bridget squeezed her eyes shut, trapping the tears that suddenly sprang up. How could Steve ever make it up to Henry? Their son was angry, frustrated, and embarrassed. Every teenage boy wants to look up his father, not hang his head in shame each time his name's mentioned. Even if Steve hadn't killed Jen, he had done irreparable damage to his family by having an affair with her.

Detective Wright scratched the side of his nose before continuing. "Henry, do you think your dad killed Jen Carson?"

Bridget let out a gasp. "You can't ask him something like that about his father. Not without a lawyer present."

Henry folded his arms in front of his chest defiantly. "I *know* he killed her."

A gleam of curiosity came into Detective Wright's eyes. "That's a pretty strong statement. Do you have any evidence to support your claim?"

Henry curled his lip. "None that I can give you."

Officer Lopez cleared his throat. "Son, you do understand that you can be prosecuted if you knowingly withhold evidence."

An uncertain look flickered across Henry's face.

"Just tell them what you know," Bridget pleaded. "You won't be in any trouble if you speak up now."

Henry brushed his knuckles across his lips nervously. "I … saw her body."

Bridget's eyes widened. She squeezed her hands together in her lap, her horrified gaze riveted on her son. What did he mean? Had he seen Jen after she'd been killed? Is that what he and Quinn had been whispering about all this time? Why had Henry not mentioned it before now?

Detective Wright and Officer Lopez exchanged a loaded look. The detective placed his hands on his thighs and leaned forward. "Where did you see her body, son?"

Henry's eyes flitted restlessly around the faces in the room. He was clearly agitated, jerking his knee up and down in place again. Bridget was torn between wanting to say something to reassure him and wanting him to hurry up and tell them the truth.

Henry opened and closed his mouth before finally choking the words out. "In the … trunk of my dad's Mercedes."

Bridget clapped her hands to her mouth, staring in horror at Henry. She wasn't the only one who'd seen Jen in the trunk of her husband's car that day. She couldn't begin to imagine how horrific a discovery that must have been for Henry. And to think he'd kept it to himself all this time.

Detective Wright scribbled furiously on his notepad. "When was this? It's very important you tell us exactly when you saw the body, Henry."

He wiped a sheen of sweat from his upper lip, unable to meet the detective's gaze. "Last Friday night."

"Why didn't you tell us about this before?" Officer Lopez asked.

Henry furrowed his brow, fidgeting with his sleeve.

Detective Wright painted a sympathetic smile on his face. "It's okay, I get it if you were trying to protect your dad."

Henry sniffed. Bridget could tell he was on the verge of tears. She really should put an end to this interview before he broke down. He was traumatized enough as it was. But she had a feeling he had more to say, and she desperately needed to hear what it was. Had he told Quinn about his discovery?

"I was only trying to help," he muttered.

"What do you mean you were only trying to help?" Detective Wright prodded. "What did you do, Henry?"

He shook his head and wiped the back of his hand across his eyes. His shoulders shook uncontrollably.

Bridget's chest tightened. A foreboding feeling crept over her skin. A part of her wanted to reach out and comfort her child, but another part of her was too numb to react.

After a moment, Detective Wright leaned back in his chair and gave a subtle nod to Officer Lopez. He excused himself and left the room. A few minutes later, he returned with an iPad. Bridget watched with mounting trepidation as he set it up on the coffee table in front of Henry and hit play. She stared at the screen, panic rising up her throat when she realized it was the footage of Jen's body being thrown into the dumpster.

"No!" she cried out. "You can't show that to him. He's only a child."

Detective Wright turned to Henry. "I think you've already seen it, haven't you, son? That's you, tossing Jen Carson's body into the dumpster, isn't it?"

*H*enry's eyes darted frantically to Bridget and back to Detective Wright. "What? No! That isn't me!"

Willing herself into action, Bridget dashed over to her son and wrapped her arms protectively around him. "It's all right, Henry, calm down." She turned and cut a glare in Detective Wright's direction. "How dare you come in here and accuse my son like that! You're frightening him!"

The detective's gaze lingered on Henry. "What did you do when you discovered Mrs. Carson's body?"

Henry wet his lips. "Nothing. I was too scared."

"Did you tell anybody what you'd found, Quinn perhaps?"

Henry shrank back, a look of horror on his face. "No, of course not."

The detective tapped a finger on his chin. "Didn't you think it was important to tell someone that there was a dead body in the trunk of your dad's car?"

Henry's lips parted but he said nothing as the color slowly drained from his face.

Bridget stood, shooting daggers at Detective Wright. "I think you'd better leave now. You came here under false pretenses. You've shown my son traumatizing footage and falsely accused him of participating in a horrendous crime, all without a lawyer present."

"I asked him a reasonable question considering the fact that he's admitted to finding Jen Carson's body in his dad's Mercedes," Detective Wright replied, unfazed.

Bridget gripped Henry more tightly. "Well you heard his answer, it wasn't him. This interview's over."

Officer Lopez reached for the iPad and got to his feet. Detective Wright nodded in Bridget's direction. "Thanks for letting us speak with Henry. We'll be in touch."

As soon as the officers had driven off, Bridget spun around to face Henry. "What in the world were you thinking, keeping that from me?"

"I didn't want to say anything. I didn't want Dad to get in trouble."

"Well you've only made matters worse, Henry. Now you're under a cloud of suspicion too."

"His eyes welled up with tears. "I'm sorry, Mom. I should have told you. I didn't want you to find out about the affair, or any of it. I knew it would kill you. I was afraid you'd divorce Dad."

Bridget swallowed back the retort on the tip of her tongue, moved by the emotion in her son's voice. Henry had meant well in trying to shield her from heartbreak. But she'd found out anyway, and it had been the kind of seismic shock you hoped you'd never have to endure in your lifetime. Bridget twisted her fingers together nervously. The only thing worse would be to find out that her son had disposed of Jen's body. Henry claimed it wasn't him in the video, but Bridget had her doubts.

The figure, easily over six-foot, had moved with the agility of a young man. She loosed a rough breath as she replayed the image of the figure trudging toward the dumpster with Jen's body wrapped in a blanket slung over one shoulder. If she had to lay a wager on it, she'd say the figure moved more like her son than her husband—and a mother knew those kinds of things. But for now, she would keep her mouth shut. If Steve had killed Jen, he could go down for disposing of her body as well, as far as Bridget was concerned. In the meantime, she had to hold her family together and carry on as best she could.

"It's almost time to leave for volleyball practice," she said, glancing at her phone. "Go get your gear together and fetch your sister."

"Do I have to go—"

"Yes!" Bridget snapped. "We still have our lives to live."

Henry gawked at her for a moment, before getting to his feet and striding out of the room.

Bridget dropped her head into her hands, her shoulders shaking with barely repressed emotion. Who was she kidding? Their lives as they'd known them were over. It didn't make any difference if Henry showed up for volleyball practice or not. He wouldn't be playing with the team in a few short weeks from now, or ever again for that matter. If Steve was charged with murder, Henry wouldn't be welcome on the team, and none of them would be welcome in the neighborhood. But for now, Bridget had to put on a brave front for the kids' sake and keep powering ahead. Maybe, just maybe, by some miracle, this would all be resolved, and Steve would come home tonight a free man, with his name cleared.

When they pulled up outside the school a short time later, Henry grabbed his sports bag and exited the car without a word.

"Don't forget it's Mrs. Dennison's turn to bring you home," Bridget called after him, but he'd already bolted out of earshot.

A couple of moms, chatting outside their cars, turned

their heads in her direction and immediately turned away again. Bridget felt a flush rise up her neck. No doubt, they'd heard the rumors. She was as good as exiled. In fact, she was surprised the coach hadn't called her this afternoon to ask her not to bring Henry tonight. Sooner or later, one of the moms was bound to call and complain that her child was being forced to play on a team with a murderer's son.

Bridget rammed the shifter into drive and peeled out of the parking lot without a backward glance.

"You're driving too fast, Mommy," Harper chided.

"Mommy's in a hurry," Bridget replied tersely.

"Why? Is Daddy coming home?"

Bridget's stomach knotted. "I'm not sure, honey. But if he is, we want to be ready for him, don't we?"

"Yup, we do. That's why I'm going to draw him a picture."

"I'm sure he'll love that. What are you going to draw for him?"

"Me, and you, and Henry, so he doesn't forget about us anymore."

Bridget's eyes blurred with tears. If only it were that simple. If only she could be sure that Steve hadn't been sleeping with Jen Carson. Maybe then she could dare to believe that he hadn't murdered her, or even helped cover up her murder. But, as it stood, she didn't know what to believe. Steve had been involved with both the Carsons on one level or another. The email evidence was all there.

Back at the house, Bridget sent Harper to tidy up her toys while she emptied out the dishwasher and reloaded it. After she'd finished cleaning up the kitchen, she unloaded the dryer and folded the kids' clothes, her thoughts circling back to the footage of the unidentified male tossing Jen's body into a dumpster. Much as she hated the thought of it being Steve, it terrified her to think that it might be Henry.

Her stomach churned with misgivings as she carried a big

pile of Henry's jeans and T-shirts into his room and started putting them away in the dresser. If she left them for him to handle, they'd still be sitting here a month from now. Glancing around the space, it occurred to her that this might be an opportune time to take a quick look around and make sure there was nothing incriminating in Henry's room. Her breathing grew shallow at the thought of what she might stumble across. What if he really had thrown Jen's body into the dumpster? He might have kept a memento, intending to give it to Quinn—her fuchsia scarf or some other item, maybe even her purse. Her heartbeat thundered in her chest. She threw a glance over her shoulder to make sure Harper wasn't lurking in the hallway and then closed the door, ready to begin.

First, she peered under the bed where Henry kept several shoeboxes stuffed full of miscellaneous items. She began sorting through them, quickly losing herself in some old birthday cards and concert tickets, and various other keepsakes. Catching herself, she hastily returned the shoe boxes to their spot beneath the foot of the bed and moved on to the bedside table. The drawer was jammed so full she could barely wrench it open. Inside, was a miscellaneous stash of coins, pens, a catapult, an old phone, and empty candy wrappers—nothing significant.

She knelt by the bed, slid her fingers underneath the mattress and ran them down both sides of it, but came up empty-handed. Getting to her feet, she peered curiously around the room looking for any other obvious hiding places. Tackling the chest of drawers next, she rummaged through the piles of T-shirts and shorts to make sure Henry hadn't hidden anything beneath his clothes. She flinched when the bedroom door rattled.

"Mommy, I'm all done," Harper said, waltzing in dressed in her fleece cat pajamas. "Will you read me a story now?"

"I'll be right there, just putting away the laundry," Bridget said nailing a chirpy tone with a hint of hysteria. "Go get your teeth cleaned."

With an air of resignation, she closed the dresser drawer and made her way to Harper's bedroom to embark on the lengthy bedtime story ritual that her daughter eagerly anticipated every night. With a bit of luck, she'd have time afterward to go back and look around in Henry's room some more.

Twenty minutes later, Bridget closed the *Who was Sacagawea?* book that Harper was currently enamored with and kissed her daughter on the forehead.

"Will Daddy be here when I wake up?" Harper asked, sounding wistful.

Bridget smiled sadly at her. "I'm not sure, sweetheart. But Mommy will be here. Mommy will always be here for you."

Harper grinned back and closed her eyes, wriggling down contentedly beneath the duvet.

Bridget closed the bedroom door behind her and leaned back against the wall, her breath coming in short, painful jabs. It was overwhelming to think she might be on the brink of becoming a single parent, solely responsible for raising Henry and Harper. Her parents would do what they could to help, of course, but there was no getting around the fact that they weren't as sprightly as they had once been. And if she was forced to move out of the area, she wouldn't even have them for support.

After composing herself, she returned to Henry's room. There weren't too many places left to look. She decided to tackle the closet next. It was a disaster zone of unwashed clothes and stinky sneakers, heaped on the floor in random piles. Tentatively, she felt along the top shelf and lifted down a couple more shoe boxes full of old photos. She took the time to flip through some of them, but they were only more innocent mementos of Henry's childhood—which should have given her some measure of relief. After all, this is what she'd been hoping to find, nothing incriminating. Nothing to suggest that her fourteen-year-old son had anything to do with the horrific murder of Jen Carson.

She regarded the discarded clothing with displeasure, and then, before she could talk herself out of it, scooped up an armful and carried it into the laundry room. Ordinarily, it was Henry's job to take care of his own dirty clothes, but after everything that had happened in the last few days, they were all behind on their chores.

After dumping the clothing on the floor, she began sorting the darks into the first load. Her hand froze mid-air when she noticed something lying at the bottom of the pile. Shaking her head in disbelief, she shrank back in horror, willing the dark shape to mold itself into something else entirely.

But there was no mistaking the black wool balaclava lying at her feet.

18

*B*ridget stood rooted to the spot, staring down in disbelief at the balaclava—a perfect match to the one the figure in the footage had been wearing. She racked her brain trying to remember if she'd ever seen it before. Maybe there was a logical explanation for it. Runners used balaclavas sometimes, cyclists too, when they were training early in the mornings or on chilly evenings. But Henry wasn't a runner, and the only time he'd been on his bicycle in the past year was last weekend when Steve had forced him to participate in a family bike ride to the park and back. She supposed the balaclava could have been part of a Halloween costume he'd worn, but none that she could recall. And of course it didn't explain what it was doing in Henry's laundry. The very fact that it was buried in the mound of dirty clothes on his floor implied he'd worn it recently.

Hesitantly, Bridget bent over and retrieved the balaclava. She turned it inside out and examined it carefully for any trace of blood or long, dark hairs, or any equally incriminating evidence. Nowadays, the police could find DNA in almost anything. Hugging the balaclava to her chest, she peered down at the rest of Henry's laundry. She could throw the offending item in with a load, wash away the evidence— if there was any—and no one would be any the wiser. She nibbled on her lip, torn between wanting to make this go away, and wanting to do the right thing this time.

No doubt, Henry had been terrified when he'd seen Jen's body, scared witless for his dad. He was convinced Steve had killed her. Henry and Quinn had observed at least one secret meeting between Jen and Steve—what else were they supposed to think? Bridget blinked back tears. In trying to help his dad by getting rid of the body, Henry had become a party to the crime. He'd tampered with the evidence. It was her fault he'd felt compelled to do something this drastic. If only she'd gone straight to the police when she'd found the body, her son would never have been put in this compromising position to begin with. Would she ever be able to forgive herself for what she'd done?

The more pressing matter at hand was what to do about the balaclava. She could get rid of it entirely—stand behind Henry's story that he'd had nothing to do with disposing of Jen's body. They could let Steve take the fall. After all, if he'd killed the woman, what difference did it make if he was convicted of disposing of her body afterward or not? It wouldn't alter much in terms of his sentencing, but it would change everything for Henry. The press would have a field day with a story like this. She could see it now—*fourteen-year-old dumps woman's body in desperate bid to protect killer dad.*

Bridget frowned as another thought occurred to her. Was it possible Steve had asked Henry to help him? She immediately dismissed the notion. If Steve had killed Jen Carson, even accidentally, he would never involve his children in helping him clean up his mess. Besides, he wouldn't have needed help. Steve was almost as tall and strong as his son, easily able to dispose of Jen's body under his own steam. No,

Henry must have come upon the body and, in a rash move, decided to get rid of it. Bridget thought back to the arguments she'd overheard between Henry and Quinn. Henry had wanted to believe that Keith killed Jen, but Quinn just as desperately wanted to believe it was Steve. No doubt, Henry hadn't been able to live with the idea of facing his best friend after the truth came out.

Bridget took a shaky breath as she pulled out a drawer in the laundry room cabinet and retrieved a Ziplock bag. She stuffed the balaclava inside and set it on the counter. Tempted as she was to get rid of it, she couldn't bring herself to do it. She hurriedly scooped up the rest of the dirty laundry from the floor and shoved it into the washing machine. After setting it to run, she took the Ziplock and made her way to the kitchen where she stashed it at the bottom of her purse. She had to do the right thing. She would call Detective Wright and turn the evidence over to him.

But first she intended to confront Henry when he came back from volleyball practice and make him admit to what he'd done. A shiver ran across her shoulders. She only hoped it wasn't a whole lot worse than she suspected. What if Henry had killed Jen Carson in a fit of rage when he'd discovered his dad was having an affair with her? She toyed with the shocking idea for a moment. It seemed to fit with Steve's staunch denial of having anything to do with Jen's murder. And it also fit with his relaxed manner the morning she'd driven his Mercedes into town, and he'd gone biking with the kids. Surely, he couldn't have exhibited such composure if he'd murdered Jen and stashed her body in the trunk of his car.

For the next hour or so, Bridget tracked the time on the kitchen clock in a daze, counting down the minutes until Henry got dropped off. The flicker of fear in her gut was steadily working itself into a wildfire. How well did she really know her son? Was his moodiness of late an indication of some deeper disturbance than the usual teenage hormonal riptides? Maybe she'd missed something, like all those other mothers of murderers who had no idea what their sons were truly capable of and remained in denial right up until the moment their children finally confessed.

Bridget startled at the sound of the front door opening. She straightened up in her chair and cast a quick glance at the kitchen counter where her purse containing the balaclava was tucked next to the toaster. She heard Henry throwing down his duffel bag in the hallway, and then a familiar tromping as he headed to the kitchen for something to eat.

He strode into the room and made a beeline for the refrigerator.

"How was practice?" Bridget asked, annoyed with herself for sounding like a tremulous schoolgirl. Her heart was fluttering around like a leaf swirling in the wind.

"Fine." Henry pulled out a tub of leftover pasta and stuck it in the microwave.

"Don't stand in front of it," Bridget said, the words spilling from her lips on autopilot. She grimaced inwardly. A few waves of radiation was hardly a consequential concern in light of the fact that her son might be packed off to juvenile hall in the next few hours.

Henry heaved out an exasperated sigh and shuffled a half-step to the right while he waited for his food to warm up. When the microwave dinged, he retrieved the Tupperware, grabbed a fork from the cutlery drawer, and slumped down at the kitchen island. Bridget got up from the table and joined him. She stood on the opposite side of the counter watching him eat for a moment.

"What?" He stopped chewing, fork halfway to his mouth,

peering up at her from beneath his brows. "Why are you staring at me like that?"

Bridget pulled out a stool and sat down. "I found something in your laundry tonight."

Henry cocked an eyebrow and stared at her quizzically. "Yeah?"

"Henry," Bridget said earnestly, "I found a black balaclava."

For a moment, he didn't react. Then, he rammed his fork into the remainder of his pasta and dropped his gaze.

"Henry, I need you to tell me the truth. Was it you in the video?"

He licked his lips nervously but didn't offer a response.

"No more lies, Henry. This is serious. Why is there a black balaclava in your laundry?"

He shoved the Tupperware aside and wiped the back of his hand across his mouth. "It was me."

The admission hit Bridget like a punch to the stomach. She shrank back in her stool and stared at her son in shock. Her child had just admitted to tossing a dead woman into a dumpster. Had she heard him right? How in the world had it come to this?

She shook her head, dumbstruck. "I … why?" She wasn't sure what she was asking him—she was too distraught to form a coherent question.

Henry looked at her, stricken, and lowered his voice. "I had to, Mom. Dad killed Jen Carson. He would have gone to prison. He might still be going there. I didn't think they'd find the body." He tugged a hand despairingly through his hair.

Bridget dropped her head into her hands. "We have to call Detective Wright. We have to tell him the truth." She swallowed back a sob and then added, "The *whole* truth this time."

"That is the whole truth, Mom," Henry said, his expression anguished. "I didn't kill her, if that's what you're getting at."

Bridget shook her head. "No, I meant I need to tell the truth too." She lifted her head and met Henry's gaze. "I saw Jen's body in your dad's car on Saturday morning when I came out of the grocery store. I drove around for a bit in shock—I guess I must have been in shock. It's the only way I can account for the fact that I didn't go directly to the police. Anyway, I'd finally resigned myself to doing the right thing, when your grandpa called to say Grandma had fallen and broken her hip. I wasn't thinking straight. I panicked and took off for the hospital—didn't get back until midnight. I figured it was too late to do anything, so I waited until the morning but—"

"By then the body was gone," Henry interjected. "I drove Dad's car to the movie theater and got rid of it during the night."

Bridget threw him a curious look. "How did you know it was in there to begin with?"

He shrugged. "By chance. I couldn't find my history book and I thought I might have left it in Dad's car when he took us to school last week. He always makes us put our back-packs in the trunk. You know how he is about buckles scraping his leather seats."

Bridget stood and walked around to the other side of the counter. She put an arm around Henry's shoulder and looked at him tenderly. "I'm going to call Detective Wright now. We need to get this resolved tonight."

"Will I be arrested?" Henry asked, a haunted expression gripping him.

Bridget winced. By all appearances, her son was a man, but inside he was still a frightened child with all the emotions that went along with that developmental stage.

"I don't know, Henry. I might even be arrested for all I know."

"What's going to happen to Harper if we're both arrested?"

"I suppose if it comes to that, she'll have to stay with Grandma and Grandpa."

Henry clenched his jaw. "You shouldn't tell the detective you saw the body too. It won't make any difference. It will only make things worse for our family, and for Harper."

"Maybe," Bridget agreed, pulling out her phone. "But that's not my decision to make."

19

*B*ridget opened the front door to Detective Wright and Officer Lopez and exchanged a terse greeting with them before ushering them inside. She led them straight to the family room where Henry was waiting and motioned to them to take a seat.

Detective Wright wasted no time pulling out his notepad. "So, Henry, your mother tells me you want to change the statement you gave us earlier."

"Yeah." He cleared his throat. "Uh, it … was me in the video."

Officer Lopez shot Bridget a glance as if seeking confirmation. She reached into her purse and pulled out the Ziplock bag containing the balaclava. Wordlessly, she set it on the coffee table between them. "He was wearing this. It was a half-baked idea, I know, but he didn't want his father—"

Detective Wright raised a palm to cut her short, a mildly irritated look on his face. "I'd prefer to hear this directly from Henry, if you don't mind."

"Of course, I'm sorry." Bridget leaned back in her chair

and folded her arms in front of her to keep herself from shaking.

Henry jerked his knee up and down. "Mom's right. I didn't want Dad going to prison."

Detective Wright's expression softened. "Do you think your dad killed Jen Carson?"

Henry gave a dejected nod. "Yeah."

"Why do you think that?"

Henry looked momentarily thrown off by the question. "She was in the trunk of his car, for starters."

A somber expression settled on Detective Wright's face. "That's true, but technically, anyone could have put the body there. Do you have any other reason to believe that your father might have killed your best friend's mother?"

"Quinn's dad told us they were having an affair."

Detective Wright scratched his chin. "Do you think Keith Carson might have felt he had a good reason to kill his wife?"

Henry's eyes darted nervously between Bridget and the two officers. "I was sure he'd killed her at first. Until I saw her body in my dad's car."

Detective Wright jotted down some notes. "Can you tell me what time you left your house with the body?"

"Two in the morning."

"How can you be so sure?"

"I set my alarm."

"And your father's Mercedes was parked in the driveway, or by the curb?"

"In the driveway."

"Had you ever driven it before?" Detective Wright raised his brows a fraction, his lips twitching imperceptibly.

Henry shrugged. "Maybe. Am I in trouble?"

"I can let that one slide," Detective Wright said. "But tampering with evidence is a serious crime. As you're still a minor, it will be up to the judge at juvenile court to decide what kind of punishment should be meted out. It's a good thing you came forward with the truth before our forensics team managed to enhance the image enough to identify you. That will work in your favor."

Detective Wright turned to Bridget. "I'm going to need Henry to come down to the station and give a formal statement."

Bridget swallowed the hard knot in her throat. She'd suspected it would come to this, but it didn't make the prospect of it any easier. "My daughter's already in bed. And Henry doesn't have a lawyer yet. Can it wait until the morning?"

Detective Wright gave an affirmative nod. "Once you sort out legal representation, call me and we'll arrange for Henry to be interviewed."

"There's something else I need to tell you," Bridget said, wringing her hands. "I'm entirely to blame for Henry's actions. I could have prevented him doing what he did. It was the choice I made earlier that day that compelled him to do it."

Detective Wright frowned. "I don't follow. What are you talking about?"

With shaking fingers, Bridget carefully tucked her hair behind her ears. "I ... I saw Jen's body in the trunk of Steve's car earlier that day. I was picking up groceries and I popped the trunk in the parking lot and—" Burying her face in her hands, she began to sob quietly.

A moment later, she felt the pressure of Henry's arm snaking around her shoulders. Drying her tears, she straightened up and blinked at Detective Wright. "I can't even begin to tell you how terrified I was. I was in shock. I couldn't think straight. I drove around for a bit trying to muster up the courage to call 911 and then my dad called to say Mom had fallen and broken her hip and was going into surgery. He needed me. It was all so overwhelming. I meant to go to the police station afterward, but by the time I got back from the hospital, it was almost midnight. I decided to wait until the morning to deal with it. Only … Henry beat me to it."

Detective Wright and Officer Lopez exchanged a loaded look.

"I wasn't intentionally trying to hide evidence. I just delayed reporting it, and by the next morning, the body was gone." Bridget rubbed the tip of her nose, sniffling as she went on, "It was hard to know what to do at that point. I didn't think the police would believe me if I told them what I'd seen. I was worried I might be in trouble—that they'd think I'd gotten rid of the body, maybe even killed her."

Officer Wright grimaced. "This is critical information. It narrows down the timeline of when the murder could have taken place."

Bridget pulled out a tissue and wiped her nose. "I suppose I need a lawyer now too."

Officer Wright shot her a sympathetic look. "A good one should be able to get you off with a plea deal if you're willing to testify. Especially given the extenuating circumstances of your mother's accident and emergency surgery. You have no prior record, and you fully intended to report it. You'll need to make a statement too. I'll expect to see you both at the station before noon tomorrow."

"What about Steve?" Bridget bit back the whimper that rose to her lips. "Is there any news?"

"Not yet," Officer Lopez chimed in. "We're detaining him overnight again for questioning. We'll know more by tomorrow."

Detective Wright pressed his lips together as he flipped his notebook closed. "Right, we'll leave it there for the time being. I appreciate you both coming forward. I'm sure you agree that the sooner we get Jen Carson's killer behind bars, the better."

THAT NIGHT, Bridget barely slept, her mind whirling her troubled thoughts like an unending wash cycle. She was still trying to come to terms with what her son had done, and what her role in his actions had been. And, of course, there was the niggling question of whether or not Henry had done more than simply dispose of the body. As horrific a thought as it was, she couldn't avoid asking herself again if he might have killed Jen Carson? Maybe he and Quinn had come up with some ill-advised plan to punish her, and it had all gone horribly wrong.

So many unanswered questions were swirling in her head. Her family was disintegrating around her, splitting at the seams. One way or another, they were all involved in this vile crime, all of them except Harper, who would pay the price for the poor decisions they had made. As innocent as her seven-year-old daughter was, she was about to be thrust into the limelight—the orphaned child of a killer family.

Giving up on sleep, Bridget belted her robe around her waist and made her way to the kitchen shortly before five to brew some coffee. She was surprised to see that Henry was already up. "Let me guess. You couldn't sleep either."

He shrugged. "I was studying for my math test."

Bridget groaned. "Is that today?"

"Yeah, third period. I don't care if I miss it. Do you think we'll get to see Dad at the station?"

"I don't know," she said, popping a coffee pod into the Breville. "But we can ask."

"What are you going to tell Harper?"

"I'll say I have to take you to an appointment this morning. I'm going to drop her off at Samantha's house. Her mom will take them both to school. That's all Harper has to know, for now." Bridget twisted her lips. "I'll tell Grandma and Grandpa the same thing in case we run late at the station and Grandpa has to pick Harper up. I hate lying to them, but I don't want to worry them needlessly. Let's wait and see if the police intend to charge us before we say anything more." She glanced at her phone and then reached for her coffee mug. "I'm going to get showered up, you should do the same."

AFTER THEY'D DROPPED Harper at her friend's house, Bridget and Henry stopped at a diner for breakfast before driving to the police station, where the lawyer Bridget had contacted was waiting.

"Bryan Miller, nice to meet you," he said, shooting an arm out to shake hands with Bridget.

"This is my son, Henry," she said, turning to introduce him.

Henry smiled tentatively as Bryan proceeded to pump his arm enthusiastically.

"All right, follow me. They've allocated us an interview room." He led them into a starkly furnished room with light gray walls and a maroon carpet and placed his briefcase on the fixed desk in front of him. "I want to run through briefly how we're going to handle the interview before Detective Wright arrives."

Bridget and Henry listened intently as Bryan covered some ground rules for the process. "Once you've given your statements, I'll follow up and find out if the police intend on pressing charges. Any questions?"

"How long do you think this will take?" Bridget asked. "My son has an important math test this afternoon."

"Assuming the police don't detain him, we'll be out of here long before—"

A sharp rap on the door interrupted them. Detective Wright stuck his head inside. "Are you ready for us?"

Bryan waved him in. "We're all set."

Officer Lopez followed behind Detective Wright and both men took a seat opposite Henry and Bridget.

"Who do you want to begin with?" Bryan inquired.

Detective Wright nodded at Henry. "Are you okay going first?"

Henry shrugged. "Sure, I guess."

Officer Lopez switched on the recording device and began by stating the date and naming those in attendance for the record.

Bridget fought the sting of impending tears as she listened to Henry explain how he'd found Jen's body while looking for his textbook, and how he'd been afraid for his dad, and also of what his friend, Quinn, would say when he found out.

"Where did the blanket come from that was wrapped around the body?" Detective Wright asked.

"I don't know," Henry said. "It was already there. Maybe it—"

"Just answer the detective's questions," Bryan cautioned. "You don't have to speculate."

"Can you describe the blanket for me, Henry?" Detective Wright continued.

"Gray and red checks, I think."

"Did you attempt to clean out the trunk after you disposed of the body?"

Henry frowned. "No, there was nothing to clean out."

Detective Wright leveled a few more questions at Henry and then switched off the recording machine and nodded to Bryan. "That concludes the first interview. Do your clients want to take a five-minute break?"

Bryan quirked an eyebrow at Bridget. She shook her

head. "No, let's just get this over with." She interlaced her fingers beneath the desk and waited for Detective Wright to begin.

"Can you state your name for the record?"

"Bridget Hartman."

"Will you please tell me in your own words what happened on the morning of January twentieth?"

Bridget took a shallow breath and began to recount her movements. "I came back out of the store with my groceries and popped the trunk. I remember seeing the tartan blanket first and thinking *that's not ours*. And then I looked at it more closely and saw that the shape beneath it looked kind of like a body. I told myself it wasn't, of course. But, some sixth sense made me cautious, nonetheless. I reached for a corner of the blanket and took a quick peek." Her voice cracked. "I'm sorry, this is just so difficult."

"Take your time, Bridget," Bryan interjected.

She heaved a heavy breath. "That's when I saw her face."

"And did you recognize who it was?" Detective Wright asked.

"No, well, yes, sort of. I thought it might have been the woman I saw coming out of my husband's office the night before. But I'd never met Quinn's mother, so I didn't know it was her."

"Did you check to make sure she was dead?"

Bridget pressed a tissue to her eyes and shook her head. "I knew she was dead. Her eyes were—"

"You don't have to answer that," Bryan interrupted.

"Why didn't you call 911 as soon as you found the body?" Detective Wright asked.

"My legs were like jelly, so I climbed into the car to think. I was debating what to do—whether to call 911 or drive straight to the police station. That's when one of the grocery store employees knocked on my window to hand me the bag of groceries I'd left in the cart. I … I panicked. I was afraid I looked suspicious sitting there. So I grabbed the bag and drove off with no real idea where I was going. I cruised around for twenty minutes or so, too scared to make a decision. Just when I'd made up my mind to head to the police station, my dad called to tell me about Mom's accident. So I drove straight to the hospital instead."

Detective Wright posed several more routine questions before ending the interview. "Okay, I think I've got everything I need for now." He got to his feet. "Thank you both for coming in this morning." He dipped his head in Bryan's direction. "We'll be in touch."

After he exited the interview room, Bridget turned to Bryan. "How do you think it went?"

"As well as can be expected. I'm not making any predictions. Now, it's just a waiting game."

They looked up at another sharp rap on the door. Officer Lopez peered inside; his genial smile firmly fixed in place. "Bail's been set for your husband. As soon as you post it, he's free to leave."

*B*ryan got up and exchanged a few muttered words with Officer Lopez before returning to the table. "It appears the prosecutor's only going to charge Steve with tampering with evidence, for now. But he isn't buying the idea that Steve had no idea Jen's body was in his car."

"For now?" Bridget echoed.

Bryan rubbed his jaw. "I don't know anything more than that. Detective Wright's coming back in to brief us."

Henry's guarded gaze slid to Bridget. "Is Dad coming home?"

She squeezed his shoulder. "Yes, we'll make bail, somehow or other." She glanced up to see Detective Wright entering the room clutching a file. He resumed his seat opposite them and flipped it open. "On the whole, it's good news. According to this report, forensics found some carpet fibers on the body that seem to indicate Jen Carson was murdered someplace other than in Steve's car. Without any more evidence, the prosecutor can't make a strong case that Steve was actually the killer. A good defense lawyer will argue that anyone could have put the body in the trunk of his car."

"You said it's good news *on the whole*," Bridget prompted. "What did you mean by that?"

Detective Wright's eyes held a discriminating glint as they darted from Bridget to Henry. "Make no mistake, we'll be thoroughly investigating the carpet fiber evidence. If it leads back to Steve, he'll be charged with murder. In the meantime, bail's been set at $15,000."

Bryan turned to Bridget. "Can you make bail, or do you need me to help you find a bondsman?"

"I think I can get the money together." Bridget reached for her purse and stood. "I'll have to go by the bank. And I need to drop Henry off at school on the way. He has an important test today that he can't miss."

Detective Wright nodded and got to his feet. "I'll have the paperwork ready when you return."

Bryan accompanied Bridget and Henry to the front door of the station. "I'll be in touch as soon as I hear something," he said, shaking their hands before striding off to his car.

"Why can't I just skip the stupid test?" Henry grumbled, as he and Bridget walked through the parking lot.

"Because you've missed enough school so far this week. Besides, I need some time to talk to your dad alone."

Henry shot her a sideways look. "You're not going to get divorced, are you?"

Bridget clenched her jaw. The thought had crossed her mind. If Steve was convicted of murder and sent to prison, would she really stick by his side? She couldn't give Henry the reassurance he wanted, not yet at any rate. There were too many unknowns, too many questions growing in the widening gap between her and Steve—a fertile breeding ground for doubt, mistrust, and suspicion.

Truth be told, she was in survival mode, mechanically going through the motions, putting one foot in front of the other as the hurdles kept getting bigger. They didn't have

$15,000 in their bank account, and Steve had made it clear that the business was struggling. She'd have to call her dad and ask for a loan. "I honestly don't know what the future holds," she said wearily. "Divorce is the least of my concerns right now. I have to stay focused on what I need to accomplish in the next few hours."

As if sensing that he'd pushed things far enough, Henry turned his attention to his phone as Bridget started the engine and pulled out of the station parking lot. After dropping Henry off at school, she called her dad who readily agreed to meet her at the bank. She only hoped he wouldn't have to give a reason for the rather large amount he'd be withdrawing from his savings account. Her nerves were already shot without the added humiliation of the bank employees knowing her shameful business.

AFTER BRIDGET HAD NAVIGATED the process at the bank with her dad, and successfully posted bail, she drove Steve straight from the police station to the Verizon store to pick up a disposable phone which he insisted he needed for work. Afterward, they drove home in stony silence. Bridget couldn't decide if she felt relieved or petrified at the idea of her husband coming home. Not knowing for sure whether he was guilty or not was eating her up inside. Once or twice, Steve attempted to start up a conversation, but each time Bridget shut him down. "I don't want to talk about it yet. My head's spinning. We'll sit down later and discuss everything."

Eventually he shrugged, leaned against the glass of the passenger window, and closed his eyes.

"I'm going to drop you home and then I need to go check on my mom," Bridget said, once they turned into their subdivision.

Steve straightened up in his seat and fixed a brooding

glare on her. "I know what you're doing, Bridget. You can't ignore what's happening. We need to talk about this."

"My head's splitting, and I have other responsibilities to take care of first."

"You mean other responsibilities that are more important than me?" Steve spat back. "I've been accused of tampering with evidence. Someone either used my car to commit a murder, or they're setting me up. Don't you care about what's happening to me?"

"Truthfully, the only thing I care about at the moment is protecting my children," Bridget answered. "You've been hiding things from me. I don't know what you did, Steve, but whatever it is, you'll have to face it in court. My opinion doesn't matter."

She turned into their driveway and parked the car, unable to meet his eyes. "Please get out. I need to go."

Steve reached for the door handle. "Where are the kids?"

"In school."

"That's just great! You couldn't even pull them out for one day." He thumped a fist on the dash. "I suppose you don't think I'm safe around our kids anymore, is that it?"

Bridget's voice rose and wobbled. "I don't know what to think. I just need for you to get out of the car."

Without another word, Steve climbed out and slammed the door. Bridget hurriedly backed down the driveway and pulled out into the road, letting out a long, tremulous breath. It was all so surreal. How could she begin to wrap her head around the idea that her husband might be a killer?

HER DAD LOOKED UP ANXIOUSLY when he opened the front door to her. "Did it go okay?"

She grimaced and nodded. "Thanks for bailing him out. I

dropped him off at home. I can't even bear to look at him right now."

"Don't jump to any conclusions. We haven't heard his side of the story, yet."

"And what side would that be?" Bridget demanded, biting back her frustration. "That it was all a big, fat accident? That he panicked and hid his lover's body in the trunk of his car?" Briny tears stung her eyes. "If he killed Jen Carson, I'm willing to bet he knew exactly what he was doing."

"I'm going to reserve judgement until we have all the facts." Her dad pressed his wrinkled lips together and accompanied her to the family room where Elise was sitting in an armchair with a fuzzy blanket draped over her knees. To Bridget's surprise, Harper was kneeling at her feet doing a jigsaw puzzle on the floor.

"What are you doing here, honey?" Bridget asked incredulously.

Harper's lips formed a petulant expression as she pressed a piece of the puzzle into place.

"The school called," Elise hastened to explain. "She was terribly upset. Some of her friends were saying mean things to her about her father."

Harper looked up at Bridget, wide-eyed. "Did Daddy get out?"

"Yes, honey, he did."

Releasing her fistful of puzzle pieces, Harper scrambled to her feet. "Where is he? I want to see him."

Bridget pinned a tight smile across her lips. "I dropped him off at home. Daddy's ... tired. He's resting."

"Awww! Not fair! I want to see him now!" Harper folded her arms in front of her and sank back down on the carpet curling her lip up at the half-finished puzzle. After a moment's hesitation, she kicked it, smashing apart the pieces she had painstakingly put together. "I don't want to do this stupid puzzle anymore."

Bridget's stomach muscles clenched. She knew Harper was only acting out because she couldn't comprehend what was going on. But how was she supposed to explain any of it to her seven-year-old?

"I understand you're upset, Harper, but that's not the right way to handle things," she scolded. "Pick up those pieces and put them back in the box so they don't get lost."

Bridget turned to her dad. "Do you need any groceries or any errands run?"

"We're all set, dear, thanks. Harper and I grabbed a few things on our way back from school, didn't we, pumpkin?"

Harper gave a tight nod. "Grandpa let me have a chocolate muffin because I was sad."

Bridget patted her on the head. "That's all right. You needed a treat. Why don't you get your things together and I'll take you home now so you can see Daddy?"

"Yeah!" Harper quickly finished tidying up the puzzle and then jumped up and ran to fetch her backpack.

"Have they charged Steve with anything?" Elise asked in a low tone.

"Tampering with evidence," Bridget replied. "They don't have enough to go on beyond that." She didn't bother bringing up the carpet fibers that had yet to be analyzed and investigated. There was no sense in adding to her parents' fears unless it was warranted.

The conversation ended abruptly when Harper came running back into the room with her thumbs looped through the straps of her silver-and-teal backpack. "I'm ready to see Daddy now. I drew him a picture at school."

Bridget reached for her daughter's hand. "I'm sure he'll love it. Say goodbye to Grandma and Grandpa."

. . .

On the drive home, Harper chatted away, giddy at the prospect of seeing her dad again and skipping the rest of the school day. Bridget mumbled the occasional appropriate response, mentally reviewing the statements she and Henry had given. Would hers be enough to clear her of any wrong-doing, or would the police see fit to prosecute her? Maybe Henry would even be charged as an accomplice. Goose-bumps pricked her arms. The press was going to have a field day once the story broke. Especially if they got their hands on the video footage. There was no getting around the fact that Henry had done an awful thing, albeit with good inten-tions—a decision that could mark him for a long time to come.

Bridget pulled into her driveway and switched off the engine. Before she had her seatbelt halfway undone, Harper was out of the car and charging to the front door. She stood on her tiptoes and rang the doorbell, skipping excitedly from one foot to the other as she waited. Gathering up her stuff, Bridget climbed out of the car and joined her on the front step.

"Get your key, Mommy!" Harper urged. "Daddy's too slow."

"Patience!" Bridget laughed as she turned her key in the door. She stepped aside to allow Harper to run past her and then hung her coat up on the wall rack.

"Daddy!" Harper shrieked. "Where are you?" A moment later, she came running back out of the kitchen and bolted down the hallway toward the master bedroom, waving the picture she'd colored for him in her right hand. "Daddy! I have a present for you."

Bridget made her way to the kitchen. She could use another strong cup of coffee before she faced the inevitable showdown with her husband. Lack of sleep was wreaking havoc with her emotions, and the last thing she wanted to do was dissolve in tears when she finally confronted him. She had to stay strong and demand the truth from him. If there was any way their marriage was going to survive this, it had to begin with him being honest about his relationship with Jen. She would start by telling Steve that she'd seen the emails they'd exchanged and make him explain what exactly had been going on between him and the Carsons.

"Daddy's not in his room," Harper wailed as she came crashing into the kitchen.

"Maybe he's in the bathroom," Bridget suggested, adding some water to the coffee machine.

"No, he isn't, I already looked." Harper slapped her drawing down on the kitchen table and slunk into a chair folding her arms dejectedly in front of her. "You said I could see Daddy."

Bridget waited until her coffee had finished brewing and then reached for the steaming mug. "Right. I'll track him down for you." She exited the kitchen and stuck her head into the family room to see if Steve had fallen asleep on the couch. Next, she walked down to the master bedroom and double checked to make sure Harper hadn't missed him. "Steve, are you in here?" She was about to exit the room when she noticed a folded piece of paper wedged between the decorative pillows on the bed. Curiously, she reached for it and opened it. The breath left her lungs as she read the only two words on the page.

I'm sorry.

ridget's breathing grew shallow as the room began to spin around her. She stared in disbelief at the note quivering between her fingers. *I'm sorry.* What did that even mean? Sorry for what, exactly? What had Steve done? Was he admitting to killing Jen Carson? And where was he? Bridget's gaze flitted haphazardly around the room, her stomach tightening as another sickening thought wormed its way into her head. Had Steve harmed himself?

Panic ricocheted through her nervous system like a fire alarm resonating through the corridors of a building. The note fluttered to the ground as she lurched across the room to their walk-in closet. Her heart drummed ominously at the terrifying thought that she might find her husband hanging on the back of the door with a tie or a belt knotted around his neck. She flung open the door, but to her relief, the closet was empty.

Still trembling uncontrollably, she dug out her phone and hit the speed dial for Steve's new number. She sank down on the bed and pressed the phone to her ear, each ring only driving dread deeper into her soul. Why wasn't he picking up? What was he thinking leaving her a note like that? The call went to voicemail and Bridget mumbled desperately into the phone.

"Steve, where are you? You're scaring me. I don't know what this note is all about. Please don't do anything stupid. I'm sorry I didn't sit down and talk with you earlier. We can sort this out. Whatever you did, we'll handle it together. Think of the kids, Steve. Please call me back as soon as you get this message."

She hung up and frantically punched in a text. She stared at her phone for several dragged-out minutes, willing Steve's response to snake across the screen, but it never came. With a despairing groan, she got up and began pacing the room, hunched over her screen. Her thoughts ping-ponged back and forth in her head as she weighed her options. Maybe she should start calling around. When people were at a crisis point, they often called or texted friends. Of course, she'd have to be deliberately vague in her message to avoid alarming anyone unnecessarily. After piecing together a generic query as to Steve's whereabouts, she sent out a handful of texts to his closest friends. Most of them responded within a few minutes, but no one had heard anything from him that morning.

Bridget flinched when Harper suddenly appeared in the doorway. "Did you find Daddy?"

"Not yet, honey. He must have gone out for a bit. I left a message on his phone. I'm sure he'll call us back real soon."

Harper considered this for a moment. "Maybe he went on a bike ride."

Bridget stared at her daughter, her brain whirring. Of course, that was it. He didn't have his car, so he'd probably taken his bike out to clear his head. After all, she'd told him she was going over to her parents to help them out. He wasn't expecting her home for hours. *I'm sorry* meant nothing cryptic; it was simply his attempt to make up with her. She hadn't given him the chance to say it. She'd shut him down every time he'd tried to talk. Relief flooded through her. She got up and hugged Harper, who was beaming at her.

"Yes, I expect you're right. I'm sure he'll be back shortly. Why don't we bake some cookies for him in the meantime?"

Harper's face lit up at the prospect. "Yeah!" she squealed, clapping her hands excitedly.

"Go wash up and I'll meet you in the kitchen," Bridget instructed her. She took a quick calming breath and then hurried out to the garage. Her heart sank at the sight of Steve's bicycle hanging upside down in its usual spot on the rack on the back wall.

"Mommy, can we make chocolate chip, *please?*" Harper pleaded, trotting up behind her. She grabbed Bridget by the hand and tugged her away from the garage door.

"Chocolate chip it is," Bridget said, her cheery air at odds with the hollow feeling inside her.

For the next half hour or so, Harper remained happily preoccupied baking the store-bought cookie dough that Bridget pulled out of the freezer. But it was only a temporary distraction. The questions would soon start up again. *Where's Daddy? Why isn't he home yet? When can I see him?*

A lawnmower sputtered to life next door, and Bridget glanced out through the kitchen window. She briefly considered going over there and asking her neighbors if they'd seen Steve leaving the house earlier, but that would require explaining the situation, and the very thought was enough to make her cringe. She was sure the neighbors were already gossiping to one another about Steve's arrest in connection with Jen Carson's murder. The last thing she wanted to do was start another unwarranted rumor that Steve had disappeared.

When he still hadn't returned by the time Henry arrived home from school, Bridget began to despair.

"How was your test?" she asked, trying to quash her burgeoning fear.

"Fine." Henry jerked his backpack from his shoulder and tossed it on the kitchen floor. "Where's Dad?"

"He's on a really, really, long bike ride," Harper said, with a dramatic sigh as she studied the picture she was coloring at the kitchen table.

Henry frowned, tossing an uncertain glance Bridget's way. "How long's he been gone?"

Bridget hesitated. "I'm not sure. He wasn't home when we got back from Grandma's and Grandpa's."

"Have you tried calling him?"

Bridget nodded, swallowing the tight knot in her throat. "It keeps going to voicemail."

The look of alarm on Henry's face intensified. "Mom, don't you think we should call the police?"

Harper stopped coloring, eyes swerving between Henry and Bridget, her mouth hanging open.

Bridget shot Henry a warning look. "Why don't you take your bike and see if he's at the park sitting on a bench or something. He didn't know we were going to be home today, so he might have gone for a walk. He probably didn't want to stay here all day by himself."

Henry bit back a retort, then winked reassuringly at Harper before striding out of the kitchen. Moments later, Bridget spotted him pushing his bike around the side of the house.

In her heart, she'd long since given up hope that Steve simply gone for a leisurely walk. She hadn't ruled out the possibility that he'd harmed himself. But a new fear to gnaw on had been growing in her gut over the past hour or so. Was it possible Steve had jumped bail? She couldn't bring herself to say the words out loud, as if that would somehow lend them credence. But, at some point, she would have to pick up the phone and inform Detective Wright, not to mention her dad. She felt sick to her stomach at the thought that he might be about to lose his savings. It was becoming increasingly clear what Steve had meant by his cryptic note. He was sorry for running away, for not facing up to what he had done, for abandoning his family, for not being man enough to face the music, his neighbors, the press, or Jen's husband and son. He was sorry for being a coward.

An icy shiver crossed Bridget's shoulders. The fact that he'd disappeared only served to confirm his guilt. If he was innocent, as he'd claimed, he wouldn't have run. He would have stayed and fought tooth and nail to prove his innocence. It was that simple. Any law-abiding person would trust the justice system to do what it was designed to do and clear their name, right? Bridget's eyes burned from the effort of holding back her tears. Now she knew why he'd insisted on swinging by Verizon to pick up a phone. She'd trusted Steve enough to bail him out, but, once again, he'd lied to her and deceived her. She gritted her teeth, vowing not to give him the chance again.

Twenty minutes later, Henry came flying up the driveway and skidded to a halt. Bridget watched as he carried his bike around to the garage and stowed it before coming back inside the house. "He's not at the park. And he didn't answer when I called him. Mom, this is serious. We need to call the police."

Harper's eyes widened. "Is Daddy in trouble *again?*"

"Yes," Henry growled, before Bridget had a chance to respond. "He's in even more trouble this time."

Bridget covered her face with her hands. How could Steve do this to their kids? He wasn't thinking straight. This wasn't the man she knew. Granted, he could be self-absorbed when it came to his work. But he wasn't a selfish man when it came to his family. He would never intentionally do anything to hurt them.

"Mom," Henry said, more gently this time. "Do you want me to call Detective Wright?"

Bridget shook her head. "No, I'll talk to him." She tilted her chin toward Harper. "Stay with your sister for a few minutes while I make the call." She slipped out of the kitchen and made her way to the family room, closing the door behind her. After sinking down on the couch, she scrolled through her contacts and pulled up Detective Wright's number. The phone rang several times, and, for a tense moment, Bridget thought he wasn't going to pick up. She flinched when his self-assured voice came over the line. "Detective Wright speaking."

"It's Bridget Hartman."

There was a brief pause and then he asked, "Is everything all right?"

"I'm … not sure." Bridget inhaled a quick breath before continuing. "The thing is, I can't find Steve, *anywhere*. And he's not answering his phone."

"How long's he been gone?" Detective Wright's tone was heavy with a new sense of urgency.

"Hours, I … don't—" Bridget's voice trailed off.

"Stay there. I'll be right over," Detective Wright said before hanging up.

Bridget took a couple of moments to compose herself before returning to the kitchen. She leaned in the doorway, observing her children for a moment. It warmed her heart to see Henry making an effort with his sister, for once. He was sitting next to her, crayon in hand, as they worked together on coloring her farmyard picture.

He looked up expectantly when Bridget stepped into the room. "What did Detective Wright say?"

"He's on his way."

"Don't worry, Mommy," Harper piped up, her attention still firmly focused on the picture in front of her. "The policemen will find Daddy."

Bridget smiled, her face slick with tears. She had no doubt the police would find him, sooner or later. It might only take a matter of days, or it could drag on for several months, but they would find him in the end. They were good at this kind of thing. And Steve wasn't a career criminal. He wouldn't last long on the run. It wasn't like he'd ever make it across the border to Mexico or Canada.

For starters, he hadn't had sufficient time to plan out how he was going to disappear. He didn't have a fake passport or a slew of alternate IDs in a secret safe like the criminals in movies always seemed to have. No, Steve was an accountant, the father of her two children, a nerd from suburbia. He was not going to get far in this reckless bid for freedom.

22

*T*rue to his word, Detective Wright showed up on Bridget's doorstep within the hour.

"I should warn you, I'm expecting a forensic technician here shortly to collect some samples," he said, as she ushered him inside. "We need to test the carpet fibers from your house to see if any of them match those found on Jen Carson's body."

"Does it have to be now?" Bridget's voice wavered. "My children are here."

Detective Wright shot her an apologetic look. "I'm afraid so. We'll be as discreet as we can. It won't take long."

"I don't care, I don't want it to be a memory the kids associate with their home. I'll ask Henry if he can take Harper to the park for a bit," Bridget said, leading Detective Wright into the kitchen. She motioned for him to sit down at the table. "Would you like some coffee, or a soda?"

"Just a water would be great."

Bridget handed him a bottle of water from the refrigerator and went in search of Henry.

She knocked on his door and peeked inside. "Do you

think you could take Harper to the park for a couple of hours? Detective Wright is sending over a forensic technician to test our carpet fibers. I don't want your sister here when they're doing it. She'll ask too many questions that call for disturbing answers."

Henry dragged a hand through his hair. "Yeah, sure. Text me when they're done."

Bridget pulled a twenty-dollar bill out of her pocket and handed it to him. "Take her for an ice cream to kill some time if you need to."

"Thanks, Mom." Henry locked eyes with her. "I know this is hard on you. I wish I could take back what I did."

"We all do, son," Bridget said, tweaking a semblance of a smile. She hugged him before making her way back to the kitchen where Detective Wright was poring over his notes. She opened the refrigerator and lifted out a water bottle. Her throat felt parched, she couldn't remember the last time she'd taken a sip of water, let alone eaten anything. "Henry's agreed to take Harper out of the house for an hour or two," she said, unscrewing the cap and taking a quick swig as she took a seat.

"Good, then let's get down to business," Detective Wright said. "I've put out a BOLO alert for your husband, but I need some more information. Do you know what he was wearing?"

Bridget shrugged. "I assume the same thing he had on this morning—jeans, tan loafers, and a gray shirt."

"And when did you first realize he was missing?"

"Around eleven-thirty. I dropped him off here and then swung by my parents' place to check on my mom. When I got back, there was no sign of him anywhere."

"And you haven't been able to get a hold of him?"

"No, his new phone goes straight to voicemail and he's not answering my texts." Bridget removed the folded note from her pocket and handed it to Detective Wright. "I found this on our bed."

He turned it over, frowning at it. "And it's his handwriting, as far as you can tell?"

Bridget nodded. "I think so."

"Any idea what it means?"

Bridget toyed with the cap on her water bottle. "Well, at first I thought it was a confession—that he was apologizing for killing Jen Carson." She let out a shuddering sigh. "But the more I thought about it, the more I started to think it might mean something else entirely—that he'd harmed himself, you know, committed suicide or something awful like that. Of course, I panicked. After I'd looked around a bit and made sure he hadn't slit his wrists in the bathroom or hung himself in the closet, it finally dawned on me what he must have meant all along." Her voice trailed off into a wistful tone.

"And what's that?" Detective Wright raised his brows and looked at her intently.

"That he was sorry for leaving—that he couldn't face what he'd done, that he wasn't coming back."

"You seem very sure of that," Detective Wright commented. "Is this something you'd expect of your husband? Is he the type to run?"

Bridget picked at the label on her water bottle as she considered the question. "Not under normal circumstances, but people do things that are out of character when they're under an inordinate amount of stress, don't they?" She gave a self-conscious shrug. "That's the only way I can explain what I did, and what Henry did."

Detective Wright's eyes kindled with understanding as he scribbled something down on his notepad. "Did you check to see if any of Steve's things are missing? Clothes, passport, anything along those lines?"

Bridget rubbed her brow. "I didn't think about that. Should I check now?"

Detective Wright gave a brusque nod. "Best do it before the forensic technician arrives."

Bridget took another quick swig of her water before making her way to the master bedroom. She steeled herself as she walked into the closet, half expecting to find Steve's side entirely cleaned out. She'd been in such a fluster earlier, fearing that he'd harmed himself, that she wouldn't have noticed if any of his clothes were missing. Her eyes scanned the rails and shelves. Everything appeared to be untouched. All his shirts were hanging in the same immaculate order he always kept them in. One-by-one, she pulled out his drawers and confirmed that the contents were as neatly organized as ever. As far as she could tell, Steve hadn't rummaged through them recently or removed any items. She walked over to the small safe at the back of their closet and pressed the touchpad with her index finger. The door swung open and she reached inside for the envelope where they kept their passports. All four of them were still there, rubber-banded together, labelled with their names on the front in Steve's fastidious fashion.

After locking the safe back up, Bridget returned to the kitchen. "There's nothing missing, to the best of my knowledge. His passport's still there. But I'm not surprised he didn't pack a bag. He knew he didn't have much time before I got back."

"What about your bank accounts?" Detective Wright asked. "Have you checked to see if any money has been withdrawn?"

Bridget's eyes widened. Another possibility that hadn't occurred to her. "I'll look right now." She retrieved her laptop from the counter and fired it up. After waiting for the bank's website to load, she tapped in her login information. "Looks like there haven't been any cash withdrawals today," she said as she scanned through her account. "The only transaction is an automatic payment for our electricity."

"Is it possible your husband had an account you don't know about?" Detective Wright suggested.

"I … suppose it's possible," Bridget conceded, her mind flitting back to the articles she'd read about cheating spouses. "After all, I didn't know he was having an affair."

Detective Wright snapped his notebook shut. "All right, I'll update the station with this information and ask Tech to follow up on tracking down any possible accounts at other local banks."

"He's in serious trouble now, isn't he?" Bridget said. "For skipping bail, I mean. Will they … will they shoot him if he refuses to turn himself in?"

Detective Wright put his fist to his mouth and coughed discreetly. "Let's not speculate on the worst-case scenario. It's not like the movies. We don't even know yet if he's gone on the run. I'd like you to try calling him again and leaving him a message asking him to contact me. Give him my direct number and tell him I'll make sure he has every opportunity to turn himself in safely if he has in fact crossed a state line and violated his conditions of bail."

Bridget swallowed back the lump in her throat as she fished her phone out of her back pocket and hit the speed dial for Steve's number. "It's me again. I'm here at the house with Detective Wright. I showed him your note. He wants to help you, we both do. I'm going to give you his direct number. It's (608) 239-1174. Please promise me you'll call him as soon as you get this. I'm so scared for the kids. I don't want this to end badly. Please, Steve, do the right thing and come home."

Detective Wright gave an approving nod when she hung

up. "Have you talked to any of your neighbors yet? Maybe one of them saw him leave."

Bridget let out a heavy sigh. "I don't want to get them involved, if at all possible. The rumors are already flying. Even the kids at school are talking about it."

"All right, I'll handle it. Officer Lopez will be here soon with the forensic technician. I'll send him to knock on a few doors."

"It's all so surreal," Bridget said wistfully. "I just keep turning over the *why* of it in my head. *Why* did Jen Carson have to die? *Why* did Steve get involved with her in the first place? *Why* did Henry do what he did?"

"We're working on getting the answers to all those questions," Detective Wright said. "But for now, we need to focus on the most pressing issue at hand, and that's locating your husband. It appears he either walked out of here, or someone picked him up."

Bridget frowned. "Who would have picked him up? I texted his friends. No one's heard from him."

"I was thinking more along the lines of an Uber ride or something of that nature. I'll have one of my guys look into it —see if anyone ordered an Uber or a taxi to this address." Detective Wright pulled out his phone and barked out a few instructions to one of the desk clerks back at the station.

The doorbell rang and Bridget flinched.

"That's probably forensics," Detective Wright said, ending his call.

Reluctantly, she got to her feet and opened the front door. Officer Lopez greeted her with an irritating ear-to-ear smile. "Forensics is here to take a few fiber samples."

Bridget looked past him to the van parked at the curb. A woman dressed in a disposable white jumpsuit climbed out and made her way up the driveway carrying her supplies in a tub.

Bridget ushered them both inside.

"Okay, we're going to need carpet samples from every room in the house," Detective Wright ordered. "Also, any walk-in closets or other small carpeted areas. Rugs too. Are you good with that?"

The forensic technician nodded and shot a quick glance into the family room. "I'll begin in here."

Detective Wright turned to Officer Lopez. "I'd like you to interview the neighbors. Ask if anyone saw Steve leaving the house this morning, either on foot or getting into a vehicle."

Officer Lopez nodded and disappeared out the front door.

Bridget watched as the forensic technician retrieved her first sample from the family room carpet. Did the police really think Jen Carson had been strangled here in her home, where she was raising her children? It was madness. There would have been signs of a struggle. And how would Steve have pulled that off with her and the kids around? If he'd killed Jen Carson, it hadn't been at this location. That much she was certain of.

Once the technician had finished collecting her samples from each room, she thanked Bridget for her cooperation before turning to address Detective Wright. "I'm on my way to the next location and then I'll take everything to the lab. I'll be in touch as soon as we have the results." She retreated out the front door and pulled it shut behind her.

"Is she going to Steve's office?" Bridget asked curiously.

"No, we've already collected samples from Bartlett and Hartman," Detective Wright explained. "She's heading to Keith Carson's house next."

Bridget rumpled her brow. "So, he's still a suspect?"

"He had motive. He also had a motive to set your husband up. What better way to take the spotlight off himself than to make sure his wife's body turns up in her lover's car?"

Bridget ran a fingertip over her cracked lips. There was nothing she'd like to believe more than that Steve had been set up. But, if he was innocent, why had he run? More importantly, why had he written her a note saying he was sorry?

23

*B*ridget went through the weekend in limbo, with not a whisper on Steve's whereabouts, and no more surprise visits from law enforcement.

The following Monday, she had just returned to the house after dropping the kids off at school when her phone rang. She swallowed the dread rising up from her gut as she slid her finger across the screen and took Detective Wright's call.

"Have you seen the news this morning?" he asked.

Bridget reached for the back of a chair, feeling as though her legs were about to buckle beneath her. "No, what now?"

"They broke the story that Steve's a fugitive on the run—wanted for Jen Carson's murder."

Bridget clapped a hand over her mouth, her stomach dangerously close to rejecting the poached egg she'd forced down earlier. "What … what are they saying?"

"The usual. They've pegged him as guilty. It's a lot more interesting to speculate that the killer's on the run than that the police are following multiple leads."

"Will this put Steve in any danger?"

"Possibly," Detective Wright conceded. "There are always the vigilantes out there who want to take matters into their own hands. It's dangerous for the public too—it's easy to mistake someone for a face on the news."

"I noticed a strange car parked opposite my house when I got back from the school run," Bridget said. "I didn't think much of it at the time, but it wouldn't surprise me if it's a reporter angling for a story."

"Get ready for the onslaught. It's only just begun," Detective Wright said grimly. "I want you to try Steve's number again. It's imperative that he reaches out to me as soon as possible, for his own safety as well as for the public's. Would you consider making an appeal to him on TV?"

Bridget sucked in an icy breath. "I'm not sure I could do that. It would be awfully hard on the kids."

"Have you given any thought to pulling them out of school for the time being?" Detective Wright asked. "Things are going to get ugly before they get better. Technically, Steve hasn't skipped bail, yet, as he hasn't missed a court appearance. But naturally the media is intent on painting the worst possible scenario."

"Steve did this to himself," Bridget said with a trace of bitterness in her voice. "It didn't have to be this way. He should have stayed here and faced the charges."

"We're in agreement there. If you want my advice, go pick up your kids from school now before the other students get wise to the story. With their smart phones, it won't be long before it's all over campus."

Bridget grimaced. "Did you get the results of the carpet fiber tests from forensics?"

"Not yet. I'll get back with you as soon as I hear anything," he said, before ending the call.

Bridget moaned softly as she climbed into her car and reversed out of the driveway. She wasn't equipped for this, but neither were her kids, and she wasn't about to leave them as chum for a feeding frenzy at school. She could only imagine the condemnatory look on the school receptionist's face when she told her she was picking her kids up. The staff had probably caught wind of the story by now. And Henry was tangled up in it. She should have asked Detective Wright if the media had mentioned his involvement. Surely the news channels couldn't release a minor child's name. Regardless, the word was out, and it wouldn't take long for the backlash to begin.

As she drove, she went over in her mind what to tell her kids. Henry could handle the truth, but could she burden Harper with something this heavy?

Steeling herself for the painful task ahead, Bridget pulled into the school parking lot and locked her car. She marched into the administration office, located between the elementary and middle school buildings, with a calculated air of confidence that didn't reflect the knot in her stomach.

"Hi, Mrs. Hartman," Debra, the receptionist, simpered. "Don't tell me Harper forgot her lunch again." She cocked her head to one side and waited, the curious gleam in her eyes telling Bridget that Steve's notorious flight from the law was already on her radar.

"I need to pick my kids up. Family emergency."

"Oh, I'm so sorry. Is your mother doing okay?"

"Fine, thank you," Bridget replied through gritted teeth. "I'll just wait over here." She turned and walked over to the visitors' seating area before Debra had a chance to grill her any further. Out of the corner of her eye, Bridget watched her pick up a phone and call through to an extension. When she was done, she scooted across the floor on her wheeled office chair and stuck her head around the edge of a cubicle. Bridget couldn't make out the running commentary that ensued. No doubt Debra was gossiping with another staff member about the situation. Bridget was beyond caring. The important thing was to get her kids out of here before the general population was turned loose on the playground.

Five minutes later, Henry and Harper came walking down the corridor toward the reception foyer. Harper broke into a run when she saw Bridget and flung her arms around her. "Mommy!"

Bridget met Henry's questioning gaze and gave a subtle shake of her head, warning him not to ask any questions within earshot of the staff, or Harper for that matter.

She escorted her kids out to the car, feeling Debra's eyes burning into her back with every step, and bundled them in before peeling out of the parking lot. As she drove, she couldn't help wondering when they would return, if ever.

"Why are we getting out of school early?" Harper asked, in a tone of barely repressed excitement.

"I thought it would be best," Bridget responded. "Some of the kids haven't been very nice to you lately. Maybe you can take a few days off. You can spend a little more time with Grandma while she recovers."

Bridget glanced in the rearview mirror to see Harper staring out of the window, poker-faced. "Is Daddy home?"

"Not yet."

"Is he ever coming home again?"

Bridget's breath caught in her throat. "Of course he is, why would you ask such a thing?"

Harper began to swing her legs and kick the back of the seat. "Samantha said he's never coming home. She said he's a bad guy and he's gonna get locked up and the policeman's gonna throw away the key."

"Honey, don't listen to her," Bridget soothed. "There will always be kids who say mean things, but it doesn't mean they're true."

"But he *is* a bad guy if he killed Quinn's mommy."

N. L. HINKENS

Bridget willed herself to remain calm even as her blood boiled in her veins. What kid had told her daughter that? They must have heard it from a parent. What was wrong with people discussing such a macabre crime within earshot of young children? "Sweetheart, we don't know what happened to Quinn's mommy. Nobody should be saying such nasty things to you. The police are still trying to figure everything out."

"I don't want Daddy to kill you," Harper whimpered.

Henry let out an audible gasp. "Harps! That's a dumb thing to say! Dad would never kill Mom."

Suppressing a weary sigh, Bridget turned down their street and then quickly slammed on the brakes, staring in horror at the sight in front of her. The news crews had arrived in full force and taken over the neighborhood. Three vans with mounted cameras aimed at her house were parked along the curb, in addition to a dozen or so other miscellaneous vehicles. A reporter stood at the bottom of Bridget's driveway talking into a mic. Several of her neighbors were leaning in their doorways, gawping at the spectacle. Some looking as if they were eagerly anticipating being invited into the fray, others wary and keeping their distance.

"What are we going to do, Mom?" Henry said in a subdued tone, sounding younger than his fourteen years.

"We can't go home. We'll have to go to Grandma's and Grandpa's for a bit." Bridget made a quick U-turn and exited the street before anyone could intercept her. She hit the speaker on her phone and dialed Detective Wright's number, relieved when he picked up on the first ring. "It's a zoo at my house," she blurted out. "I don't know what to do. I can't get near the place. Are they allowed to surround my house like that?"

"I'll send a squad car over to check things out," Detective Wright responded. "So long as they're on public sidewalks and streets, they're not doing anything illegal, but I'll see if I can't disperse them. Hold on a minute, Lopez is signaling to me."

The line went quiet for a moment and then Detective Wright came back on. "That was forensics. The fibers from your house weren't a match."

"Well, that's one piece of good news, I suppose," Bridget said.

"Yes and no," Detective Wright said. "The fibers didn't match any of the carpets in the Carsons' house either. It doesn't rule Keith or your husband out as suspects. It only confirms that Jen Carson wasn't strangled in either home. Whoever killed her could have done it in a hotel room, for all we know. Where are you at the moment?"

"I'm on my way to my parents' house. I can't stay here. Half my neighbors are out on their lawns ogling the news crews." Bridget hesitated. "Did Officer Lopez find out anything useful from any of the neighbors?"

"No one saw Steve leave. Most of them were at work at that time of day. We followed up with Uber, and the cab companies too, and no one ordered a ride to pick up from your address. But we'll keep digging. I'll let you know if we get a hit on anything."

When he ended the call, Bridget released a frazzled sigh.

"What did the policeman say, Mommy?" Harper pried.

"They're still looking for Daddy," Bridget replied, keeping her tone upbeat. "How about we pick up some pizza for lunch and bring it over to Grandma's and Grandpa's? What flavor would you like?"

"Hawaiian, please!" Harper squealed.

"Pepperoni," Henry added.

"All right," Bridget said. "Quiet down while I call Grandpa and let him know we're on our way."

Forty-five minutes later, they pulled up at her parents'

house with two large pizzas in hand. Bridget mustered her resolve as she rang the doorbell. She would have to find a way to tell her parents what she and Henry had done—or not done, in her case. Now that all the news channels were covering the story, it was going to come out, sooner or later. She would have to give it some thought as to how best to break it to her parents gently. What Henry, in particular, had done would devastate them.

"Oh my, that's a lot of pizza," Elise said, when they descended on her in the family room.

"It's probably overkill," Bridget agreed.

"Nuh-uh! I can eat a whole one myself," Henry protested.

Elise chuckled. "I'm sure you can!"

"Thanks for letting us stay here tonight," Bridget said.

"You know you're always welcome," her dad chimed in, his brow trenched with concern. "I'm worried about your safety."

"We shouldn't discuss that right now." Bridget gave a meaningful tilt of her chin in Harper's direction.

"*Please*, can we eat our pizza?" Harper pleaded.

Bridget smiled. "It's kind of early for lunch, but, sure, if you're hungry. What about you, Henry?"

"I'll wait and eat with you guys later," he said, sinking down in an armchair facing the television."

Bridget accompanied Harper into the kitchen and set her up at the table with two slices of pizza and then put the rest in the refrigerator. She walked back into the family room and sat down next to her mom. "I feel like I've been neglecting you these past couple of days."

"Nonsense." Elise patted her leg. "With everything you have going on, I can't believe you're holding it together as well as you are."

Bridget grimaced. "Only on the outside. I have to keep

going for the kids' sake. I can't think about what's happening too much or the tears start flowing."

She glanced across at the television in the corner of the room. The volume was turned down low, but it was tuned to the local news channel. She froze when all of a sudden Steve's face filled the screen. She couldn't hear what the newscaster was saying, but it was obvious they were reporting on his disappearance. The camera slowly panned to a shot of her house. The crowd outside had only swelled in the past hour or so. Bridget's eyes widened when she realized the reporter was interviewing their next-door neighbor. "Turn that up, Henry," she hissed, flapping a hand at the television.

He reached for the remote on the coffee table in front of him and pointed it at the screen.

"I'm here with Steve Hartman's next-door neighbor, Bart Rasmussen," the reporter announced. "Bart, what's your reaction to the news this morning that Steve Hartman— allegedly wanted for the murder of Jen Carson, the mother of his son's best friend—has skipped bail?"

Bart shook his head in a disbelieving manner. "It's shocking in a neighborhood like ours. He always seemed like such a nice guy, hard worker too. Guess you never really know a person. Turns my stomach to think I was living next door to a killer." He hesitated and looked straight at the camera. "And to think that boy of his was in on it with him. Piece of trash tossed that poor woman's body into a dumpster."

24

*E*lise twisted around in her chair, mouth agape. "Are they talking about ... Henry?"

"Mom ... I wanted to—" Bridget startled at a rustling sound behind her. She swung around and let out a gasp of dismay. Harper stood in the doorway, her piercing stare fixed on the television screen. Bridget leapt out of her chair and hurried over to her daughter, wrapping her up in her arms. "How long have you been standing there, honey?"

Harper shrugged her tiny shoulders. Her eyes darted to Henry.

He shifted uncomfortably in his seat, fastening a pleading look on Bridget.

Her breath came in short, sharp jabs which felt like someone was stabbing her chest. Her dad reached for her mom's hand and then turned to Bridget expectantly. It seemed everyone was counting on her to say something, to come up with an answer to make things better, to make this go away. But how could she? Henry had made his choice, just like Steve had. And now she was stuck in the middle trying to reassure her seven-year-old on one end and dispel her aging parents' fears on the other. The truth was, she couldn't shield her parents any longer, and she couldn't cushion her fourteen-year-old son from the consequences of his rash decision, but she still had to fight to protect her daughter's innocence as best she could.

"You can't trust the news," Bridget said briskly. "They make up outrageous stories to get people to tune in. You need to ignore everything people are saying, on the news and at school. Do you understand me, Harper?"

Her daughter stared back at her with a look in her eyes Bridget hadn't seen before. She looked so much older than her seven years. As if she sensed her mother was lying to protect her, even if cognitively she couldn't quite grasp why. Bridget blinked back tears. The age of innocence was over. No matter how hard she fought for her family, things would never be the same for any of them again.

John motioned to Henry to hand him the remote control. "How about we watch a movie together, Harps?" he suggested, as he pulled up the menu on the TV screen. "Here we go, we've got The Princess Diaries, Toy Story, oh and here's that Frozen movie you love."

Harper shook her head. "No thanks, Grandpa. I'm just going to play with my Barbies."

Bridget's heart broke as she watched her daughter beat a retreat down the hallway to the guest room dragging her little backpack behind her. Harper was missing her Daddy desperately. In the interim, she had latched on to Henry, but now, all of a sudden, her faith in her brother had been shattered in a way that was incomprehensible to a seven-year-old.

Bridget got to her feet. "I need to go and talk to her."

"Why don't you let her be for a bit?" her mom soothed. "Give her some time and then she'll be more ready to talk."

Bridget glanced across at Henry. He rubbed the back of

his hand over his eyes. "I'll never forgive myself for doing this to her."

John furrowed his brow. "Doing … what to her?" His eyes jerked uneasily to Bridget. "Is it … true … what they're saying?"

She squeezed her eyes shut and took a steadying breath. It was time to come clean and fill her parents in on everything that had happened.

When she'd finished going over what she and Henry had already confessed to Detective Wright, John got up and shuffled over to his grandson. He put an arm around him and squeezed him tightly. "It doesn't do any good to keep beating yourself up, Henry. I understand why you did what you did. It wasn't the right decision, but you didn't do it out of a bad motive. You were only trying to protect your dad. Harper may be too young to grasp that, but one day she will."

"It was still the wrong thing to do, no matter his motive." Bridget gave a despondent shake of her head. "He potentially messed up a crime scene, and the police don't look kindly on things like that."

Elise's fingers fluttered nervously over her face. "But he's only a boy. It breaks my heart to think that poor Henry was only trying to keep his dad out of trouble. Surely they won't lock him up for that."

Bridget pulled a strand of hair back from her forehead. "We don't know anything yet, Mom. He won't go to prison. Juvenile hall, maybe."

She startled when her phone began to ring. Glancing down at the screen, she saw an incoming call from Bryan, their lawyer. "I need to take this," she said, getting to her feet and exiting the room. She hurried to the kitchen and sank down in a chair at the table.

"I have good news and bad news," Bryan began without preamble.

"Please tell me they're not going to prosecute Henry," Bridget muttered. "That's all I care about right now."

"The good news is they're not going to prosecute you," Bryan replied. "The county prosecutor doesn't feel it would benefit anyone given the mitigating circumstances and given the fact that you volunteered the information."

"And Henry?"

There was a weighted pause on the other end of the line and then Bryan cleared his throat. "There's no real way for them to let it slide. The public's hungry for blood, especially now that Steve's disappeared. In his absence, Henry's become the sacrificial lamb, so to speak. The prosecutor is dead set on taking this all the way. He'd like to try Henry as an adult, if he can."

"Can he do that?" Bridget whispered.

"He can try to do anything he wants. Naturally, I'll do my very best to circumvent any such attempt and ask to have the petition filed with the juvenile court instead. Henry has no prior record and his motive was only to protect his father, not to cover up his own crime, so that will stand in his favor. There'll be a preliminary hearing tomorrow, at which time the judge will determine whether or not to transfer the case to adult court."

"So now what?"

"Henry will have to turn himself in. The police will charge him and release him." Bryan explained. "If he doesn't turn himself in voluntarily, he'll be arrested, and I'm sure you'd rather not have to deal with all the news crews, and the bedlam of an arrest."

Bridget shut her eyes and groaned inwardly. Just when she'd thought things couldn't get any worse. In the space of a couple of days, she'd gone from a law-abiding citizen to the wife of a fugitive and the mother of a criminal. "All right. I'll bring him down to the station now."

"Great, I'll meet you there," Bryan responded and hung up.

Bridget sank her head down on the table, the strength seeping from her limbs. She wasn't sure she could keep going. For one crazy moment she contemplated ushering her kids into the car and simply driving away. But it wouldn't fix anything. She was no more equipped to go on the run than Steve was. She didn't know the first thing about hiding from the police. The only way out of this was to move forward. She had to make sure Henry complied with the arrest warrant and then she'd work her way through the process. She needed to have a little faith that the judge would look favorably on their situation and allow Henry to be tried in juvenile court where he belonged.

Wearily, she rose from the table and trod back into the family room, her feet like leaden blocks beneath her.

Her mom blinked quizzically at her. "Everything all right, dear?"

"No, that was our lawyer. The prosecutor wants to file charges against Henry."

Henry's brows twitched up in alarm. "Am I going to prison?"

"No, of course not," Bridget replied hastily. "But we need to go down to the station and fill out some paperwork. It's only a formality. They'll give us a hearing date and you'll have to go before a judge."

"Oh, the poor child," her mom exclaimed. "You do have a good lawyer, don't you Bridget, dear?"

"We'll find out," she said through gritted teeth. "If it's all right with you, I'll leave Harper here. She's traumatized enough as it is without me dragging her down to the police station."

"Of course," her mom soothed. "Don't worry about her."

Bridget nodded her thanks. "I'll let her know I need to

run an errand with Henry." She exited the room and returned a few minutes later. "She's fast asleep on the bed, poor thing. Probably best to leave her be. We'll be back as soon as we can. Do you need anything from the store while we're out?"

Her dad scratched his head. "Why don't you pick up a gallon of milk and some cereal for the kids in the morning?"

WHEN THEY ARRIVED at the station, Bryan was waiting for them in the reception area. "I've reviewed the paperwork. Everything's in order. You'll both need to sign it." He handed it to Bridget first and threw Henry a sympathetic smile. "Don't worry, they're not going to keep you in custody. You're not considered a threat to yourself or others."

Bridget looked up as Detective Wright approached them. "I'm sorry it came to this," he said, grimacing. "I tried to advocate for him in my report, but ultimately, it's not my decision."

"Thanks for trying," Bridget replied. "I appreciate everything you've done to help us."

Detective Wright nodded. "I should tell you that we have a new lead on Steve. A dog walker in your neighborhood reported seeing a silver Audi parked at the curb near your house on Friday morning. He didn't get a number or anything, but he stopped to admire it as it was one of those new luxury sedans. We're trying to follow up on it right now."

Bridget furrowed her brow. "So someone did come to the house. Do you think they picked Steve up?"

"That's our best guess at this point. We'd very much like to speak to that individual, as you can imagine."

"I don't think any of Dad's friends have a new Audi," Henry chimed in. "I'd have noticed something like that."

"Yeah, it's pretty much been a dead-end so far on that front," Detective Wright replied. "But we're still going through our databases. I'll keep you posted on any developments." He nodded goodbye to Bryan and then strode off toward his office.

"You're free to go for now," Bryan said, slipping a copy of the paperwork they'd signed into his briefcase. "I'll see you both at the hearing tomorrow. You have my number if you have any questions in the meantime."

Bridget and Henry exited the police station and walked back to the car together. "So far so good," Bridget said, unlocking it and climbing in. "At least they didn't detain you until the hearing. I'm not sure I could have handled losing you too." She placed both hands on the steering wheel and looked across at Henry. "I'm proud of you, son. You've stepped up to the plate these past couple of days. Helping out with Harper and all."

"I don't know what you're so proud of," Henry groaned. "I've messed up everything."

"You're not a coward, Henry. You're facing up to what you did. I'm proud of you for that reason for starters." Bridget grimaced as she turned the key in the ignition. *Unlike your father.*

On their way back, they swung by the grocery store and picked up a few breakfast items. Once they reached her parents' house, Henry carried the groceries inside to the kitchen and began putting them away. Bridget left him to it and joined her parents in the family room.

"How did everything go?" her dad asked, wringing his hands.

"So far so good. The hearing's tomorrow. The judge will decide whether it goes to adult court or stays in juvenile court." Bridget chewed on the inside of her cheek. "To be honest, I'm not optimistic. This is turning out to be a high-profile case thanks to Steve's reckless decision to run."

"I'm happy to give a character reference if it helps with the court hearing," her dad said, smoothing a hand over his thinning hair.

Bridget gave him a rueful smile. "Thanks, Dad. I'll ask Bryan about it next time he calls." She got to her feet. "Is Harper still asleep."

Her dad nodded. "I checked on her a little while ago."

"I'm going to put the kettle on," Bridget said. "Does anyone want a cup of tea?"

"Yes, please," her mom answered. "A cup of tea sounds good."

Bridget stepped into the kitchen to put the kettle on to boil. Henry was seated at the table, watching YouTube videos on his phone.

"Thanks for putting the groceries away," she said, squeezing his shoulder, before making her way down to the guest bedroom to check on Harper. She opened the door quietly and stuck her head in. She took in the scene with a vague sense of unease. The bed was rumpled but Harper was gone.

25

———

*B*ridget stepped inside the bedroom, searched around, and then made her way over to the adjoining bathroom. "Harper, are you in there, honey?" She turned the handle and walked into another empty room. A dull gong began to sound somewhere in the pit of her stomach, but she quickly quelled it. The events of the past few days had frayed her nerves to the point where she was jumping to the worst possible conclusions before she'd exhausted any more reasonable explanations. She hurried back up to the family room where her parents had just tuned into an episode of Jeopardy.

"Dad! Harper's not in the guest bedroom," she blurted out. "I don't see her backpack either. Are you sure she was there when you checked earlier?"

John got to his feet, a concerned look darting across his face. "Absolutely, I put a blanket over her. She must have just woken up in the last thirty minutes or so. She was out cold when I looked in on her."

"Did you check under the bed?" Elise suggested. "She was upset earlier at that news report. You know how little kids like to find a hiding spot to curl up in when they're upset."

Bridget shook her head. "She's not there."

"I'll help you look for her," John said, leading the way back down the hallway. "She might have fallen asleep some-place else."

Together, they combed through the bedrooms and bath-rooms, peeking into closets and searching under all the beds.

"I just don't understand it," John said, scratching his head. "She wouldn't have gone outside without telling us. She must be somewhere in the house." They made their way back down to the kitchen where Henry was still engrossed in his phone. "Have you seen Harper?" Bridget asked.

Henry looked up sharply, catching the urgency in her tone. "No, why?"

"She's not in the guest room, or any of the other bedrooms."

Henry stood abruptly, the chair screeching on the hard-wood floor beneath him. "I bet she hid when she heard us come back. She's mad at me."

With Henry's help, they searched through the laundry room, the mudroom, and the garage, but there was no trace of Harper anywhere.

Bridget's blood ran cold as several terrifying possibilities came to mind. She tried not to dwell on them, ignoring the increasingly painful, staccato beat of her pulse in her temples. She had to consider the possibility that Harper had wandered outside without telling her grandparents. She ran a hand distractedly through her hair, her stomach knotting at the thought. Bryan had indicated that the public was crying out for blood now that Steve had disappeared. What if someone had snatched her daughter? Would people go so far as to harm her children because of what her husband had done?

"Henry! Dad!" Bridget called out, as she headed to the front door. "I'm going to walk up and down the street in case Harper wandered outside. Can you start knocking on doors and asking the neighbors if they've seen her?"

Without waiting for an answer, Bridget dashed outside and scanned the road, desperately searching for a familiar tiny figure with a silver-and-teal backpack. She jogged down the front steps and set off down the road at a brisk pace, her hands stuffed into her pockets for warmth. She kept telling herself that Harper had to be close by. She might have woken up and been upset when she realized that Bridget and Henry had left her alone with her grandparents again. She hadn't been acting like herself lately. Her sweet spirit had been hit hard by everything that had happened in the past couple of days. She was confused by the shocking allegations against her brother and traumatized by the mean taunts of the kids at school.

In a haze of dread, Bridget peered behind every hedge, circled around parked cars, and asked everyone she bumped into if they'd seen a little girl with a backpack. Every so often, she called out Harper's name, blinking back blinding tears when her voice echoed into silence. Harper didn't even know how to cross a neighborhood street safely by herself. How on earth was she going to navigate junctions with traffic lights? And where was she headed to—if she even knew herself? Bridget swallowed back her trepidation. She had to stay calm for her daughter's sake, and for Henry's sake. She could tell he blamed himself now that Harper was missing. After all, it was the news report about him tossing Jen Carson's body in the dumpster that had upset his sister.

"Mom!"

She swung around at the sound of her son's voice, hopeful for one split second that she'd see Harper at his side.

"Any sign of her?" Henry yelled, jogging up to her.

She shook her head, watching disappointment leak into his face. "She has to be close by. She can't have gone far. We'll keep looking."

"Grandpa's checking with the neighbors," Henry said. "I'll scout around the places she used to play hide and go seek. Maybe she's holed up somewhere."

Bridget gave a distracted nod. She cleared her throat trying to keep her voice from wavering. "Good idea." She didn't want Henry to realize the depth of her panic. But Harper couldn't simply have vanished into thin air. Someone might have recognized her as Steve's daughter—some crazy vigilante who'd possibly decided to hold her hostage until Steve turned himself in.

"Mom," Henry said, suddenly grabbing her by the arms. "It's going to be all right."

Instantly, Bridget's eyes pooled with tears. She sniffed and fished out a tissue. Evidently, she wasn't fooling him.

He pulled her into a clumsy hug and then released her. "I'll find her, I promise." He turned and broke into a jog, wheeling down a side street up ahead.

Bridget shivered as she watched him disappear. What if something happened to Henry too? She shook her head free of the disturbing thought. No one was going to snatch a young, six-foot-two male in broad daylight. She needed to get a grip and keep her focus on finding her daughter, instead of speculating on grim scenarios that hadn't tran- spired. Every minute Harper was missing increased the danger of something happening to her.

"Excuse me!" Bridget called to an elderly woman kneeling in her front yard.

When the woman didn't respond, Bridget opened the wrought-iron gate at the end of the pathway and walked up to her. "Excuse me," she gasped. "Have you seen a little girl, seven-years-old, with a silver-and-teal backpack?"

The woman glanced up, a confused look in her rheumy eyes. She brushed a strand of silver hair behind her ear, exposing a hearing aid, and shook her head. "I haven't seen any children. Aren't they all in school this time of day?"

Bridget grimaced. Another stark reminder that this was no ordinary day in her kids' lives. They weren't in school this morning because the media had just announced to the world that their father was a killer on the run. Not that she was about to explain all that to a frail, elderly woman whose only concern was the weeds in her flowerbeds. Bridget thanked her and moved on, feeling as if she was operating in some other dimension. Was this really happening? Was her daughter actually missing now too?

Her flustered thoughts flew in circles as she continued her search through the entire neighborhood, half-jogging at times, sweat gathering in her armpits and beneath her collar. Anger boiled in her gut that Steve wasn't here to help her. She needed him now more than ever. Their young daughter had vanished, and he was nowhere to be found. How could he have done this to her—left her with only a pathetic hand-scrawled note? *I'm sorry.* He wasn't sorry, he was only sorry he'd been caught. He wasn't sorry about what his actions had prompted his son to do. He wasn't sorry about the shame his family was facing, or how Harper was being bullied at school. If he was sorry, he would have been here for them.

Bridget scrunched her eyes shut. What if she never saw her daughter again? This was an unbearable twist in an already unspeakable nightmare. She came to a sudden halt and grabbed an iron railing for support. Her mind flailed this way and that, trying to think of what to do next. She needed help. If Steve wasn't available, she'd have to call on someone who was.

After a moment's thought, she dug out her phone and scrolled through her contacts for Detective Wright's number. He would know what to do. He could figure out if Harper's disappearance was connected to the case or not. With trembling fingers, she dialed the number and pressed the phone to her ear. Her voice stuck in her throat when he answered.

"Hi … it's Bridget … Hartman. Harper's missing. I don't know what to do. I … I'm afraid someone might have taken her … we can't find her anywhere."

"Okay, slow down," Detective Wright said. "Where are you?"

"At my parents' place. We're canvassing the neighborhood trying to find her. My dad's knocking on doors. Henry's out here too looking for her. I'm so afraid—" She trailed off, swallowing back a despairing sob.

"How long has she been missing?" Detective Wright inquired.

"At least an hour. She was sleeping in the guest bedroom when Henry and I left to go down to the station. I went to check on her when we got back, and she wasn't there. She must have slipped out of the house. My parents are elderly, and with the television on, they wouldn't have heard her opening the door."

She scrunched her eyes shut as another thought hit. What if the police went after her parents for negligence? Maybe she shouldn't have mentioned the fact that she'd left Harper alone with them. Things were going from bad to worse. But she couldn't think about any more dire scenarios now. The important thing was to find Harper.

"Can you give me a description of what she was wearing?" Detective Wright asked.

Bridget swallowed the lump in her throat. He was taking this seriously, which was both good and bad at the same time. Apparently, he agreed with her that Harper might be in danger. "A white sweater with a puppy on the front. Pink jeans. Tennis shoes, and I think she took her backpack. It's silver and teal."

"All right I'm going to put out a BOLO. I'll send an officer your way. He'll be there in a few minutes."

"Thank you." Bridget slid the phone back into her pocket and picked up her pace. She wasn't going to stand around and do nothing while she waited on the officer to make an appearance. A middle-aged man walking two menacing-looking muzzled dogs approached on the other side of the street. She waved frantically and darted across to him. "Excuse me, have you seen a little girl walking along here? Seven-years-old with a backpack."

The man scowled and shook his head, barely breaking pace. Bridget clenched her hands into fists. How could people be so unfeeling? Wasn't her distress obvious? Then again, he probably thought she was just some overprotective mother. He wasn't to know the girl's father was an alleged killer on the run and that she might have been abducted.

Bridget crossed back to the other side of the street and continued searching in front yards and behind parked vehicles in driveways and along the curb. She didn't waste time stopping to ring doorbells. Most people were likely at work anyway. Interviewing the neighbors would be a job for the police if she couldn't find Harper. A sob escaped her lips. She wouldn't be able to stand it if anything happened to her daughter. It didn't bear thinking about. And it was all Steve's fault. His actions had shattered their family in more ways than one. She pulled out a tissue and wiped at the tears dangling from her lashes.

A shout from farther down the street caught her attention. She blinked through her tears and peered into the distance. Racing toward her was Henry. Clinging to his chest like a limpet on a rock was Harper.

*B*ridget collapsed to her knees on the sidewalk, sobbing with relief.

Henry ran up to her and laid a hand on her shoulder, panting hard. Scrambling to her feet, Bridget held out her arms for her daughter. "Is she all right?"

"She's fine." Henry heaved for breath as he tried in vain to peel his sister from his chest and hand her off.

"No!" Harper screamed, burrowing further into Henry's chest.

Resigned to her daughter's resistance, Bridget settled for wrapping her arms tightly around both of her children, whimpering with relief. "Where ... where did you find her?"

Henry took another sharp breath before answering. "I searched all our old hiding places. She was behind the electrical utility box at the end of the street."

Bridget rubbed her hand in gentle circles over her daughter's back. "You scared Mommy, Harper. I didn't know where you were. I'm so glad you're safe."

"Do you wanna go to Mom now?" Henry asked.

Harper shook her head against his chest, still not looking up at either of them.

Bridget and Henry exchanged a defeated look.

"Let's go back to Grandma's and Grandpa's," Bridget suggested. "They're bound to be worried sick."

As they approached the house, she caught sight of her dad dialoguing with one of the neighbors. She waved and called out to him, while Henry whistled loudly. The neighbor tapped John on the shoulder and pointed in their direction. Without a moment's hesitation, he abandoned his conversation and hurried down the path to meet them.

"Thank goodness you're safe, pumpkin," he said, kissing the back of Harper's head tenderly. "Where were you? You should have told Grandpa you were going outside. We—"

Bridget frowned and shook her head to warn him not to press the issue.

"Well, the main thing is you're okay," he continued brightly. "Let's go back inside and let Grandma know."

Five minutes later, a police officer showed up on the front doorstep. "We found her," Bridget explained when she opened the door to him. "She was hiding behind an electrical utility box at the end of the street. I'm sorry for making you come all the way out here, but I was afraid something might have happened to her." She hesitated and furrowed her brow. "You know, in light of my husband disappearing and everything. People are angry, and they can be unpredictable."

"You did the right thing to call it in," the officer reassured her, reaching for his walkie-talkie. "I'll cancel the BOLO and let Detective Wright know your daughter's safe."

After the officer left, Bridget returned to the family room where everyone was gathered. Harper was still sitting on Henry's lap, but she'd finally unlatched herself from his neck. Her eyes followed Bridget as she walked across the room and sat down on the chair opposite her. "Honey," Bridget began. "Why were you hiding?"

Harper's eyes darted to her grandparents and then back to her mom. "I didn't want anyone to find me."

"But why not?" Bridget persisted. "We were all really worried about you."

"I wanted to look for Daddy."

"Poor little angel," Elise tutted. "Don't you worry about your daddy, pumpkin. The police will find him."

Harper stuck out her bottom lip. "I don't want them to find him. I don't want Daddy to go to prison."

Henry squeezed his sister in his arms. "Don't worry about Daddy. I'm here for you in the meantime."

Bridget smiled gratefully at Henry. She didn't know what she would have done without his help. He'd turned out to be a real hero in this situation. Who else would have known where to begin to look for Harper? Her daughter desperately needed some daddy love, and, as young as he was, Henry seemed to realize that and was stepping up to the role. If only Steve could see him now, he'd be so proud of him.

BREAKFAST THE FOLLOWING morning was a subdued affair. Bridget hadn't slept well on the somewhat lumpy guest room mattress she'd shared with Harper, tossing and turning as her mind sifted through everything she needed to take care of in the coming days, beginning with this morning's hearing. She chewed on a piece of toast, steeling herself to break the news to Harper that she and Henry had to take off once more. Truth be told, she was terrified at the thought of leaving Harper with her parents again, but she couldn't in good conscience subject her to a court hearing on whether or not her brother would be tried as an adult.

Bridget wasn't entirely clear yet what Henry would be

charged with—tampering with evidence, or improperly disposing of a body? She took a long sip of black coffee, weighing her words carefully. "Harper, honey, I have to run an errand with Henry this morning. We won't be gone long, but I need you to stay with Grandma and Grandpa. It's very important you don't leave the house this time."

Harper stopped eating her Fruit Loops, spoon in midair. "But I want to go with you. I don't want to stay here."

"I know, but Mommy needs to talk to Henry's lawyer and it's not for little kids. Tell you what, if you're good for Grandma and Grandpa, Henry and I will bring back some ice cream and we can make sundaes this afternoon. How does that sound?"

Harper gave an enthusiastic nod. "Can we have gummy bears and sprinkles on them?"

"Yes," Bridget said with an inward sigh of relief. "We certainly can."

After they'd finished breakfast, Bridget and Henry hugged Harper goodbye and left for the court hearing. Bridget ran an approving eye over Henry's outfit. He was smartly dressed in a shirt and slacks in muted colors borrowed from her dad. For her part, she wore a floral wrap dress she hadn't seen her mother don in years. Bryan had advised them to look professional and respectful, but they'd had to make do with whatever clothing her parents had available to them.

"Are you nervous?" Bridget asked as they drove to the courthouse.

Henry shrugged. "I know this kid at our school who went to juvenile hall. He said it wasn't that bad."

Bridget's stomach twisted at the thought of her son going to juvenile hall. The very fact that he was even thinking about it broke her heart. "You don't know yet what's going to happen. The judge might throw out your case or order you to do community service or something. It's not like you're up for murder."

"You don't know that," Henry responded glumly. "They might charge me with that too."

Bridget shot him a sideways glance. "Much as I hate to admit it, the obvious suspect is your father. As far as the police are concerned, it was always either him or Keith Carson. They never considered you a suspect."

A few minutes later, they arrived at the courthouse parking structure and retrieved a ticket from the meter before pulling into a spot on the lower level.

"Ready?" Bridget turned to look at Henry.

He nodded and climbed out of the car, rubbing his hands on the unfamiliar slacks he was wearing.

Bryan was waiting for them at the top of the courthouse steps. "Doing okay, Henry?"

"Yeah," he answered, stuffing his hands into his pockets.

Bryan gave a reproving shake of his head. "Hands out of your pockets. The court's a serious place so don't smile or joke around when you're inside. Just be respectful when the judge addresses you and you'll be fine."

"Will I have to tell them what I did?" Henry asked, scratching at his jaw in an agitated fashion.

"No, you won't have to say much at all at this hearing, just answer a few basic questions." Bryan glanced at his watch. "The only decision being made today is whether or not to transfer this case to adult court. It will be up to me to convince the judge to keep it in juvenile court. Any other questions?"

Henry raised his brows at Bridget and then shook his head.

At the door, Bryan turned to them. "One more thing before we go in, turn off your cell phones. Judges don't take kindly to ringtones interrupting the proceedings."

In a somber procession of sorts, they followed Bryan into the courtroom and took their seats as directed. Bridget surveyed the room silently. The wood-paneled space was a hive of activity, the plastic water bottles and laptops dotted around the place at odds with the austere old-world charm of the rich wood. The judge, a middle-aged, bespectacled woman seated in a black leather chair, was in the process of reviewing the case ahead of them—a fifteen-year-old caught in the act of robbery.

"Mr. Steadman, you are charged with warrant 107495806, breaking into a motor vehicle," the judge said. "Do you understand these charges?"

"Yes, your honor," the defendant replied.

Bridget chewed nervously on her lip. The teenage defendant was five-seven or eight in height at most, which made him seem particularly vulnerable standing in the middle of the imposing courtroom surrounded by a bevy of adults typing furiously on laptops, or consulting their notes, while armed security guards in tan pants and black shirts milled around, eyes constantly roving the room's occupants.

"You have a right to an attorney, if you cannot afford one, one will be appointed for you," the judge droned on. "You also have a right to have this expunged from your record. If you are found not guilty, this charge will be dismissed."

Bridget zoned out, her thoughts drifting back to the moment she'd seen Jen Carson exiting Steve's office. If only she'd had the courage to confront the woman there and then, maybe none of this would have happened. She could have circumvented a murder. Instead, she'd acted like a coward and skulked away in the darkness to lick her wounds. She was no better than Steve running from his problems. With a grimace, she vowed to fight for Henry no matter what it took. When it came to her children, she would not back down.

"Mom," Henry whispered, nudging her in the ribs. "It's our turn."

Bridget blinked her eyes back into focus and turned to Bryan who gave her a confirming nod. She got to her feet and followed him and Henry up to the front of the courtroom. The judge shuffled some paperwork around on her desk before addressing them.

"Mr. Miller, our hearing today is regarding the charge against Mr. Henry Hartman relating to penal code 75-03-C and whether or not this case should be adjudicated in juvenile court or transferred to adult court."

"Yes, your honor. I move that the case remain in juvenile court due to my client's young age and the fact that he has no prior record. Furthermore, his motive was not to cover up a crime that he had committed, but rather a misguided attempt to protect his father."

The judge peered down over her spectacles at Henry. Her expression was impassive, and Bridget couldn't tell which direction she was leaning. More than anything, she wanted to jump in and beg for clemency for Henry—to tell the judge what an amazing and smart young man he was, and how kind he was being to his sister through all of this, and how he was really just a gentle giant despite his intimidating size. But she managed to bite her tongue. The judge wouldn't be swayed by a mother's biased opinion. Bridget needed to trust that Bryan's professional efforts would get the job done.

For a long moment there was silence, broken only by the rustling of papers and the tapping of fingernails on keyboards. Then, the judge cleared her throat. "I'm willing to keep this case in juvenile court given the extenuating circumstances your lawyer has outlined, Mr. Hartman. Your court date will be one week from today. You are not to leave the state, you will stay out of trouble, and you will appear for your court date as directed. In addition, you are to have no contact with Mr. Carson or any other members of the victim's family. Is that clear?"

"Yes your honor. Thank you, ma'am." Henry mumbled.

Bridget passed a trembling hand over her forehead, a torrent of relief rushing through her. Her heart was racing so fast she feared she might pass out. She glanced across at Bryan and mouthed her thanks. Whatever Henry's fate, at least he wouldn't have to face the full fury of an adult court judge and jury.

Her husband, on the other hand, was a different story—whenever his day came, a jury of his peers would not look kindly on a murdering coward.

"Well that went as well as we could possibly have hoped for," Bryan remarked when they convened outside the courthouse afterward. "Next step will be the adjudication hearing."

Bridget furrowed her brow. "What does that entail?"

"That's the trial, so to speak. The judge will read the prosecutor's petition and I'll present our case. I'll need to meet with you ahead of time to prepare for that. Call my office and set up an appointment sometime in the next day or two."

"What's going to happen to me after the trial?" Henry asked.

"I can't speculate on that," Bryan replied. "It's up to the discretion of the juvenile court judge. He could give you a reprimand, or order you to complete community service, or he could elect to detain you and send you to juvenile hall. I'll do my best to convince them to dismiss the petition. In the meantime, I'm going to advise you not to give any interviews to the press and, should your father return, I strongly recommend that you distance yourself from him until your trial is over. The more you're associated with an alleged killer, the less sympathy you're going to elicit from the judge or the public."

"Okay," Henry responded, sounding uncertain.

"Thank you," Bridget added. "I'll call your office later on this afternoon and make that appointment."

With a final wave, Bryan strode off to the parking structure elevator. Bridget and Henry made their way back to their car on the lower level.

"I'm glad that's over," Henry said, sinking down in the passenger seat.

"Me too," Bridget agreed, turning the key in the ignition. "Time to focus on something else now. Let's swing by the store and pick up those sundae supplies for Harper."

"And some cookie dough ice cream. Grandma only ever has vanilla," Henry said, pulling out his phone.

Bridget's lips twitched in a melancholy grin as she veered out of the parking structure. Her son really was still just a big kid at heart.

As she drove, Henry scrolled through his apps for several minutes before letting out an aggravated gasp. "You gotta be kidding me!"

"What's wrong?" Bridget threw him a scant glance before returning her attention to the road ahead.

"I'll show you once we're stopped," he said, sounding dejected. "You're not gonna like it."

"Just tell me what's going on, *please*," Bridget insisted, anxiety beginning to swirl up from her gut again. "Are kids saying mean stuff on social media?"

"They've been doing that for days," Henry retorted. "But now they've taken it up a notch."

Bridget swung into the grocery store parking lot and pulled into the first empty spot she found. She switched off the engine, turned to Henry, and held out her hand for his phone. "Let me see."

He sighed and passed it to her. "Scroll through all the pictures to the end."

Bridget stared at the first image on the screen, her stomach muscles clenching at the distressing sight. Their house had been egged. Dozens of close-up pictures were being shared and liked all over Instagram. The front door was stained with yoke, and remnants of shells were scattered all over the steps and down the pathway leading to the side-walk. Hardened egg trailed down the windowpanes like bird poop, and sodden cardboard egg cartons were strewn across the lawn. Bridget grimaced as she continued scrolling through the pictures. The house and yard were a complete mess. The whole front of the house would have to be hosed off—possibly power washed. It remained to be seen if the back had received the same treatment.

With a beleaguered sigh, she returned the phone to Henry. "Do you know who did this?"

He kept his eyes forward, his expression rigid.

"Henry! Do you know who's behind this?" Bridget repeated.

"A bunch of kids from school," he muttered angrily. "They've been threatening to do something like this, but I didn't think they'd go through with it, so I didn't say anything. I'm pretty sure Quinn was in on it, too."

"Quinn?" Bridget gawked at him, horrified. "Are you sure? Why would he do that after everything we've done for him?"

Henry studied her, his face twisted in pain. "You mean like kill his mom? It kind of wipes out everything we've ever done for him, don't you think?"

Bridget opened and closed her mouth before turning away and looking out the window at the shoppers bustling to and fro with overflowing carts and screaming kids in tow. Of course, Henry was right. Egging their house paled in

N. L. HINKENS

comparison to what they had put Quinn and his family through. What Steve had done was unforgivable.

Wearily, she reached for her purse and pulled the keys from the ignition. "I thought you said Quinn hated his mother."

"He kinda did because she didn't pay him any attention. But he still loved her."

Bridget rubbed her aching forehead. In a convoluted way, that made perfect sense. Volatile teenage emotions could swing from love to hate and back again in half a heartbeat.

"What are we going to do about our house?" Henry asked.

Bridget twisted her lips. "I'll have to hire a crew to clean it. I'll report it to Detective Wright first. Technically, it's vandalism. It's hard to believe no one saw it happen with the amount of people who've been hanging around our place lately."

"They did it in the middle of the night," Henry said. "A few kids posted about it."

"You need to screenshot all those posts so I can turn them over to Detective Wright."

Henry scowled. "I'm not gonna do that. They'll just take it out on me if I do. Anyway, most of the posts were on Snapchat and they've already been deleted."

"All right, we'll just send the Instagram pictures." Bridget pulled out her phone and dialed Detective Wright.

He answered after the first ring. "Hi, Bridget. Glad to hear you found Harper safe and sound. Is she all right?"

"She's fine, thanks. But I'm calling about something else. My house was egged last night. It's all over social media. Henry says it was a bunch of kids from his school. Some of them have been bragging about it."

"Do you want to press charges?" Detective Wright asked.

Bridget hesitated. "I don't think so. Henry's worried about the repercussions if we do. I just want to make sure it's on

204

record in case the harassment doesn't stop, and we have to take action later."

"Fair enough. Send me any photos or screenshots you have, and I'll start the process. I assume you're not planning on going back home any time soon. If you want to get any stuff out of your house, I can send Officer Lopez around to meet you there."

"That would be great—I do need to pick up some things. How about this evening, maybe around eight or so? Hopefully, the crowd will have dispersed by then."

"Sounds good, I'll put in a request." After a moment's pause, he added. "I assume you haven't heard anything from Steve?"

"Not a breath," Bridget replied. "No leads on your end either, I take it."

"I wish I had better news, but no luck so far. We're still working on the Audi tip. I've got a couple more dealerships within a hundred-mile radius to call. I'll keep you posted. In the meantime, keep trying to reach your husband."

"I will, thanks." Bridget hung up and stashed her phone in her purse before turning to Henry. "Come on, let's go get those supplies for your sister."

Armed with everything they needed to make ice cream sundaes à la Harper style, Bridget and Henry returned to her parents' house. Harper greeted them at the door, a huge smile stretched across her face. Bridget was heartened to see that she seemed to be back to her usual cheery self, even if it was only a temporary reprieve. She'd warned Henry not to mention what had happened to their house. She'd tell her parents about it later, but her daughter had enough on her small shoulders for now.

For the next half hour or so, Harper was happily occupied making exotic concoctions for every member of the family and proudly carrying each one into the family room to surprise them. "Yours is a *get-well sundae*, Grandma," she announced, as she handed Elise a glass dish piled high with three different flavors of ice cream and covered in gummy bears. "Those are your vitamins, so you have to eat them all." Harper hovered at her grandmother's side, eagerly waiting for her to take a bite.

"Mmm, this is delicious," Elise said. "You make the best ice cream sundaes."

Harper let out a dramatic sigh, her little chest rising and falling. "Daddy makes the best ice cream sundaes *and* the best pancakes."

Bridget gritted her teeth. Despite the best diversionary tactics, Steve was never far from his daughter's thoughts. This was not going to be an easy road ahead for them, no matter how things played out.

When Harper had finally finished dishing up the sundaes and presenting each one with a flourish, she disappeared into the kitchen to begin cleaning up her mess.

Bridget set down her napkin and turned to her parents. "Our house was egged last night. Henry showed me the pictures on social media."

Elise blinked across at her, a perturbed expression on her face. "Egged? You mean, people threw eggs at your house?"

"That's exactly what they did," Bridget said. "They're all over the windows and front door, and the shells are scattered across the pathway. And they even dumped the empty cartons on the front lawn."

John jerked his chin at Henry, his face creased with concern. "Let's see those pictures, son."

Henry pulled them back up on his phone and handed it to his grandfather. He reached for his reading glasses and studied the photos for a long moment before passing the phone to Elise. She pursed her lips and shook her head in disbelief as she peered at the pictures. "I can't believe the cruelty of some people. Who would behave in such a vindictive way?"

"It was kids from school," Henry said. "They've been threatening to do something like this. I think they talked Quinn into getting on board."

"Can't you have a word with him and put an end to it?" Elise asked. "He's your best friend, after all."

Henry shot Bridget an uncertain look. "I'm not supposed to talk to him until after my trial."

She gave a small shrug. "It doesn't mean I can't talk to him. I've half a mind to go around to his house myself. Maybe if I apologize to him and explain how distraught we all are over his mom's death, he might tell the kids to back off."

"Are you sure that's wise?" John asked.

"I don't know if it's wise," Bridget conceded. "But it would be a step in the right direction. Maybe I'll even get a chance to talk to Keith while I'm there. I feel awful for suspecting him."

"I'll go with you," John said.

Bridget shook her head. "I think it would be for the best if I talk to them on my own."

"Then I'll wait in the car," her father replied firmly. "But I'm not about to let you go around there by yourself. After what happened at your house, you should be prepared for trouble wherever you go."

*S*hortly before seven-thirty, Bridget left her parents' place to drive to her house and meet Officer Lopez. She'd made an extensive list of everything she needed to pick up for herself and the kids, fully aware that her mind was far too frazzled to think on the spot, and that it could be days before she made it back to her house again. For all she knew, they mightn't be able to return at all. Vandals might not stop at an egging spree. They could decide to take radical action and burn the whole place down. She intended to take full advantage of Officer Lopez' presence and protection while she had it and spend whatever time it took at the house gathering up as much of their stuff as possible.

As she drove, she tried calling Steve's disposable phone again. She had no real expectation that he would answer, but at least she could assure Detective Wright she was still trying to reach him. She desperately wanted Steve to turn himself in. As much as what he had done sickened her, the thought of him being shot to death in a stakeout with the police pained her heart. At the end of the day, he was still her husband and her children's father, and she couldn't easily erase the lifetime of memories they had made together.

Bridget pulled onto her street at five minutes to eight, her stomach heaving in anticipation of what awaited her. To her relief, the news crews vans were gone. Only two unmarked vehicles remained. Of course, there was no guarantee they weren't waiting to notify the news crews of her arrival. But at least she'd be able to get into her house without a circus erupting around her.

She swung into her driveway and sat for a moment in her car, wondering whether she should make a run for it or wait for Officer Lopez to arrive. The issue was resolved when the driver's door to one of the unmarked vehicles opened and Officer Lopez stepped out. Bridget exhaled in relief. Thankfully, he'd had the sense to come in an inconspicuous vehicle. A squad car would have been a sure indication something was afoot and would almost certainly have attracted the reporters back for another feeding frenzy.

"Thanks for meeting me here," Bridget said. "I wasn't sure what to expect."

"No problem." Officer Lopez graced her with one of his perfectly calibrated smiles. "Let's get this done and blaze a trail out of here before it gets too dark. That's when troublemakers typically show up." He kept an eye on their surroundings while she fumbled with the key in the front door, trying not to inhale the rotten odor coming from the dried-out eggs plastered everywhere.

She pushed the door open and stepped inside, looking around her home with fresh eyes. Signs of happier days and childhood memories in the making were scattered along the hall—a pair of dirty tennis shoes, an abandoned volleyball bag, a textbook, a lunchbox that had yet to be emptied judging by the all-too-familiar smell of an overripe banana wafting from it. It broke Bridget's heart to think her children might never return to the only home they'd ever known.

Officer Lopez closed and bolted the front door behind them before turning to her. "What can I help with?"

She set down her purse on the console table and rubbed her arms as she contemplated how best to go about the packing job. "I'll gather up a few boxes and plastic tubs from the garage to haul my stuff in. Maybe you can start putting the kids' clothes in some black trash bags while I load up the other essentials."

They worked steadily for the next hour or so, ignoring the repeated ringing of the doorbell that had commenced less than five minutes after their arrival. Bridget peered discreetly through the family room window and confirmed that a handful of people had gathered out on the street again, including a reporter with a microphone. A neighbor had been recruited to ring the doorbell, ensuring the reporter wasn't breaking any laws.

Bridget dreaded the moment when she'd have to open her front door and start carrying the loaded boxes and bags out to her car. Despite Officer Lopez's assurances that no one was permitted to step onto her property, he wouldn't be able to stop them from hurling abuse at her. Questions from reporters were inevitable, but she shuddered at the thought of enduring vitriolic taunts and disparaging comments aimed at her and her family.

After she'd packed her personal items, she went into Steve's office and took a quick look around. There was nothing here that she needed. She frowned at the empty spot where Steve's desktop computer usually sat. The police hadn't mentioned anything about the Tech team finding the emails between Keith and Steve. Maybe she should give Detective Wright a quick call and see what he'd made of them. She sat down at the desk and dialed his number.

"I'm at my house with Officer Lopez packing up my stuff," she said when he answered. "I just wondered if the Tech team had found the emails between Keith and Steve on his computer?"

"As a matter of fact, I got a printout of them an hour or so ago," Detective Wright replied. "Naturally, I'd love to be able to talk to Steve about the contents. So far, I've only got Keith's side of the story."

Bridget dragged a hand through her hair. "What did he have to say about threatening my husband?"

"He insists he wasn't threatening him, just spouting off—angry because Steve refused to admit he was having an affair with his wife and helping her siphon money from the company."

"How did he explain Steve asking him what he'd done to his wife?" Bridget asked. "Surely that's an indication Steve suspected Keith had harmed her."

"Keith's theory is that Steve had already killed Jen by then and was trying to throw everyone off the scent."

Bridget considered this for a moment. "If that's the case, why did Keith arrange to meet up with Steve instead of going straight to the police with his suspicions?"

"The way he tells it, it was all about the money. He was afraid the company would go under and he would lose everything. He wanted Steve to own up to where he and Jen had stashed the money. And then he was going to turn him in for her murder."

"Do you believe him?" Bridget asked.

Detective Wright sighed. "If your husband's innocent, he's not doing himself any favors by running. These emails could help his defense, but only if he shows up to face the charges."

Bridget nibbled on a ragged fingernail. She was right back to where she'd started with her own suspicions—if Steve was innocent, why had he run? "I tried calling him again a little while ago. Still no answer."

"All right, keep at it. He might come to his senses yet. Without hearing Steve's side of the story, Keith Carson has free rein to interpret the emails in a way that puts him in the best light. In fact, he's holding a press conference tomorrow at noon."

Bridget's blood turned to ice in her veins. What exactly was Keith planning to say? This could put her kids in more danger than ever. She had to talk to him beforehand—apologize and try and persuade him to appeal to the public to leave them alone. Detective Wright might not approve of her plan, but he didn't need to know. "I'd better get going," she said. "I should bail out of here before it gets too late."

She made a final sweep of the house before hunting down Officer Lopez and letting him know she had everything she needed.

He made his way to the front door, where they'd stacked up the boxes they were taking, and took a quick peek outside to assess the situation. "There are several reporters out there now. It might be best if I load the car and you wait inside until we're ready to leave."

"Are you sure?" Bridget slid a guilty gaze his way. "I feel bad about leaving you to haul all the boxes."

"It's not that much," Officer Lopez assured her. "It will make my job easier if I don't have to worry about your safety."

Bridget raised her brows. "I thought you said no one's allowed to step on my property."

"They're not," he confirmed. "But there's no guarantee the mob mentality won't result in something being lobbed your way. A decent-sized rock on the side of the head would be enough to knock you out."

Bridget scratched at her cheek nervously. "What about you?"

Officer Lopez dismissed her concern with a wave of his hand as he reached for a plastic tub of toiletries. "They won't mess with an armed police officer. If there's any indication of trouble, I'll call for back up."

Bridget gave a dubious nod and stepped away from the door, concealing herself from view as Officer Lopez carried the first load out to the car. She cringed at the barrage of questions and comments that trailed him.

"Officer! Is the killer's wife going to be arrested?"

"Will the fourteen-year-old be charged as an adult?"

"Sickos, the lot of them!"

"Can you comment on whether the girl's been placed in foster care?"

"The kid did it! Fry him!"

"Is it true it was really the fourteen-year-old who was having an affair with Jen Carson?"

Bridget squeezed her eyes shut and retreated to the kitchen. She couldn't listen to the putrid bombardment any longer. It was clear her entire family had been tried and condemned along with Steve. As usual, the public had dispensed with the facts and run with a far more titillating adaptation, going so far as to speculate that Henry had been both Jen's lover and killer.

Bridget sank down at the dining table and ran her hands over her face. She would go to the Carsons' place tomorrow and try to reach out to them. Maybe Keith would take pity on her. After all, they'd both lost their spouses, in one sense or another. She would express to him and Quinn how terribly sorry she was for what Steve had done, and maybe they would reciprocate with a sliver of sympathy. Hopefully, Quinn would agree to tell the kids at school to back off, and Keith might even be willing to address the issue with the media and ask everyone to restrain from venting their rage on Steve's family, who were also victims. Of course, it was a stretch to say Henry was merely a victim. She had to admit he'd done something reprehensible in the eyes of the community, and now they were all paying the price for it.

"Okay, your car's loaded up," Officer Lopez said, coming back into the room. "If you're ready, I'll escort you out and follow you to your parents' place."

"That's really not necessary," Bridget said. "You've done more than enough already."

"I'd feel better knowing you made it there safely. Besides, if anyone attempts to follow us, I can call it in and have them pulled over."

Bridget nodded her thanks. What he was saying made sense. It didn't do her or her family any good if the hostile crowd outside simply relocated to her parents' neighborhood.

Steeling herself for the walk of shame from her front door to her car, she exited the house at Officer Lopez's side. Keeping her head down, she hustled over to her car and wrenched open the door, ignoring the feverish volley of questions and jeers. Quaking, she slid behind the wheel and gripped it tightly with her left hand as she turned the key in the ignition. Glancing in her rearview mirror, she saw that Officer Lopez had positioned himself at the bottom of her driveway and was guiding her out. She backed out slowly, half afraid the crowd would swarm the trunk of her car and start hammering on it with their fists. She crawled off down the street, thankful to see Officer Lopez's vehicle in close pursuit. As he'd predicted, one of the reporters jumped in her car and did a U-turn in the street, intent on following them.

Within minutes, a squad car with flashing lights was on her tail and pulled her over. Bridget swallowed back the bile in her throat, thankful for police protection, but nauseated at how vulnerable she'd become. Was this to be her life from now on? Hunted and exiled—an outcast in her own community? The only saving grace was that the public's attention span was short. As morbid a thought as it was, she couldn't help hoping it wouldn't be long before they latched onto their next victim and left her and her children in peace.

29

---

*A*t her parents' house, Officer Lopez helped Bridget and Henry unload the car and carry all their bits and pieces inside.

"I really appreciate all your help," Bridget said, when he got ready to take off.

"My pleasure. Don't hesitate to call if you feel threatened again in any way." He tipped his fingers to his head and strode back down the driveway to his car.

"I'm thankful Officer Lopez was there at the house with me," Bridget commented to Henry as they watched him drive away.

Henry turned to her. "Was it really bad?"

Bridget nodded. "Not so much the questions from the reporters, more the ugly comments and jabs." She squeezed Henry's arm and led him back inside the house, reluctant to elaborate on the malicious gibes she'd overheard that pertained to him.

"Why don't you go put your things away," she suggested. "I want to talk to Grandma and Grandpa alone for a few minutes."

216

"I don't have to go to school tomorrow, do I?" Henry asked.

"No, I'm keeping you and Harper home from school in the meantime. We'll talk about your options after the trial when we know where we stand."

Bridget grabbed a water bottle from the refrigerator in the kitchen and joined her parents in the family room. "Did Harper go to bed without kicking up a fuss?"

"She was no trouble at all," Elise assured her. "Poor little thing was exhausted. How was it at the house?"

Bridget pulled a face. "I suppose it could have been worse. At least nobody threw anything at me. I was prepared for anything."

John let out a sigh. "I'm so sorry you're going through this, dear. It's not right. Whatever Steve's done, he should have stayed and faced it."

"I just found out that Keith Carson's holding a press conference tomorrow at noon," Bridget said. "I'm going to go around there first thing in the morning. Maybe I can persuade Keith to appeal to everyone to leave both of our families alone. If nothing else, I need to let him and Quinn know how sorry I am."

"I'm not sure that's such a great idea. If it doesn't go well, Keith could use the press conference to make things worse for you." John rubbed his brow disconcertedly. "If he threatened his wife before, he has a temper."

"I have to try," Bridget insisted. "Besides, Quinn left his house key at our place and I need to return it to him. It will be a good excuse to see how receptive Keith is to hearing me out."

"I can tell I'm not going be able to talk you out of it," John conceded. "What time do you want to go over there?"

"Let's say eight. I don't know for sure if Keith will be there, but at least I can have a chat with Quinn—he won't be at school, he posted something about being out for the rest of the week."

John got to his feet, a stiff crust of resignation on his face as he walked over to help Elise up. "All right, it's settled. I'll see you bright and early."

THE NEXT MORNING, Bridget drank a black coffee while her dad ate a plateful of scrambled eggs. She didn't trust her stomach to handle any food, at least not until after she had this uncomfortable conversation with Quinn and his father behind her. She didn't particularly like what she knew of Keith Carson, but she'd come to the unhappy conclusion that even though he'd threatened his wife on multiple occasions, he wasn't the one ultimately responsible for her murder—there was no getting around the fact that Steve was the man on the run.

Her dad got to his feet and took his plate over to the sink. "I'll just let your mother know we're leaving and then I'll be right out."

Bridget reached for her purse and checked her messages as she made her way to her car. Still no response from Steve. Her heart sank. She couldn't help fearing the worst—what if he'd taken his life, overcome with guilt? If that were the case, the police might never find him. She grimaced, wondering how people managed to live out their lives with no conclusive answers about their loved one's fate. Wherever Steve was, whatever he had done, she would rather know the agonizing truth than be left to speculate for years on end.

A few moments later, her dad shuffled out to the car. They drove the short distance to the Carsons' house making small talk and avoiding alluding to the uncomfortable task Bridget had set herself. She parked along the street and turned to her dad. "Please, promise me you'll stay in the car."

"I won't move unless you text me otherwise," he assured her.

Bridget kissed him on the cheek before making her way up the path to the front door and ringing the doorbell. She waited anxiously for a minute or two before Maria opened the door to her. A flicker of consternation crossed her brow. "Bridget! I didn't expect to see you here."

"Hi, Maria, I was hoping to talk to Quinn, and Keith too, if he's home."

The housekeeper cast a quick glance up and down the street and then ushered Bridget inside. "Keith went to the office to take care of a few things. Quinn's here though." She led Bridget through to the kitchen. "Would you like a cup of coffee?"

"Sure, that would be great," Bridget replied. She'd already had more than enough caffeine to set her teeth on edge but holding a mug would give her something to do with her shaking hands.

Maria poured her a coffee and refilled her own mug before joining her at the table. "I take it you still haven't heard anything from your husband."

Bridget shook her head. "That's why I'm here, actually. I wanted to tell Quinn face-to-face how sorry I am. I didn't want to believe at first that my husband could be behind something so awful, but the facts don't lie." She stared morosely into her coffee mug.

Maria reached over and put a hand on her arm. "That's just it, Bridget. You don't have all the facts. You're assuming you know what happened."

Bridget twisted her lips. "I realize that Keith and his wife weren't getting along, and I know that people in unhappy marriages say a lot of ugly things to each other. But Keith's not the one on the run, Maria. Evidently, my husband has something to hide."

Before the housekeeper had a chance to respond, Quinn strode into the kitchen. He came to a sudden halt, clearly taken aback at finding Bridget sitting at the table.

She got to her feet and walked over to him, embracing him before he could get away. "Quinn, I'm so sorry about your mom. If I could make this right, believe me I would."

He gave an embarrassed nod. "I know. You've always been kind to me, Mrs. Hartman. I wish my mom had been more like you."

Bridget blinked back tears. It broke her heart to hear the anguished resentment in his voice.

"Do you want some breakfast?" Maria asked him.

He shook his head as he slid into a chair. "I'm not hungry."

For a moment there was an awkward silence, and then Quinn fastened a stricken gaze on Bridget. "Mrs. Hartman, I'm sorry about what happened to your house. I didn't want any part of it, but these kids at school, they were going on and on about it and—"

"It's all right," Bridget interrupted. "We've all made mistakes. Believe me, yours is the least of them."

Quinn sniffed, scratching one arm nervously. "It won't happen again. I told the other kids I'd go to the police if they don't leave you alone."

"I appreciate that, Quinn." Bridget gave him a tentative smile. "It's one thing when people are saying ugly things about you, but when it gets physical, it's terrifying. Especially without Steve being here to—" Her voice trailed off.

Quinn looked at her curiously. "Do you really not know where he is?"

Bridget drew her brows together and shook her head. "He left a note saying *I'm sorry*. That's it. No indication of where he was going or why. He won't answer his phone or respond to any of my messages."

Quinn rubbed a hand over his jaw. "Me and Henry argued about it a lot. I didn't want to admit it, but I thought all along it was my dad who did it—he threatened Mom enough times."

"Quinn," Bridget said gently. "Why did you lie to Detective Wright about that? Why did you tell him your mom threatened your dad?"

Quinn shot a frightened glance from Bridget to Maria and back. "Dad told me to. He said the police were trying to frame him for Mom's murder."

Bridget closed her eyes briefly, contemplating whether or not to press him on the issue. Maybe she could persuade him to retract his statement and tell Detective Wright the truth. She startled at the sound of footsteps coming into the room, turning her head to see Keith looming over them.

"Bridget! What's going on in here?" he demanded.

She scooted her chair out from the table and stood. "I wanted to come over here in person and tell you how terribly sorry I am. If there was any way at all I could make this right, believe me I would."

Keith appeared to size her up for a moment before responding. "They still haven't eliminated me as a suspect."

"I know, and I'm sorry for what you've been put through," Bridget responded. "I didn't want to believe my husband was capable of doing something so awful, but the evidence speaks for itself."

"It appears so," Keith agreed, his brow furrowed.

"I … also wanted to apologize for my son's role in all of this," Bridget continued. "He wasn't thinking straight—he was scared for his dad. I know it was rash and stupid, and Henry deeply regrets it."

Keith cleared his throat. "I imagine this isn't easy for you either. I know what they've been saying about you and your family."

"It's been very hard—a nightmare, to be honest," Bridget admitted. "We've had to move out of our house for the foreseeable future."

"If there's anything I can do, let me know," Keith said, with a helpless shrug.

"Detective Wright told me you're holding a press conference at noon," Bridget replied, seizing the opening. "Maybe you could appeal to the public to leave both of our families alone."

Keith gave a curt nod. "I'll see what I can do."

Bridget smiled her thanks. "I should get back to my kids. I appreciate you hearing me out."

Maria got up from the table and escorted her to the front door. "Don't trust that man," she said in a low tone, her gaze locked on Bridget. "He wanted his wife dead, and he got his wish. I don't believe for one minute that's a coincidence."

30

*B*ridget's dad peered across at her anxiously when she climbed back into the car. "How did it go?"

"Better than I expected. I don't think Quinn holds what Steve did against me, or against Henry either, for that matter. And he was bummed about what the kids did to our house."

"I saw Keith pull into the garage a few minutes ago. How did he react?" her dad asked.

"I told him how sorry I was. He knows how stressful this has been for us too. I'm optimistic he'll appeal to the public to leave both of our families in peace."

"That's a relief to hear. It was brave of you to talk to him."

"I had to try for Quinn's sake—he's like a second son to me. He's spent a lot of time at our house lately. I can't even imagine the pain he's going through right now. It's bad enough watching Henry suffer—he's essentially lost a parent also."

John pressed his lips together. "The whole situation's a crying shame if you ask me."

Bridget nodded despondently as she started up the car

and shifted into drive. "Let's go home and check on Mom and the kids."

As she drove, she mused over Maria's words, mumbling appropriate responses to her dad's occasional remarks. It wasn't the first time Maria had strongly hinted that Keith had something to do with his wife's death. Bridget hadn't entirely dismissed the notion that he might have blackmailed Steve into getting rid of Jen's body in exchange for keeping his mouth shut about Steve's and Jen's affair. And then there was the money Keith was so desperate to recover. What role had Steve played in that?

An uncomfortable nagging at the back of Bridget's mind grew stronger. If Steve had been helping Jen siphon off money from Keith's company, it was possible he'd bought himself safe passage across the border and was already a long way from here reaping the rewards of his cunning scheme. As outrageous as it sounded, it was all beginning to make sense. It appeared her husband was a better liar, and a whole lot cleverer, than she'd ever given him credit for. He was definitely not the man she thought she'd married.

By the time they got back to the house, Harper was bouncing off the walls. "Henry says we don't have to go to school today *again*!"

"He's right," Bridget replied. She turned to her son with a pleading look in her eyes. "Maybe you can take your sister to the park when it warms up and let her burn off some of that energy."

"Sure." He shuffled his feet, looking awkward. "Did you … talk to Quinn?"

"Yes, he's really sorry about what happened to our house. I get the impression the other kids strong-armed him into it."

Henry looked relieved. "I knew he'd feel bad about it afterward."

Bridget pulled her phone out of her purse. "I'm going to

call your lawyer now to make that appointment about the hearing." She wandered into the kitchen and began unloading the dishwasher while she waited for Bryan's office to pick up.

"Miller and Saarloos legal services," a young female voice chirped. "How can I help you?"

"Yes, this is Bridget Hartman. I need to make a pre-hearing appointment with Bryan Miller for my son, Henry Hartman."

"What date is the hearing scheduled for?"

"Tuesday the twenty-second," Bridget answered.

"Ah yes, here it is. Bryan actually has a cancellation this morning if you can come in at ten?"

"I think that will work," Bridget said, scrambling to remember if she'd committed to anything else this morning. She wanted to watch the press conference at noon, but the meeting with Bryan would be over before that.

"Great, we'll see you in a bit." The woman hung up and Bridget went to look for Henry.

"Bryan Miller wants to meet with us at ten o'clock this morning," she said when she found him sprawled in a bean bag in the guest room, scrolling through his phone.

"What about taking Harper to the park? I promised her."

"We won't be gone long. You can take her when we get back." Bridget didn't add that it would be a good thing if the kids were out of the house when Keith Carson's press conference aired. She would prefer it if they didn't hear him answering questions about his dead wife and how her body had been discovered in a dumpster, tossed there by his son's friend. A shiver ran across Bridget's shoulders. It was still hard for her to comprehend that her son had done something so egregious.

.   .   .

THEY ARRIVED at Bryan Miller's office a few minutes early and sat down to wait in the elegantly appointed lounge area. Henry was clearly agitated, bouncing his knee up and down and twisting his hands in his lap. Bridget could hardly blame him. He faced the very real possibility that an unsympathetic judge might elect to incarcerate him. After all, it wasn't as though he'd dumped a bag of trash illegally, or something equally innocuous.

"There's no need to be nervous," Bridget assured him. "Bryan's on our side. He'll do his best to convince the judge to be lenient with you."

"Mrs. Hartman," the receptionist called over to them. "Bryan will see you now."

The receptionist led them into a wood-paneled office and quietly closed the door behind them.

Bryan got to his feet and shook hands with Bridget and Henry. "Glad you could make it this morning. How are you feeling about the adjudication hearing?" He addressed the question to no one in particular, but his gaze settled on Henry who gave a non-committal shrug. "Okay, I guess."

"The presiding judge is a father himself," Bryan said. "That may help us in our plea for clemency."

He flicked open the file in front of him and glanced through it. "Basically, the same rules apply as last time. Dress smart and be respectful. Don't speak unless you're asked a question." He looked pointedly at Bridget. "That especially applies to you. You're only there to accompany your minor child. The judge probably won't address you at all. You might have to bite your tongue at times, but it would be in Henry's best interest if you don't jump in. The judge isn't going to want to see you answering questions on your son's behalf."

Bryan turned his attention back to Henry. "The judge will want to see genuine remorse on your part. I can only do so much in terms of pleading your case, but in the end, it comes down to the impression you make."

Henry scratched his cheek, looking nervous. "What kind of impression are you talking about?"

"Just be yourself," Bryan replied. "Don't be cocky. Tell the judge honestly what you told me and your mother. You were afraid for your dad. You panicked and tried to help him. You meant well, but you just made a bad decision in the heat of the moment, and afterward, you didn't know how to fix it. You're very sorry and you feel terrible about what you did."

Bryan went on to explain exactly what would take place at the hearing and then handed each of them a printout of his instructions. "Don't hesitate to call if you have any additional questions in the interim," he said as he got to his feet at the end of their meeting. "Oh, and make sure you're on time. Judge Peterschick is a stickler for punctuality." He ushered them out to the reception area and shook hands with them as they took their leave.

"Do you feel better about the hearing now?" Bridget asked, as she and Henry walked back to the car.

He let loose a nervous laugh. "I'll feel better when it's over."

Bridget put an arm around his shoulder and hugged him. "We both will."

BACK AT THE HOUSE, Harper was frothing at the mouth to get to the park. Henry grabbed a banana-nut muffin from the kitchen and took her by the hand, waving goodbye to Bridget on their way out. "We'll be back for lunch."

"Wait!" Bridget rummaged in her purse and pressed some money into Henry's fist. "Why don't you take your sister to McDonalds?"

"Yay! Thank you, Mommy!" Harper jumped up and down, tugging on her brother's hand. "Hurry, Henry!"

He rolled his eyes as he let her lead him out the door.

Bridget busied herself checking the contents of the refrigerator and the pantry, making a quick grocery list while she brewed some more coffee.

"Mmm, smells good in here," her dad said, walking into the kitchen.

Bridget smiled and poured him a mug. "Is Mom up yet?"

"She's getting dressed. She flat wore herself out at physical therapy yesterday."

"She's making great progress. I didn't expect her to be this mobile already."

They glanced up at the sound of a walker squeaking its way down the hallway.

"I'm such a slow poke." Elise tinkled a laugh as she appeared in the doorway. "Takes me forever to get dressed." She shuffled over to the table where John helped ease her into a seat.

"What would you like for breakfast?" he asked. "Although it's almost lunchtime."

Elise swatted a hand in his direction. "Don't remind me. Just some toast and a cup of tea would be great." She pinned a questioning gaze on Bridget. "How did everything go at the Carsons?"

"I think it went well. Quinn's upset, of course, about his mother and sorry about what happened to our house. Keith's holding a press conference at noon, and he plans on addressing the harassment and asking the public to leave both our families alone."

"That's good news." Elise took a long draught of her tea. "Still no word on Steve's whereabouts, I take it?"

Bridget shook her head despairingly. "I have a sinking feeling he's disappeared with Keith's money. I just hope Keith doesn't sue me down the line. I'm sure his lawyers will encourage it."

"But you did nothing wrong," Elise protested.

Bridget grimaced. "He could still go after Steve's business. And if he does, our whole world will crumble like a stack of cards. I can't support myself and the kids and pay the mortgage and all the other bills on a shift supervisor's salary. We could end up losing the house."

Her dad squeezed her arm. "You're not going to end up homeless, not as long as we're here to help you." He glanced at the clock on the wall. "It's eleven-forty-five. Almost time for that press conference."

Elise drained the rest of her tea and then reached for her walker and struggled to her feet. After she'd navigated her way down the hallway, they settled themselves in the family room and John turned on the television. Bridget interlaced her fingers around her mug, her thoughts drifting to the upcoming hearing, while her parents caught the tail end of a home decorating show.

At noon, John tuned into the local news channel. The newscaster introduced the lead story and then the camera panned to the press conference. The police chief stepped forward to the multitude of microphones and addressed the crowd first. "Our attempts to locate Steve Hartman are ongoing and we are exhausting every possible avenue and exploring every lead. Rest assured, he will be found, and he will be tried for the charges he's facing."

Bridget frowned. As far as she was aware, the only charge he was facing was tampering with evidence. Evidently, his flight had served to confirm in the eyes of law enforcement that he was the killer.

After a few minutes, the police chief moved aside, and Keith Carson stepped up to the podium."I want to thank everyone for their support at this extraordinarily difficult time for myself and my son." He gestured to his right where Quinn sat on a chair next to his grandfather, his eyes avoiding the camera.

"While the investigation into my wife's murder is ongoing, I have no doubt that Steve Hartman, the man she was having an affair with, is responsible for killing her. As we know, his son has admitted to dumping … Jen's body." He hesitated, choking up, and then looked straight at the camera. "It's clear that Steve Hartman's family is willing to go to any length to help cover up his crime. My family has suffered enough. I'm appealing to the Hartman family to do the right thing—to come forward and tell the police where Steve is hiding out."

he police chief stepped back up to the podium and took a few questions before ending the press conference. The footage returned to the studio where the newscaster swiftly moved on to the next story.

Bridget sat in stunned silence on the couch, trying to digest what she'd just witnessed. Keith Carson had completely blindsided her. She'd left his house this morning convinced they had an understanding, both reeling from the pain of being cheated on, both bereft of their spouses. But Maria had been right about him after all. He was not to be trusted.

"I'd like to give him a piece of my mind," John said, his face like thunder. "How dare he accuse us of helping Steve run from the law!"

Elise turned to Bridget. "He must know we would never do any such thing."

Bridget rubbed her throbbing temple with her fingertips, trying to collect her thoughts and make sense of it. "To be fair, if the shoe were on the other foot, I suppose I might suspect Keith's family of helping him flee. I don't hold it against him that he doubts me. I hold it against him that he was too spineless to say it to my face when I was at his house earlier."

Elise adjusted her glasses and peered anxiously at her husband. "John, you don't think we'll have any trouble here now, do you?"

He let out a snort. "I'm sure we will! What's to stop the neighbors thinking we were in on helping Steve disappear?"

Bridget dropped her head into her hands. "I'm sorry I brought this on you. We should have gone to a hotel instead."

"Nonsense!" her mom retorted. "We'll get through this, one step at a time. Anyone who knows us won't believe for one minute that we helped Steve evade justice."

"I'm not so sure," Bridget responded, getting to her feet. "They know Henry tried to cover up the crime. And kids learn things from their parents. It's not too much of a stretch for the public to conclude we were all in on it. I think it's time we faced the fact that we're in for a PR nightmare."

THE DAYS LEADING up to Henry's trial proved to be equally as difficult as Bridget had feared. It pained her to no end to see her dad snubbed at the grocery store and neighbors cutting off contact. Even some of her parents' close friends had resorted to giving them the cold shoulder. Nobody wanted to be associated with a killer's family, especially when that family was under suspicion of harboring a fugitive.

On Monday, Bridget made a quick trip to the school to pick up some work that Henry's and Harper's teachers had assigned them. She was still unsure at this point whether the kids would return to their school or not, but it was important to keep up with the semester's work in the meantime. Not to mention the fact that they needed something to do to distract them from everything that was going on. Bridget entered the foyer of the administration building and gave Debra, the receptionist, a stiff smile. "I'm here to pick up some work for Henry and Harper Hartman," she explained, trying to sound more composed than she felt.

Debra ran her eye unabashedly over Bridget. "Let me see if I have anything for them." She got to her feet and retreated to the shelving at the back of the office, making a show of looking through various slots for the kids' assignments. Bridget had a feeling she knew exactly where the work packets were located. No doubt she'd had a good gossip with the kids' teachers when they'd handed them over.

"Mrs. Hartman," a voice behind her said.

She wheeled around to see Mr. Barker, Henry's English teacher, standing behind her.

"I wonder if I might have a quick word," he added, stroking his goatee.

"Of course," Bridget replied, a feeling of mild panic circling in the pit of her stomach.

He gestured to the seating area in the corner of the foyer. She followed him over there and sat down in a vinyl lounge chair.

"As you can imagine," he stated, "this has all been very traumatic for my students."

Bridget stared at him coldly. "I don't need to imagine the trauma, Mr. Barker. This has been extremely hard on our family."

"Indeed." He blinked rapidly behind his glasses. "Well, I'm going to get right to it, Mrs. Hartman. Henry is one of my best students, but some of the parents have expressed reservations about him being in the class with their children, on account of his … recent actions."

"That seems a bit extreme, don't you think?" Bridget shot back. "He made a mistake. He acted instinctively to protect his dad."

233

"He threw a woman's body in a dumpster—his friend's mother whom he believed his father had killed," Mr. Barker responded, an incredulous note in his voice. "Some of the parents see his actions as those of a disturbed child, Mrs. Hartman. It puts me in an extremely difficult position."

"Henry's not disturbed," Bridget retorted. "He's a teenager who did something rash and impetuous. He deeply regrets his actions." She reached for her purse and got to her feet. "However, if that's the kind of judgment he faces at this school, perhaps it would be best for his sake if he didn't return."

Abandoning her plans to pick up her kids' assignments, Bridget stormed out the front door and down the steps, shaking as she made her way back to her car. It seemed no one was prepared to offer her a scrap of empathy or support, or ask if there was anything they could do for her or her kids. They were simply collateral damage in this horrendous situation that Steve had instigated. She thumped on her steering wheel in frustration as she raced out of the parking lot. It wasn't fair! What Steve had done to his own family—not to mention to the Carsons—was unforgivable.

BRIDGET BARELY SLEPT THAT NIGHT, between agonizing over what Mr. Barker had said and sweating over what the hearing the following day would bring. In many ways, it would be harder for her to watch her son on trial than her husband—if it ever came to that. She was beginning to fear the police would never catch up with Steve.

Shortly before eleven the next morning, Henry came into the kitchen dressed in a white shirt, chinos, and a jacket. The dark circles under his eyes told Bridget he hadn't slept much either.

"You look very presentable," she said, mustering up a

smile. "Just make sure you don't spill your breakfast on that shirt."

Henry slid into a chair at the table. "I'm not hungry." He rested his elbows in front of him and rubbed his hands together. "I just want to get this over with, whatever way it goes."

"Have a little faith in Bryan," Bridget assured him. "He's an excellent lawyer."

"I texted Quinn earlier," Henry said. "He went to school today—he couldn't bear to stay home alone anymore. He wished me luck."

Bridget stabbed at a piece of poached egg. She couldn't forgive what Keith Carson had done to them. In an instant, he'd managed to erase whatever little support they'd had in the community, turning the tide of popular opinion firmly against them. Still, it wasn't a valid reason to hold a grudge against Quinn. The boy had only ever been a pawn in his parents' hands.

"I'm glad you two made up," Bridget said, taking a quick sip of her coffee. She pushed her plate aside. "I still think you should eat something before we go. We could be stuck at the courthouse for several hours. I'm not sure how many other cases are ahead of us."

Henry curled his lip. "Can't. I'd only toss it back up."

THE RIDE to the courthouse was tense as Bridget tried to come up with innocuous topics to talk about, while Henry answered in monosyllables. Eventually, she gave up and concentrated on getting them there on time.

Once again, Bryan Miller was waiting for them on the courthouse steps. He was smartly dressed in a gray suit and pale blue tie, but his expression was more strained than usual.

"Is everything all right?" Bridget asked.

"Let's hope so," he replied. "The media hasn't put a favorable spin on Henry's role in all of this. Still, the judge is a professional. I have to trust he'll assess the case objectively."

Bridget and Henry followed Bryan into a waiting room with several rows of padded chairs. A bailiff stood by the door leading into the courtroom. Bridget counted six other minors, with their parents and counsel, waiting to be called in.

"Each case will be heard individually, so we may have to wait a while," Bryan told them. "All hearings involving minors are confidential."

As it turned out, it was almost one o'clock before Henry's name was called. Bryan stood and gave Bridget a curt nod. "All right, let's do this." They followed the bailiff into the courtroom and sat down at the desk assigned to them, glancing nervously around. Bryan handed Bridget a sheaf of stapled pages. "This is a copy of the petition. It details the charges Henry's facing, or the allegations, as they're referred to here. The judge will likely allude to the petition at various points during the proceedings."

Bridget set down the paperwork and glanced apprehensively around the room. The court reporter was in position, poised to begin typing.

"All rise," the bailiff announced. "The third district juvenile court is now in session. The Honorable Judge Ryan Peterschick presiding."

Bridget watched as the judge entered the courtroom and took his seat at the bench. Bryan had assured her that in juvenile court a judge's first priority was rehabilitation, but it was still a terrifying proposition to find herself in front of one with her fourteen-year-old son.

"Mr. Hartman," the judge began, "do you understand the

allegation of tampering with evidence that is being brought against you today?"

Henry glanced uncertainly at Bryan who leaned over and whispered something to him.

"Yes," Henry mumbled.

"Speak up, son," the judge said.

"Yes, your honor."

"And do you admit to disposing of the deceased's body, one Jen Carson, into a dumpster in the area of Glenwood Lane and Pine Street at two-thirty-seven on the morning of January fourteenth?"

Once again, Henry glanced at Bryan before responding, "Yes, your honor."

The judge rested his chin on his hand, perusing the paperwork on the desk in front of him for a moment or two. When he was done, he removed his glasses and addressed Henry again. "There are several rehabilitation options available to me. I will consider all of these carefully before the disposition hearing at which time I will inform you of my decision. However, due to the serious nature of your crime, and the fact that your father is allegedly a fugitive from the law, it is my belief that flight risk is a high probability in your case."

Bridget dug her nails into the palms of her hands, dread rising up from her gut.

Bryan got to his feet. "Your honor, my client is extremely remorseful for his actions. He has no knowledge of his father's whereabouts, nor any desire to emulate his actions. I don't believe him to be a flight risk in any shape or form."

"Duly noted, Mr. Miller. However, due to the public outcry about this crime, it would be in Mr. Hartman's best interests for his own safety that he be detained in a juvenile facility until the disposition hearing."

"No!" Bridget jumped to her feet. "Please, your honor, he—"

Bryan yanked on her arm. "Sit down!" he hissed.

The judge ran a disapproving eye over her. "I hereby order Mr. Hartman to be detained at the regional juvenile detention center until the disposition hearing on Friday. Perhaps, Mrs. Hartman, the public will be safer that way too."

Before she could respond, he slammed his gavel down and dismissed the case.

32

*B*ridget watched in horror as a bailiff with a holstered weapon on his waist approached Henry and handcuffed him before escorting him out of the courtroom. "Can't you stop this?" she implored, her voice rising as she grabbed Bryan by the arm. "File a petition or something?"

He grimaced. "I can't overturn the judge's decision. But the detainment's only until the disposition hearing. It doesn't mean it will be part of Henry's sentencing."

"But it doesn't bode well for the judge's decision, does it?" Bridget cried. "What if he sends Henry to juvenile hall until he's twenty-five or something?"

"Let's not get ahead of ourselves," Bryan soothed. "That's an unlikely scenario. It's not as if Henry's being sentenced for murder."

Bridget pressed her fingers to her face. "If the judge puts Henry away, this will follow him for the rest of his life."

Bryan's expression softened. "Not necessarily. There's a possibility he can go back to court and have his case sealed, which means it would be removed from his record. First things first, we have to concentrate on getting through the disposition hearing."

"Can I at least visit my son between now and then?" Bridget choked out.

"Absolutely," Bryan replied. "There are visiting hours every other day. You'll need to verify the schedule. And feel free to call me anytime if you run into any problems. I'll see you both here again on Friday morning."

Back in the privacy of her car, Bridget leaned her head on the steering wheel, moaning as the adrenaline that had carried her through the hearing slowly leaked from her system. This was not how she'd envisioned things playing out. If anything, she'd been hoping the judge would throw out the case, recognizing that Henry had no other motive than wanting to protect his father.

After a moment, Bridget drew herself up in the seat, squaring her shoulders. She couldn't allow herself to go down this path of despair and hopelessness. She wouldn't give up now. She had to keep fighting for Henry—putting one foot in front of the other until this was over. Somehow she'd get through the next few days.

HER PARENTS WERE FLABBERGASTED when she relayed the news to them.

"But he's only fourteen-years-old," Elise stammered, her hand fluttering nervously around her face. "How could the judge do such a thing to our Henry? He's no criminal."

Bridget gave a melancholy shrug. "He committed a crime. That's the definition of a criminal. Believe me, I'm devastated. But, in retrospect, I can't fault the judge for doing his job. He felt Henry might be a flight risk with his father on the run."

John frowned, scratching his scalp. "What are you going to tell Harper?"

Bridget sighed. "I'll have to tell her the truth. She's going to hear it from someone, sooner or later. I don't want to lose her trust by continuing to lie to her about all of this."

"She's going to take it hard." Elise gave a sad shake of her head. "She's been very attached to Henry ever since Steve disappeared."

"I know," Bridget agreed. "But she still has us. We'll just have to make sure she gets plenty of love and affection over the next few days. The last thing I need is for Harper to run away again."

John got up and wrapped his arms around her. "My poor Bridget. This is a terrible blow for you, on top of everything else. Just remember, your mother and I are here for you no matter what."

Bridget wiped her eyes with the back of her hand. "Thanks, Dad. I feel so bad that this is falling on your shoulders while Mom's still recovering from surgery."

"Now don't be worrying about us," Elise said. "We're enjoying the company. Obviously, I wish it wasn't under these circumstances, but you know how much I love having you all here with me."

Bridget got to her feet. "I'm going to have a talk with Harper. I can't put it off any longer."

She made her way back to the guest bedroom, dread gnawing at her gut with every step. She wasn't sure how much more Harper could handle. Maybe she should take her to see a therapist. Considering what she'd been subjected to in the last few days, it was probably a good call. But, right now, it seemed like one more thing to worry about on her already overloaded plate.

"Hey honey," Bridget said, knocking on the door as she turned the handle. "What are you up to?"

"Nothing, just playing." Harper continued combing her doll's hair. The remainder of her Barbies were seated in a circle in front of her with a pile of Cheerios in the middle.

Bridget grinned at her daughter. "Do you think they're going to be able to eat all those Cheerios, or can I have one?"

"They're not Cheerios, they're donuts, silly," Harper admonished her. "They're having a picnic."

"Got it! Well, it looks like fun."

Harper gave a non-committal shrug. "I miss my room. You didn't bring all my stuff over."

"I know, but Mommy could only bring so much. The rest of your toys will be waiting for you when we go back."

"I want to go home now." Harper tossed the doll's hair-brush aside and folded her arms in front of her.

Bridget inhaled and exhaled softly. "We all want to go home. But we have to stay at Grandma's and Grandpa's for a few more days."

Harper scrambled to her feet. "I'm bored. I wanna go to the park with Henry now."

Bridget reached for her arm and pulled her into her lap. "Honey, there's something I need to tell you."

Harper looked up at her wide-eyed.

"Henry had to go away for a few days."

Harper's brow furrowed. "But why? He said he'd take me to the park. I don't want Henry to go away!"

"I know, and Mommy doesn't want him to go away either, but it's only for a few days." Bridget's stomach twisted even as the words fell from her lips. She had no idea how accurate that was. Henry might be coming home with them after the hearing on Friday, or he might be going to juvenile hall for years on end, or his fate might lie somewhere in between— some type of community service, perhaps. The truth was, she didn't know how long Harper would be parted from her brother, and she couldn't control the outcome.

"Did Henry put Quinn's mommy in a dumpster?" Harper asked, looking Bridget directly in the eye.

She made an incoherent sound, as she fought to summon her courage. If she didn't tell her the truth, Harper mightn't trust her going forward. She needed to come clean, and then handle her daughter's reaction as best she could. "Yes, he did. He was very scared, and he made the wrong choice. He should have called the police, or told me, or another adult. He's really sorry for what he did."

Harper blinked contemplatively. "But was she dead?"

"Yes," Bridget said firmly. "She was already dead." That much she could answer with conviction. She'd seen Jen's lifeless body in her husband's car with her own eyes. "I can promise you Henry did not kill Quinn's mommy."

"I know." Harper leaned her head against Bridget's chest. "Daddy killed her."

Bridget's breath caught in her throat. It was earth-shattering to hear her daughter utter those terrible words. And the worst part about it was that she couldn't refute them. She hugged her daughter close. Little children shouldn't have to grow up believing their parents were killers. It was unnatural to think the people they trusted most to protect them in this world, could actually turn out to be monsters.

"Let's go make some peanut butter and jelly sandwiches for lunch," Bridget suggested. "How does that sound?"

Harper nodded. "Can I make some for my Barbies too?"

Bridget reached for her daughter's hand as they got to their feet. "Of course, you can. Maybe you can take them outside, and they can have a real picnic in the backyard."

She was rewarded with one of Harper's winning smiles as they made their way to the kitchen.

· · ·

Bridget had just come in from the backyard when Detective Wright called.

Her heart lurched as she stared at the screen. Now what? She set down the paper plates she was carrying and took the call.

"Is this a good time to talk?" Detective Wright asked.

"Have you … found Steve?" Bridget's voice faltered.

"No, not yet," Detective Wright replied, "I wanted to call and give you a quick update on the investigation. As you know, we confiscated Steve's computers and phone when we arrested him. We've finished going through everything, and the Tech team has been comparing the emails between Keith Carson and Steve to the emails between Jen Carson and Steve, hoping they might shed some light on what was going on with the money."

"Keith's convinced Steve was helping Jen siphon money from his company and move it into a new account," Bridget said. "He claimed they were planning to run off together—at least that's what he told Quinn."

"So far the Tech team's been unable to confirm that Steve moved any of the company's money on Jen's behalf. It appears he was advising her against doing that before her divorce."

"Yes, Steve told me the same thing," Bridget replied. "But he said Jen ignored his advice and went ahead and hired some disreputable company to help her move the money offshore."

"We're still trying to track down that money," Detective Wright confirmed. "It was definitely transferred out of the company's accounts, which in theory gives Keith Carson a motive to kill his wife."

"But it still doesn't explain why Steve fled," Bridget said.

"Which brings me to that lead from a couple of days ago."

"What lead?" Bridget asked, her head spinning.

"The silver Audi that was parked outside your house the morning Steve disappeared."

Bridget's heart began to race, her thoughts flying in several different directions at once. Had they found it abandoned somewhere across the border? Or worse, wrecked at the bottom of a canyon? But then, Detective Wright said they hadn't found Steve yet, so he couldn't be dead, could he? She needed to calm down and not get ahead of herself. "Do you know who the car belongs to?"

"We can't confirm it as we don't have a license plate number. But we did find out that Keith Carson's company leased a brand new, silver Audi A3 last month."

33

*B*ridget clapped a hand to the nape of her neck, trying to process what Detective Wright was telling her. It couldn't be a coincidence. It seemed to indicate something she'd feared deep down but had been too afraid to voice—that Keith Carson and her husband were in cahoots with one another. The only question remaining in Bridget's mind was to what degree blackmail had played into the crime. "So it could have been Keith who picked Steve up in the Audi?"

"We're looking into that angle," Detective Wright said. "Especially now that we know about their clandestine meeting in The Muddy Cup the day after Jen's body was discovered."

Bridget rubbed her brow, still reeling from the bombshell news. "I can't believe Keith held a press conference and accused me of knowing Steve's whereabouts and keeping it from the police."

"A clever ploy to throw us off their trail," Detective Wright conceded. "At this point, we're going to explore the option that Keith and Steve were working together."

"Are you going to arrest Keith?"

"Not yet, we don't want to alert him to our suspicions. First, we need to locate the Audi. Interestingly enough, he hasn't been driving it around. Neither his son nor his house-keeper have ever seen it."

Bridget's pulse thudded in her temples as she tried to fathom the notion that Steve and Keith Carson had conspired together. What could have induced Steve to assist Keith in such a hideous crime? There had to be more to it. Keith Carson must have some kind of hold over Steve. Was it about money? After all, the accounting practice was floundering. Had Keith offered Steve money to dispose of his wife's body?

Bridget grimaced. Maria had been right about Keith. He'd wanted his wife dead, and he'd got his wish—hardly a coincidence. And if he had killed her, blackmailed Steve into disposing of the body, and helped him disappear while pinning the crime on him, then he was a very clever and dangerous man indeed.

"It's odd that Keith would help Steve flee if he wanted him to go down for the murder," Bridget said.

"He might have been afraid Steve would crack under interrogation and rat him out—nail him for Jen's murder," Detective Wright answered. "It's all speculation at this point, we have a lot of unanswered questions. We still haven't confirmed it was Keith's Audi at your house. Officer Lopez and I are heading over to the Carsons' company right now to try and track down the vehicle. I just wanted to give you a heads up on where we're at with everything."

"Thanks," Bridget said. "I appreciate it."

"I'll let you know as soon as we find out anything more," Detective Wright added. "If I don't call, it's because I don't have any news."

Bridget hung up and sank down in the kitchen chair. Her

phone buzzed again almost immediately, and she glanced down at it, frowning at the unknown number. She slid a shaking finger across the screen, wondering if it could possibly be Steve.

"Mom!"

"Henry!" Bridget's heart jolted at the welcome sound of her son's voice. "Are you all right?"

"I'm fine. They let me make a call. I just wanted to tell you not to worry about me."

Bridget moaned softly. "I'm so sorry it came to this, Henry. I never dreamed the judge would detain you."

"One of the corrections officers said it's because it's a high-profile case. Even though I didn't commit the murder, I helped cover it up. And the killer got away. So it looks bad, and the judge doesn't know for sure how much I know. He can't take a risk and let me walk." He paused before adding, "I miss you, Mom."

"I'll come visit you tomorrow," Bridget promised.

There was silence on the other end of the phone for a moment. "Can you bring Harper with you, please?"

Bridget scrunched her eyes shut. She didn't want her daughter's childhood marred by ugly memories of juvenile hall, or ever even associating Henry with such a place, for that matter. "I don't know, Henry. She's so young and impressionable."

"Is Henry on the phone?" Harper cried, running into the kitchen.

Bridget flashed her a startled look. "Yes, do you want to talk to him?"

She nodded vigorously, holding out her hand for the phone. Bridget hit the speaker button and set it on the table between them.

"Hi, Henry." Harper said, twisting shyly to and fro while clutching the edge of the kitchen table. "Where are you?"

"Well, it's kind of like a boarding school where you get to sleep over," Henry said. "I have my own room here so at least I don't have to share with you at Grandma's and Grandpa's."

"Lucky!" Harper stared at the phone intently. "When are you coming home?"

"I'm not sure yet. What are you doing?"

"A Barbie picnic with real peanut butter and jelly sandwiches."

Henry laughed. "Sounds good. I'm starving. You better make me some when I get back."

"Okay," Harper said. "See you later." She turned and skipped back outside, humming to herself.

"I think she feels better after talking to you," Bridget said, picking up the phone. "She was really upset when I told her earlier that you weren't coming home."

"Then bring her with you when you visit," Henry urged. "There's nothing scary here—it's not like prison. We might as well face it. This could be the rest of her childhood, visiting me in this place. Better get used to the idea."

Bridget ended the call with a sick feeling in the pit of her stomach. She could not—would not—allow Henry to spend the rest of his childhood in juvenile hall. Slipping her phone back into her purse, she frowned when it chinked against something. She rummaged around inside her purse for a moment and then pulled out Quinn's house key. Her jaw dropped. She'd meant to give it back to him when she'd stopped by, but she'd completely forgotten about it.

As she twisted the key between her thumb and forefinger, the idea that had begun brewing in her head when she'd first found the key came back to mind. Why not pay a visit to the Carsons' place when no one was home and take a quick look around, on the pretext of returning the key? She wasn't sure what exactly she hoped to find, but maybe there would be something there that proved Keith Carson had helped Steve escape—hotel reservations, airplane ticket receipts, perhaps?

Her mind made up, Bridget slung her purse over her shoulder and went into the family room to look for her dad. He glanced up from the newspaper he was perusing. "Is Harper doing all right?"

Bridget nodded. "Henry called and she got to talk to him for a couple of minutes. I think it reassured her that he hadn't disappeared into thin air like Steve did. Is Mom still napping?"

"Yeah, she didn't sleep too well last night. She's upset about Henry."

Bridget pressed her lips together and gave a shallow nod. "We all are. I need to run a few errands. Is it all right if I leave Harper here? She's playing with her Barbies in the backyard."

"Sure," John replied, folding up his newspaper. "I'll go out there and keep an eye on her."

Bridget wasted no time grabbing her coat and heading out to her car. She switched on the engine and reversed down the driveway, guilt churning in her stomach. She felt bad about deceiving her dad. Trespassing was hardly a legitimate errand, but there was no way she could tell him what she was really intending to do. He would only try and stop her. The last thing he needed was another member of his family being handcuffed and loaded into a squad car. Bridget ignored the voice of reason in her head telling her she could still turn back. If she was caught, she would say she'd gone inside to return Quinn's key, thinking the housekeeper was home.

A few minutes later, she pulled up on the Carsons' street and parked a short distance from their house. She didn't want anyone remembering seeing her vehicle outside. She threw up the hood of her sweatshirt, climbed out of her car and strolled nonchalantly down the sidewalk. When she reached the bottom of the brick pathway leading to their front door, she cast a quick glance up and down the street to make sure no one was around before walking briskly up to the door.

Fingers shaking, she put the key in the lock and turned it. She stepped inside and quickly closed the door behind her. For several minutes, she stood with her back to it, listening for any sounds emanating from within the house. But all she could hear was the thud of her heartbeat in her chest. Maria normally worked mornings, so Bridget was fairly certain she had the house to herself until Quinn got back from school.

Adjusting the strap on her purse, she headed to the kitchen first. After taking a quick look around, she peered into the laundry room, before checking the family room to make sure no one was there. It was an eerie feeling to be in someone else's house, uninvited. Every house had its own aura, and this one had a decidedly gloomy one, almost as if the walls themselves had picked up on the animosity between the parties who lived here.

After taking a quick breath to center herself, Bridget padded up the stairs to the second floor. Butterflies swirled in dizzying circles in her gut as she made her way toward the master suite. She stepped inside the opulent space decorated in gray, silver and white, and checked the bathroom to make sure Maria wasn't cleaning it, before moving on to the other bedrooms. Inside Quinn's room, she paused for a moment, leaning against the wall as she took in the menagerie of electronics, sports equipment, concert posters and teenage boy paraphernalia covering every inch of floor and wall space. She felt sick to her stomach about everything Quinn had gone through in the past week and was still going through. His life would never be the same again. She turned and exited the room, wishing there was some way she could roll back time and make this all go away.

Satisfied there was no one in the house, Bridget returned to the master suite to begin searching in earnest for some kind of evidence of a connection between Keith Carson and Steve. She worked methodically, pulling out drawers, combing through the contents, and going through the closet from top to bottom. There was a small desk in one corner of the master suite, but it was apparent from the lack of files and cabinets that Keith didn't work from home.

She reached up to a shelf above the desk and lifted down a photo album. As she flicked through it, she was struck again by how beautiful a woman Jen Carson had been. Quinn had got his luxurious dark locks from her, as well as his magnetic green eyes. Bridget's stomach twisted at the sheer joy in Jen's expression as she held her young son on her lap in a lounge chair by the pool at some hotel. It was heartbreaking to think Quinn had lost his mother before he was fully grown.

After a few minutes, Bridget returned the photo album to the shelf and grabbed another one. She sat down on the edge of the bed to peruse it. The Carsons had traveled a lot—Egypt, Switzerland, Australia—even an African safari vacation. Bridget browsed through the photos until she came upon some Christmas pictures in which Quinn looked to be about twelve. Bridget couldn't help smiling at the exuberant look on his face as he clutched an Xbox in his arms and beamed at the camera.

She flipped through several more pages, and then came to a sudden halt at a photo of the Carson family proudly displaying their gifts in front of an enormous Christmas tree, dripping with glittering ornaments. Her blood froze. She slipped the photo out from behind the plastic sleeve and scrutinized it.

There was no mistaking what she was looking at. The charcoal and red tartan blanket that Quinn's grandfather was holding up to the camera was an exact match to the one Jen's body had been wrapped in.

34

The photo album slid from Bridget's lap to the floor with an ominous thud. She stared down at it for a moment, and then covered her face with her hands, trembling all over. It was definitely the blanket Jen's body had been wrapped in—she was sure of it. This changed everything. This was enough to throw reasonable doubt on the theory that Steve had killed Jen Carson. It must have been Keith. The only remaining question was where the murder had taken place. The police had ruled out Keith's house as a possible crime scene, but the forensic pathologist had found some kind of carpet fibers on Jen's body—a hotel room, perhaps?

A sound outside the bedroom door startled her. Her breath froze. She got to her feet just as Quinn's grandfather, Jack, strode into the room. When he saw her standing at the bottom of the bed, he came to a sudden stop. A confused scowl blazed across his face.

Bridget blinked at him, scrambling to come up with an excuse to explain what she was doing in Keith's bedroom. "Hi, Jack, I … I was hoping I'd catch someone at home." She reached into her purse and fished out the front door key. "Quinn left this at our house last week. I wanted to return it."

Jack continued to stare at her coldly for a long, uncomfortable moment. His gaze dropped to the floor where the photo album was lying. He walked over and picked it up, studying the Christmas pictures contemplatively. His eyes radiated a chill when he asked, "Did you get what you came for?"

"I ... I'm sorry," Bridget stuttered. "I just came upstairs to see if Quinn was in his room. I decided to wait around for a few minutes in case he showed up and then I wandered in here and spotted the photo albums." She gestured apologetically with her hands, before setting the key down on the desk. "Maybe you can return this to Quinn for me. I should get going." She made a beeline for the bedroom door, but Jack stepped in front of her. "I'm afraid that won't be possible."

Bridget gaped at him, taken aback by his intimidating posturing. "What are you talking about?"

"I mean I can't let you leave."

A chilly tremor rippled down Bridget's spine. "I ... don't understand."

Jack quietly closed the bedroom door behind him. "I think you understand perfectly. You stuck your nose in where it wasn't wanted, took the liberty of trespassing in my son's house, and browsing through personal photos. I have a right to know why."

Bridget's voice shook. "I told you already, I was waiting for Quinn to come home."

"Is that what you normally do, let yourself in to other people's houses when they're not home, give yourself a private tour, and root through their personal possessions?"

"I admit I was out of line," Bridget said in a placating tone.

"I was curious about Quinn's mother, that's all. Quinn's like a second son to me."

"But he's not your son, and you're not his mother, and your husband isn't entitled to our money."

Bridget wet her lips as she appraised Jack nervously. *Our money.* Where was he going with this? He'd founded the company, maybe he was still an invested party. "My husband has no interest in your money. He never did."

Jack threw back his head and guffawed. "Is that what he told you? Do you really think he was only interested in Jen for her feminine charms?"

Bridget shrugged. "It wouldn't be the first time a man fell for a beautiful woman. Jen looks like a model in some of those pictures."

Jack eyed her thoughtfully. "What else did you learn from our family photos?"

"Nothing," Bridget said, her voice wavering despite her best attempt to sound nonchalant. "Other than that the Carson family liked to travel."

Jack jabbed at a photo in the album with his forefinger, his voice sharp as steel. "I'll wager you paid close attention to a particular Christmas gift in this picture, did you not?" When he looked over at Bridget again, the expression in his eyes was oddly detached.

Her knees knocked together in fear. "I don't know what you mean."

Jack let out a snort of disgust. "Let's not play games with one another. Neither one of us is an idiot. You think you recognize the blanket in this photo, don't you, Bridget? You desperately want to believe that your husband didn't kill my daughter-in-law, and you're willing to latch on to any alternative theory no matter how far-fetched."

"I'm desperate for the truth, whatever that is," she replied defensively. "Aren't you? Or would you rather let your murdering son walk free while my husband pays for a crime he didn't commit? I know Keith blackmailed Steve into helping him dispose of Jen's body by threatening to expose their affair."

Jack raised his eyebrows in a bemused manner. "You don't actually believe your husband agreed to dispose of Jen's body in exchange for Keith's silence, do you? The affair was no secret. Your son and Quinn followed Jen to your husband's office on multiple occasions." A malicious chuckle slipped from his lips. "But then they say the wife's always the last to know. No, Keith wasn't in the business of blackmailing. Your husband was a very clever man, Bridget. He even had Jen fooled. All he was after was the money. And now he's disappeared with it."

Bridget shook her head. "I don't believe it! Steve was never interested in your company's money. He counseled Jen against moving any assets before the divorce. She went against his advice."

Jack twisted his lips sardonically. "Did your husband also tell you that his company was struggling, possibly in danger of going under?"

Bridget swallowed hard. It was true Steve had admitted to money problems. But he would never steal money from another company to resolve them. And he would never have absconded with the money and abandoned his family. No, he had gone on the run fearing he would be indicted as a murderer. But the blanket in the Christmas photo proved otherwise, and Jack knew it—he was covering for his son.

"Steve didn't kill your daughter-in-law," Bridget said, holding Jack's gaze. "You and I both know it. That photograph proves it. The blanket came from this house. Your son's going to face justice, sooner or later. If you don't turn him in, I will."

"Yeah, I was afraid you might say that." Jack tossed the

photo album onto the bed and let out a heavy sigh. He reached into his pocket and pulled out a pair of black, leather gloves. Bridget watched with a heightening sense of terror as he put them on, meticulously adjusting each finger.

He took a step toward her, a cool smile flicking across his lips as she retreated.

"What are you doing?" she cried. "Are you insane?"

He cocked his head to one side as if weighing the possibility. "Not in the clinical sense. You, on the other hand, are insanely focused on ruining my son's life, and I can't allow that to happen."

In a flash, he closed the gap between them, and lunged for Bridget. She ducked beneath his grasp and tried to make a run for the door. But, seconds later, she felt the weight of his huge hand on her shoulder, and then a violent tug as he wrenched her backward. She tumbled to the ground, scrabbling to make her escape, but he was on her in a heartbeat, pinning her arms to the floor.

"You think you're quite the clever little detective, don't you? Spying on your husband, calling the City Crime Line, stealing Quinn's key, poring through our photos and searching for evidence. In fact, I bet you were feeling pretty proud of yourself right up until the point when I walked into the room. The thing is, Nancy Drew, you've got it all wrong." He paused, a feral grin sliding across his face. "Keith didn't kill Jen. Oh, he wanted to kill her all right, but he's a hothead. He would have gone about it all wrong, left a trail of evidence. Unlike your level-headed, number-crunching husband who executed a near-perfect crime."

Bridget's eyes widened in horror as Jack's words sank in. She writhed beneath his weight, desperate to knock him off. But he was much too strong and muscular— a far cry from the ailing man Keith had made him out to be. Her mind thrashed about, trying to make sense of what he was telling her, lining it up with everything that had transpired since Jen's body was discovered.

"You were never ill at all, were you?" she spat out. "That little episode at the hospital was all a ruse to distract the police from investigating Keith."

Jack let out a contemptuous laugh. "Maybe you're not such a lousy detective after all. Which is why, I'm afraid, you're too much of a threat to keep around any longer." His lip curled as he released her arms, and then put his gloved hands around her neck and began to squeeze.

Bridget gasped and gurgled, every basic survival instinct kicking in. Her brain screamed at her to breathe, her body unable to respond. Adrenaline flooded her system as the terror of knowing she had only seconds before her body would be rendered helpless, gripped her. The pain of Jack's muscular hands squeezing her neck was lost in the agony of being starved of oxygen. Every failing brain synapse urged her to fight on for even the smallest puff of air. Her hands flailed around as she sought purchase—skin, hair, anything. Her nails made contact and she clawed wildly at Jack's face. He roared in pain when she jabbed him in the eye, but her vision was blurring, and he easily moved out of range.

She willed her brain to direct her body to continue to thrash, but Jack managed to pin one of her arms beneath his knee. She was vaguely aware that her movements had become little more than those of a hapless fish flopping around on dry land. Her eyes felt as though they were about to pop out of her head. A sense of impending doom took over. Seconds had passed since Jack had put his hands around her neck, but it felt like she'd been fighting for hours underwater.

She was losing the battle to live, unable to speak or swallow. Every lifeline to the outside world was shutting down. All she could think about was trying to breathe. Her mind was consumed with the desperate need to fill her lungs with oxygen.

But Jack's flushed face loomed over her, lined with an equally ferocious concentration as he directed all his energy into finishing her off.

3 5

Just when Bridget was sure the darkness was about to overtake her, she heard a shout. Seconds later, the chokehold around her neck released and the crushing weight was lifted off her body. She heaved in breath after agonizing breath, her raw throat gasping life back into her body as she rolled onto her side, her fingers instinctively reaching for her throbbing neck. She was vaguely aware of a scuffle of some description, a dull thud, and a muted cry, but she couldn't open her eyes to take in what was happening around her. Every muscle in her body ached. Her mind was gripped with only one thought —*keep breathing*. When her system was finally flooded with sufficient oxygen, she shakily pulled herself into a sitting position. Her vision was still blurry, but she could just about make out Jack prostrate on the floor.

"Are you all right, Mrs. Hartman?" a muffled voice inquired.

Bridget frowned, the room spinning every which way. She forced her eyes to focus on the person kneeling at her side. *Quinn!* When had he arrived? She opened her mouth to respond, but nothing came out other than a peculiar rasping sound that filled her with fear. A wave of nausea coursed through her. What had Jack done to her?

"It's okay, don't try and talk," Quinn said, looking as scared as she felt. "I called 911."

Bridget sank back to the floor, sucking in one slow, painful breath after another. Air had never felt so precious.

Quinn watched her with an uneasy expression on his face. "Do you want some water?"

Bridget attempted to nod, wincing at the pain in her throat. Quinn disappeared into the bathroom and returned a moment later, with a glass of water in hand. He cradled her head in his arms and held the glass to her lips. She tried to take a sip, but the muscles in her neck felt like jelly, and most of the water dribbled down her chin. Her head flopped back, the mere effort of trying to swallow draining the last of her energy.

She lost all track of time as she waited for the ambulance to arrive. To his credit, Quinn never left her side. Every time her eyelids fluttered open, he was anxiously peering down at her, making sure she was all right.

At the sound of the doorbell, Bridget flinched out of a semi-conscious state. All of a sudden, the room was filled with a blur of color, activity, and snatches of terse conversation.

"Ma'am, can you hear me?" a female voice asked.

"She can't speak," Quinn answered on her behalf.

"Did she lose consciousness at all?"

"I ... don't think so," Quinn said. "I don't know for sure."

"All right, we'll take it from here."

Bridget was dimly aware of walkie-talkies warbling, and uniforms moving in and out of her field of vision, and then she felt herself being hoisted onto a gurney. She wondered briefly where Jack was. Had they taken him out already? Her stomach churned at the possibility of coming face to face with him again in the emergency room. She wished she could ask the paramedics about him, but she had neither the energy nor the ability to talk.

When she opened her eyes again, she was being wheeled into the hospital. The first face she recognized in the ER was her father's.

Her lips mouthed the word, *Dad*, but the only sound that came out was a weak wheezing. It sounded like air was leaking through her windpipe. She desperately wanted to ask him where Harper was. He'd probably had to leave Elise and Harper to fend for themselves. It wasn't as if any of the neighbors were likely to offer to help given the cold shoulder they'd been meting out of late.

"Don't try and speak, sweetheart," her dad said, rubbing her arm. "Your throat's badly swollen."

Bridget bit back tears of relief and trepidation. Everything felt tender, bruised, and raw, and her ears were ringing. She was terrified at the thought of the damage Jack might have done to her throat. But she was alive, and he hadn't left her brain damaged—she could understand everything her dad was saying, surely that was a good sign.

A solitary tear trickled down the side of her cheek and into her ear when she thought of how Jen Carson must have suffered at Keith's hands, how she'd undoubtedly experienced those same desperate feelings of wanting to fight for every last breath—only Jen hadn't been so lucky. What must she have thought, looking into the eyes of her husband as he'd strangled her to death?

The next few hours went by in a mindless blur as Bridget was subjected to a barrage of tests and x-rays to rule out any serious internal injuries or bleeding. By the time Detective Wright showed up, she was sitting up in bed and had managed to swallow a few drops of water. Her throat was still too painful to attempt to speak so Detective Wright handed her a legal pad to write on.

"How are you feeling?" he asked.

Sore. Thankful Quinn arrived home when he did.

Detective Wright gave a sympathetic nod. "What were you doing in the Carsons' house?"

Looking for evidence that Keith helped Steve flee—an airplane ticket receipt or something like that. Yes, I know I was trespassing. Is Jack here?

"He was. He's been discharged and taken into custody."

He said Steve killed Jen.

"He wanted you to die believing that." Detective Wright grimaced. He interlaced his fingers and leaned forward. "That's why I'm here. I wanted to tell you in person. Jack's confessed to strangling Jen and hiding her body in your husband's car."

Bridget's eyes widened and a rasping sound escaped her lips. A thousand thoughts fired through her brain at once. *So Steve wasn't trying to dispose of Jen's body?*

"No. Jack was trying to pin the murder on him. The tampering with evidence charge against Steve has been dropped. He's a free man whenever he decides to show his face again."

Bridget furrowed her brow. *I don't understand why he ran. It doesn't make sense.*

Detective Wright rubbed his chin, looking uncomfortable. "The money's still missing from Keith's company. It always comes back to the money, I'm afraid."

Bridget grimaced inwardly. Loathe as she was to entertain the possibility that Steve had made off with the money, there really didn't seem to be any other explanation for his disappearance at this point. She reached for the legal pad again. *Why did Jack kill Jen?*

Detective Wright leaned back in his chair and folded his

arms in front of him. "He overheard Jen and Keith arguing about their impending divorce and splitting up their assets. Jack was afraid Jen was going to ruin the company. Keith had threatened to kill her on more than one occasion, and Jack knew there was a good chance he would do it in a blind rage and end up in prison. So he decided to come up with a more carefully orchestrated plan to pin the murder on Steve—he knew Jen had been secretly meeting with him."

Bridget lifted her pen. *Where does this leave Henry?*

"I'm afraid he'll still have to go to his disposition hearing on Friday. The fact remains that he tampered with evidence. However, my guess is that the judge will be more lenient once he hears that Henry's father had nothing to do with Jen's murder."

Did Keith know about his father's plan?

"He says he didn't. Naturally, we're skeptical that he was entirely clueless. We're bringing him in for questioning, and I intend to put plenty of pressure on him. We'll also ask him about the silver Audi and whether or not he picked Steve up that morning. If he denies it, we'll impound the vehicle and have forensics test it to see if Steve was ever in it."

Bridget glanced up at the sound of footsteps approaching the room.

"Mommy!" Harper yelled as she darted into the room, followed by her grandfather.

Bridget's heart lurched in her chest as she wrapped her arms around her daughter and buried her face in her lavender-scented hair. "Hi, honey," she managed to croak.

Detective Wright got to his feet. "I'll leave you to catch up with your family. I need to get back to the station to interview Keith Carson." He nodded goodbye to John and exited the room.

Bridget reached for the yellow legal pad that had slipped beneath the sheet. *Does Henry know what happened to me?*

Her dad shook his head. "Not yet."

Don't say anything to him. I'll tell him myself tomorrow.

"Are you sure you're going to be up to visiting him?"

Bridget nodded. *They're only keeping me overnight for observation.*

"Mommy, I'm sorry a bad guy hurt you," Harper whispered, stroking her arm softly.

Bridget threw her dad a questioning look.

"That's why you never talk to strangers," he said cryptically.

Bridget smiled her thanks at him. It was better that Harper didn't know it was Quinn's grandfather who'd tried to strangle her and killed Jen. Bridget didn't want Harper developing a fear of her own grandfather in return. She scribbled another question on the pad. *Is Mom okay on her own?*

"She's not on her own. Our next-door neighbors came over and offered to stay with her. They were deeply apologetic for not being more supportive. They were afraid to get tangled up in the situation when they thought Steve was the killer. Apparently, there were rumors we were hiding him in our house."

Bridget gave a rueful smile. She couldn't help wondering if the school would be as remorseful about how they'd treated her children when they learned the truth. A familiar voice drifted down the corridor, interrupting her musing. A moment later, Quinn and Maria entered the room carrying a huge bouquet of flowers.

Quinn set the flowers down on the table next to Bridget's bed. "I'm so sorry about what happened to you, Mrs. Hartman."

My hero, Bridget mouthed to him.

"I would have warned you away from Jack, but I was

completely blindsided," Maria said, shaking her head. "I was certain Keith was behind it."

"The police still think Dad might have had a hand in it," Quinn added, stuffing his fists into his pockets.

Bridget smiled sadly at him as she reached for her pen. *I'm so sorry for everything you've gone through with your parents.*

He read what she'd written and gave an awkward shrug. "Thanks. I'm lucky I have Maria."

"Can we have Maria as our housekeeper too?" Harper piped up.

Maria chuckled. "Your mom doesn't need me when she has a helper like you."

Harper puffed out her chest. "I can make peanut butter and jelly sandwiches."

"Well, there you go," Maria said. "You can make your mom lunch when she comes home."

"When's Henry getting out?" Quinn asked.

"We're not sure yet," John answered. "His disposition hearing is on Friday."

"We should get going and let you rest, Bridget," Maria said. "Quinn just wanted to stop by and drop off these flowers."

Bridget reached for his hand and squeezed it gratefully.

Maria and Quinn hugged Harper goodbye and shook hands with John before taking off.

A moment later, Bridget's phone rang. She glanced down to see Detective Wright's number appear on the screen. She hit the speaker and gestured to her dad to answer it.

"Hello, this is John, Bridget's father."

"Detective Wright here. Can Bridget hear me?"

"Yes," John replied. "Harper's here too."

"Okay, thanks for the heads up. I just wanted to let you know that we've finished interviewing Keith Carson. He denies having anything to do with Jen's murder, but he's admitted to picking Steve up in his Audi the morning he disappeared."

John shot Bridget a quick look before asking, "Did he say where Steve was headed?"

Detective Wright cleared his throat. "He didn't get very far. Turns out Keith Carson's been holding him hostage in one of his storage facilities."

*B*ridget let out a strangled rasp and reached for the pen and pad lying next to her. *Is Steve all right?*

Her dad read the question aloud for Detective Wright.

"We think so," the detective responded. "I've dispatched a squad car to the storage facility. Apparently, Keith was trying to pressure Steve into revealing the account Jen moved the company's assets to. Rest assured, Keith Carson will be going to prison for a long time."

A thousand thoughts flooded Bridget's mind at once. Steve hadn't gone on the run at all—more importantly, he hadn't abandoned them. He'd been kidnapped and held hostage by Keith Carson in a desperate bid to force him to reveal information he didn't have to begin with. Her eyes flooded with tears of relief and shame. All this time she'd believed the worst about her husband—suspected him of murdering his lover, then covering up the crime, and fleeing with the money. But he hadn't killed Jen Carson, and he hadn't tampered with the evidence either. His only mistake had been to try and talk her out of moving the Carsons' company assets illegally.

A wave of guilt washed over Bridget. Steve hadn't lied to her about any of it. Her thoughts flitted back to the night she'd seen Jen exiting his office. Nothing was how it seemed. In fact, the more she thought about it, the more unlikely it was that Steve had been having an affair with Jen at all— maybe he'd simply been helping out an old friend as he'd claimed all along.

Harper tugged on Bridget's sleeve, pulling her out of her reverie. "Is Daddy coming home?"

Bridget nodded, squeezing back more tears. "Yes," she wheezed. "Daddy's coming home now."

IT WAS several hours later before an unshaven and haggard-looking Steve appeared at Bridget's bedside. The swelling in her throat had subsided a little and she was finally able to converse in a hoarse whisper. "Honey, I'm so sorry."

"For what?" Steve raised his brows in bafflement.

"For everything. For doubting you." She traced her fingers slowly along his cheek, taking stock of the bruises on his face. "And for what happened to you—it looks like Keith roughed you up."

"Forget it, it's nothing compared to what you went through." Steve's forehead puckered. "It's me who should be saying sorry. It's my fault you ended up in the hospital. I should never have agreed to counsel Jen behind her husband's back. I should have sent her someplace else. It's not like she couldn't have afforded to hire a skilled accountant and a good divorce attorney."

Bridget smiled sympathetically at her husband and squeezed his hand. "It's hard to say no to a beautiful woman in distress."

A haunted look crossed Steve's face. "I'm not going to deny that some part of me was flattered when she reached out to me for help—we all had a crush on Jen back in high school. But I could never be unfaithful to you, Bridget. You must know by now how much I love you and the kids. I would never do anything to jeopardize what we have. I realize I was giving all the wrong signals by working longer and longer hours, but I was honestly just trying to keep the company afloat so that none of you would have to suffer."

Bridget dropped her gaze, trying desperately to hold stinging tears at bay. "I know that now. I didn't mean to add to your burden by nagging you about spending more time with me and the kids—I just didn't want you to miss out."

"You had every right to nag me," Steve said. "Going forward, I intend to make some much-needed changes. If I have to downsize the company, then that's what I'll do. Henry will be out of the house in a few short years and it will be too late to build a relationship with him then."

"I'm so worried about him," Bridget croaked. "His disposition hearing is on Friday."

"I talked to his lawyer a little while ago. He's optimistic the judge will be more lenient now that the charges against me have been dropped, not to mention the fact that Henry has a loving, two-parent family to come home to. Bryan says the juvenile court judges prefer to send kids home with their families than to juvenile hall, if at all possible."

"I hope he's right about that. I don't think I could stand it if Henry's sent back to juvenile hall," Bridget said. "At least we're allowed to visit him tomorrow."

Steve slid an arm around her shoulders. "And we will, together, just like we're going to get through everything from now on." He kissed her softly on the forehead. "It's time for you to get some rest."

. . .

271

THE FOLLOWING MORNING, Bridget was discharged with a list of instructions on how to care for her throat, along with a follow up appointment with an ENT doctor to make sure she was healing properly. Steve escorted her out to the parking lot, supporting her as if she were a waif about to collapse of malnutrition at any minute.

"My legs work fine. You do know that, don't you?" Bridget said with a faint chuckle, wincing at the pain that immediately radiated through her neck. Whispering was just about tolerable, but laughing and coughing were still beyond a manageable pain threshold.

Steve grinned as he opened the car door for her. "Make the most of it. Pack horse duties will resume before you know it."

"Did you stay at my parents' house last night?" Bridget asked.

"No, I was down at the station with Detective Wright until the early hours. The police are still trying to trace the Carsons' money, but there's a chance they'll never find it now that Jen's dead. I ran home to shower and change and grab a couple of hours sleep before coming here to pick you up. Our neighbors are getting together this morning to clean the exterior of the house. There's nothing stopping us all going back home today, after we visit Henry, of course. Harper will have to stay with your parents until we get back. They don't allow minor siblings at juvenile hall."

"I'd like that. It's time to go home and be a family again," Bridget said smiling across at Steve as he clicked in his seat-belt. "And Harper's more than ready. She misses her room and her toys."

"Then it's settled." Steve turned the key in the ignition. "Let's go by your parents' place and pack up your gear. I want to see my little girl."

. . .

Bridget's parents were ecstatic when she and Steve walked into the house a short time later.

"My poor baby!" Elise exclaimed. "How are you feeling?"

"A lot better today," Bridget whispered, sinking down in the chair next to her. "Steve got roughed up pretty badly too."

"It's nothing, only a few bruises," Steve said.

"Mommy!" Harper shrieked, tearing into the room like a tornado. She came to a sudden halt and stared at Steve for a split second before hurtling toward him and wrapping her arms tightly around his legs. He picked her up and cradled her to his chest where she snuggled contentedly. A tingling warmth of happiness spread through Bridget's veins. It seemed like only yesterday that Harper was born. From the very beginning, she'd always slept peacefully next to Steve's heart.

"We're going to gather up our stuff and then head back home after we visit Henry," Bridget said.

"Are you sure about that, dear?" Elise asked dubiously. "Don't you want to stay here for a few more days until you recover first. I hate to think of you having to deal with all those reporters when you can barely talk. I imagine it's stressful enough, even if you can yell at them."

Bridget gave a small huff of amusement, taking care not to tax her throat. "I have Steve to do that for me. We need to go home and be together again. It's the best thing for Harper, too. I can't thank you both enough for everything you've done for us."

"Let me at least make you a cup of tea," her dad said, getting to his feet. "I was just about to put the kettle on."

While Bridget sipped on a lukewarm lemon and honey tea, Harper enthusiastically helped Steve load up the car with their belongings.

"Daddy's ready, Mommy," Harper announced a short time later. "Time to go see Henry."

Bridget got to her feet and hugged her daughter. "Be good for your grandparents. We'll be back to pick you up in a couple of hours."

Bridget kissed her parents goodbye and headed out to the driveway where Steve was waiting with the engine running. "When are you getting your car back?" she asked as she climbed in.

"Not for another week or so. I'll line up a rental in the meantime." He turned to Bridget, a broad smile deepening the hollows of his cheeks. "Ready to see our son?"

She nodded. "I'm ready to bring him home too."

THE JUVENILE DETENTION center proved to be every bit as inhospitable as Bridget had envisioned. She felt like a criminal herself as a hawk-eyed guard scrutinized her ID and subjected her to a thorough search before allowing her to pass through the security gate. Along with a small group of other equally uncomfortable-looking parents, they followed the juvenile corrections officer assigned to them through several more steel security doors, cameras tracking their every move.

The officer took them into a large white room that resembled a school cafeteria. Round tables with benches secured to the ground dotted the space, most of them occupied by detached or sullen-looking teenagers. Bridget sucked in her breath when she caught sight of Henry, dressed in an orange jumpsuit and white T-shirt, seated at a table in the far corner of the room.

Hand-in-hand with Steve, she wove her way through the sea of tables.

"Dad!" Henry burst out, jumping up and enveloping Steve in a huge hug. "Where have you been?"

"It's a long story," Steve said. "The good news is that the police have dropped all the charges against me."

He seated himself at the table while Henry turned to hug Bridget.

"It's so good to see you, son," she rasped.

A look of alarm flashed across Henry's face. "Mom! What's wrong with your voice?"

His eyes swerved anxiously to Steve as Bridget sat down next to him.

"Quinn's grandfather tried to strangle her," Steve explained. "He's confessed to killing Jen too."

Henry's jaw dropped. "What? Are you okay, Mom?"

"I'm fine, just a little sore. How are you doing?" Bridget rubbed a hand over his orange jumpsuit. "This is colorful."

Henry twisted his lips. "The worst part is the used skivvies they give you when you arrive."

"That's gross." Bridget shot Steve a horrified look. The sooner they got Henry out of this place, the better. She didn't want to contemplate the sheer volume of germs that must be floating around a facility like this.

"It's not so bad here," Henry said, wearing a bright smile, but not meeting Bridget's eyes. "They have classrooms and a proper school, so at least I won't fall behind on anything. And you get to decorate your room whatever way you want —Harper would love that. She'd have Barbies riding unicorns all over the walls."

Bridget hitched her lips up into a smile. She could tell Henry was trying hard to put a brave face on things while inwardly dreading the idea of spending any length of time here. "You won't be in this place long enough to start school," she assured him. "Bryan's confident the judge will go easy on you now that the charges against Steve have been dropped."

. . .

ALL TOO SOON, visiting hours were up, and Bridget and Steve found themselves hugging Henry goodbye. Despite her best efforts, Bridget couldn't keep the tears from falling, and her throat from choking up. "We'll see you on Friday, it will be here before you know it."

"Keep your chin up, son," Steve added, patting him on the back. "You're going to come out the other side of this real soon."

Bridget leaned her head on Steve's shoulder as they walked back to the car together, marveling at the stunning turn of events that had retuned her husband to her. As hard as the visit to juvenile hall had been, it was that much easier with Steve back at her side where he belonged.

AFTER THEY PICKED HARPER UP, they did their best to prepare her on the drive home for what awaited them. Bridget's stomach churned as they approached the house and saw the vans camped outside again. No doubt they were more eager than ever for a story now that news had broken of Steve's return, and the arrest of the Carson father and son duo.

"Brace yourself," Bridget said to Steve as they climbed out of the car and into the instant melee swarming them.

"Steve, how does it feel to have the charges against you dropped?"

"Can you comment on the arrests of Jack and Keith Carson?"

"Has your incarcerated son been informed of your return?"

"Do you intend to sue the Carsons?"

Steve smiled genially for the cameras, carrying Harper in one arm, the other draped protectively around Bridget. "It feels great to be back with my family. I have no other comments at this time." With that, he ducked his head down and swept Bridget up the path to the front door.

Safely inside, Harper darted off to her room. Bridget let out a sharp sigh of relief as she shrugged out of her coat. "How long do you think we're going to have to put up with that barrage of media?"

Steve batted a hand dismissively through the air. "They'll be gone before you know it. They're like hound dogs always after a new scent. Tomorrow something else will pop up on their radar and they'll hightail it out of here."

"Poor Quinn," Bridget whispered. "I hope they're not hounding him too. I wonder if he has any other family he can move in with."

Steve hung up their coats on the hall rack and led the way to the kitchen. "Jen has a sister, but I think she lives in Florida."

Bridget sat down at the table, drumming her nails. "We could offer Quinn a place to live."

Steve retrieved a couple of water bottles from the fridge and joined her. "You mean, ask him to move in with us long-term?"

Bridget nodded. "I've always jokingly referred to him as my second son, and I know he loves being with our family. I would hate for him to have to leave all his friends behind and move out of state now that he's lost both his parents."

"You're serious about this?" Steve asked.

Bridget fixed a solemn gaze on her husband. "Absolutely. Quinn saved my life—this is my chance to save him."

Steve took a long swig of water before answering. "I'm a lucky guy to be married to someone as big-hearted as you, Bridget Hartman. You always did put relationships before stuff, and I need to be reminded of that on a daily basis. If Quinn's your second son, then he's mine too."

*B*ridget climbed out of bed on Friday morning and got ready for Henry's disposition hearing under a cloud of apprehension. Despite Bryan's assurances, and Steve's bravado, there was no guarantee Henry wasn't about to be sentenced to hard time in juvenile hall. She couldn't stomach the thought of making a weekly pilgrimage to that bleak building, waiting in line as correctional officers rummaged through her purse searching for contraband and weapons.

Even worse, she couldn't stand the thought of her son being confined within its walls, twisting and turning on a paltry mattress pad, and eating substandard food in a cafeteria that was a far cry from her standards of cleanliness. More than anything, she dreaded what any such sentence would do to Henry's spirit. Surely a child couldn't spend any length of time in an institution without it changing them forever, and not in a good way.

And then of course there was Harper to think of. How would she be affected if her older brother was confined to juvenile hall for years on end? She would miss him dreadfully, for starters, and she'd be forced to endure her fair share of bigotry and ridicule from kids at school. Bridget's brain ached as she contemplated the inevitable consequences her family would face. She might end up having to homeschool Harper, and that would mean giving up her job which would put them under even more financial pressure than they were already facing. But, as usual, she was getting ahead of herself. It was pointless to worry about any of it before it had happened. Today, she needed to put her best foot forward and maintain a spirit of optimism for Henry's sake.

After dropping Harper off once again at her parents' house, Bridget and Steve headed for the courthouse. It was the third time Bridget had met Bryan at the top of the courthouse steps, and she fervently hoped it would be the last. The lawyer shook hands with Steve and introduced himself, before leading them both inside the building. "It's Judge Peterschick presiding again today," he said as they entered the courtroom.

"Is that a good thing or a bad thing?" Steve asked.

Bridget whipped her head toward him. "He's the one who sent Henry to juvenile hall in the first place—he considered him a flight risk."

"All the more reason for him to show leniency today," Bryan remarked tersely as he ushered them to their seats. "And it's good that Steve's in the courtroom too. Juvenile court judges don't like splitting up intact families."

Minutes later, Henry was escorted into the room by a bailiff and seated next to Bryan. Bridget leaned forward and smiled encouragingly at him. Steve gave him a thumbs up and he smiled tentatively in return.

Bridget's heart thudded in her chest as Judge Peterschick made his entrance and took up his position at the front of the courtroom. He positioned his glasses on the end of his nose and glanced over the paperwork in front of him.

"Mr. Miller," he began, "did you wish to present any information to the court."

"Thank you, your honor," Bryan responded, getting to his feet. "I would like to remind the court that Henry pleaded guilty at the first opportunity, and that he is very remorseful for his actions. His parents are with him today to show how supportive they are of their son and how concerned they are for his future going forward."

"Mr. Hartman," the judge said, shifting his gaze and addressing Henry, "do you understand why we are here today and what the purpose of a disposition hearing is?"

Henry swallowed tentatively. "Yes, your honor."

"In your case," the judge continued, "evidence of your crime in the form of CCTV footage has been admitted to the court, a crime to which you have confessed. Do you stand by that confession?"

"Yes, your honor."

Bridget pressed her knuckles to her lips, watching, with morbid fascination, as the court reporter's fingers flew up and down on her stenograph machine, recording Henry's fate. A surreal haze settled over the courtroom as Bridget felt her control over her son's life slipping away.

The judge adjusted his robes and surveyed the room. "I've studied the probation officer's report and recommendations and taken into account Detective Wright's comments on the situation. Furthermore, Mr. Hartman, your attorney has requested leniency on your behalf based on new facts that came to light as recently as yesterday." The judge leaned forward and peered over his glasses at Steve. "I understand all charges against you have been dropped, Mr. Hartman."

"That's correct, your honor," Steve replied.

"It would appear Henry has plenty of support in the home environment, if he were to commit to a program of rehabilitation."

"Absolutely," Steve said.

The judge reached for a piece of paper on his desk and held it up briefly. "I'm also compelled to take into consideration a letter I received this morning from Henry's schoolteacher, a Mr. William Barker."

Bridget's eyes widened. Her pulse raced in trepidation of what was coming next. Surely Mr. Barker wasn't going to try and persuade the judge that it would be a bad idea to allow Henry back into the classroom. Her fingernails dug into Steve's arm as she waited breathlessly for the judge to continue.

He pushed his wire-rimmed glasses up his nose and began to read aloud.

I am writing in reference to Henry Hartman who is appearing before your court on a tampering with evidence charge.

It has been my privilege to be Henry's English teacher this year, and I can attest to the fact that he is a hard-working, conscientious, respectful, and intelligent young man. While I appreciate the serious nature of the crime he has confessed to committing, I would like to point out that this is completely out of character for him and was obviously done under great duress. The Hartmans are a loving, close-knit, and supportive family, and Henry was no doubt devastated at the thought of his father possibly going to prison for a crime for which he had been set up to take the fall. As the real criminals in this situation have now been apprehended and will serve time for their crimes, I would contend that justice has been adequately served. As a result, I ask for leniency for Henry and his family who have already been put through so much as a result of the despicable actions of Jack and Keith Carson.

I have no doubt that Henry has learned from his mistakes. I would like to add that the school will do whatever it can to support him in any form of community service you might see fit to assign as a form of rehabilitation in lieu of a penalty that would deprive a good student like Henry of his current educational situation and a loving family, which he needs now more than ever.

Sincerely yours,
William F. Barker

THE JUDGE SET down the letter and peered down at Henry. "Evidently, you've made quite an impression on your teacher. It would be a shame to deprive you of such an intelligent and supportive educator going forward. I have given careful consideration to his comments and concur that your family has suffered greatly as a result of the vile actions of others. This whole situation came about because the perpetrators of Jen Carson's murder tried to frame your father. While I do not wish to downplay the errancy of the course of action you chose to embark on, I agree with your teacher that incarcerating you any longer in juvenile hall has little value, and that a more suitable and proportionate disposal would be preferable. Therefore, I am sentencing you to one-hundred hours of community service at your local school in whatever form your teachers decide. In addition, I am placing you on a six-month probation, the conditions of which include a curfew, a victim awareness class, and counseling."

Bridget clapped a hand to her mouth, tears of relief billowing down her face. She fumbled for a tissue and mopped at her eyes, blinking through blurry vision at Steve who was smiling broadly at her.

"Thank you, your honor," Henry said, looking like he was about to dissolve into tears himself.

The judge gave a curt nod in his direction and then slammed down his gavel.

Bryan stood and turned to face Bridget and Steve. "That's it, it's over. You're free to take Henry home. We'll pick up a copy of the paperwork on the way out."

Henry covered his face with his hands, his shoulders shaking. Steve stood and wrapped his arms around him, holding him close. Bridget bit her lip—it was the most beautiful sight she'd seen in a long time, her husband and her son safe, exonerated, and free.

The ride back to her parents' place was a very different affair to the sober drive they'd taken to the courthouse earlier that morning. Henry was both exuberant and incredulous. "I just can't believe it," he marveled, running his hands through his hair for the umpteenth time. "I was sure Judge Peterschick was going to send me back to juvenile hall. I thought I'd be spending years of my life in that place."

"Well, you'll never have to spend another night there, and I won't have to see the inside of a prison cell either," Steve said. "It's happy endings all around."

"Except for Quinn," Bridget said, throwing a meaningful look Steve's way.

He raised his brows and glanced at Henry in the rearview mirror. "Your mother and I have been talking about offering Quinn a place to live, if you're agreeable. He's almost fifteen now, so legally he has a voice in where he goes. He has an aunt who lives out of state, but I don't think he'll want to leave all his friends behind."

"Is this for real?" Henry looked from Bridget to Steve. "You'd let Quinn come and live with us?"

Bridget nodded. "You know I've always had a soft spot for him. The poor kid has never had things easy."

Henry's grin grew even wider. He shook his head in disbelief. "I didn't think this day could get any better, but this is seriously the best news ever."

"Let's hope your sister shares your enthusiasm," Bridget said. "She might be a tad jealous of Quinn coming to live with us. You know how much she likes to keep you wrapped around her little finger."

. . .

HENRY'S GRANDPARENTS were overjoyed when they returned from the hearing with their good news. John hugged his grandson tightly, tears flowing in rivulets down the crevices in his wrinkled face. "I kept hoping for the best," he said, "but I have to admit, it's been a tough few days on your grandmother and me."

Henry kissed his grandmother and threw himself down on the couch. Harper immediately crawled up into his lap and put her arms around his neck. "I'm glad you don't have to live in the hall with your own room anymore."

"Me too," Henry said. "And guess what?"

"What?" Harper asked, her little hands tugging at his neck impatiently.

"Mom and Dad are going to invite Quinn to come and live with us."

Harper opened her mouth wide and stared at Henry. "Forever and ever?"

Henry laughed. "Well, at least until he's grown up. What do you think about that?"

"Then I can have two big brothers." Harper cocked her head to one side contemplatively. "Mommy!" she called across to Bridget. "Can Maria be our housekeeper when Quinn comes to live with us?"

Bridget smiled, trying hard not to laugh and hurt her throat again. "Maybe. We can certainly ask her."

Henry narrowed his eyes teasingly at his sister. "But only if you promise to tidy up your Barbies every day so she doesn't trip on them."

Across the room, Bridget met her husband's gaze. *I love you*, she mouthed to him.

He pressed his fingertips to his lips and blew her a kiss in return.

Gratitude welled up inside her for the family she'd been blessed with—the family she'd almost lost thanks to a fatal hesitation, an undelivered dinner, followed by a string of false assumptions, bad decisions, and terrifying outcomes. There and then, she vowed to never again doubt the motives of the man who'd been faithful to her throughout their marriage. Their relationship was far from perfect, but it wasn't the mess she'd thought she would have to mop up either. It was a matter of knowing what to hold on to and what to let go of. And that had become a whole lot clearer over the past few days.

Their story wasn't over. She looked forward to turning a new page, cherishing the next chapter, and growing old together.

The other woman hadn't been so lucky when Jack's hands closed around her neck, but Bridget had been given a second chance. And she intended to seize it.

YOU WILL NEVER LEAVE

Ready for another suspense-filled read with shocking plot twists and turns along the way? Check out my psychological thriller *You Will Never Leave* on Amazon!

Some of us are hiding secrets. All of us are lying.

After Matt returns from a harrowing deployment in Afghanistan, he and his wife, Blair, take off around the States in his father's camping trailer for what they hope will be a tranquil trip. But when torrential rain derails their plans, they, along with a handful of other travelers, seek shelter at a remote campground. Things take a disturbing turn when they stumble upon a body.

And then the unthinkable happens. A horrific mudslide overnight washes out the only access road in and out of the campground, leaving them cut off from the outside world— and at the mercy of an unknown killer. But when one of the campers mysteriously disappears from her trailer, their fear quickly turns inward.
Is someone stalking the camp, or is the killer one of them?

- A nail-biting thriller that will leave you guessing to the very end! -

Do you enjoy reading across genres? I also write young adult science fiction and fantasy thrillers. You can find out more about those titles at **www.normahinkens.com**.

A QUICK FAVOR

Dear Reader,

I hope you enjoyed reading *The Other Woman* as much as I enjoyed writing it. Thank you for taking the time to check out my books and I would appreciate it from the bottom of my heart if you would leave a review, long or short, on Amazon as it makes a HUGE difference in helping new readers find the series. Thank you!

To be the first to hear about my upcoming book releases, sales, and fun giveaways, sign up for my newsletter at **www.normahinkens.com** and follow me on Twitter, Instagram and Facebook. Feel free to email me at norma@normahinkens.com with any feedback or comments. I LOVE hearing from readers. YOU are the reason I keep going through the tough times.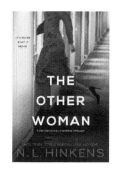

All my best,

Norma

BIOGRAPHY

NYT and USA Today bestselling author Norma Hinkens writes twisty psychological suspense thrillers, as well as fast-paced science fiction and fantasy about spunky heroines and epic adventures in dangerous worlds. She's also a travel junkie, legend lover, and idea wrangler, in no particular order. She grew up in Ireland, land of make-believe and the original little green man.

Find out more about her books on her website.
www.normahinkens.com

Follow her on Facebook for funnies, giveaways, cool stuff & more!

ALSO BY N. L. HINKENS

Head to my website to find out more about my other psychological
suspense thrillers.

www.normahinkens.com/books

- The Silent Surrogate
- I Know What You Did
- The Lies She Told
- Her Last Steps
- The Other Woman
- You Will Never Leave
- The Cabin Below
- The Class Reunion
- Never Tell Them

BOOKS BY NORMA HINKENS

I also write young adult science fiction and fantasy thrillers under Norma Hinkens.

www.normahinkens.com/books

THE UNDERGROUNDERS SERIES - POST-APOCALYPTIC
Immurement
Embattlement
Judgement

THE EXPULSION PROJECT - SCIENCE FICTION
Girl of Fire
Girl of Stone
Girl of Blood

THE KEEPERS CHRONICLES - EPIC FANTASY
Opal of Light
Onyx of Darkness
Opus of Doom

FOLLOW NORMA:

Sign up for her newsletter:

https://books.normahinkens.com/VIPReaderClub

Website:

https://normahinkens.com/

Facebook:

https://www.facebook.com/NormaHinkensAuthor/

Twitter

https://twitter.com/NormaHinkens

Instagram

https://www.instagram.com/normahinkensauthor/

Pinterest:

https://www.pinterest.com/normahinkens/